D1596921

DON'T CLOSE YOUR EYES

Also by Emily Kazmierski

Don't Look Series
Don't Look Behind You
Don't Look Too Close (a prequel novella)

Embassy Academy Trilogy
Deadly First Day
Lethal Queen Bee
Killer Final Exams

Ivory Tower Spies Series
For Your Ears Only
The Walk-in Agent (a Julep Short Story)
The Eyes of Spies
Spy Your Heart Out
Spy Got Your Tongue
Over My Dead Body

Other Novels
Malignant
All-American Liars

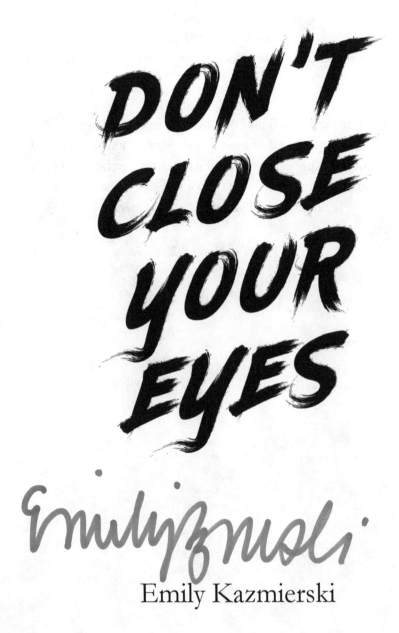

DON'T CLOSE YOUR EYES

Emily Kazmierski

For you.
You rock.

DON'T CLOSE YOUR EYES

Chapter 1

Day 239, Friday

Audrey

FBI Agent Justin Chambers is trying to murder me. That's the only explanation.

Never mind that I've already survived a serial killer's deranged obsession. Being torn apart by the death of my parents. Kidnapping at the hands of a favorite teacher. Almost losing my twin, Taryn, forever. You know, the usual.

But this dinner? It is awkward with a capital A.

Agent Karen Biel and her boyfriend and partner Justin invited all of us out to the diner for Friday night dinner instead of ordering takeout to the old house we call home. We've all gone out once or twice since Karen instituted Friday night dinners all together, saying she wants to be more involved in our lives now that we're not hiding out. Get to know Taryn's and my boyfriends, not that Noah's my boyfriend. But the buzzing under my skin tells me this evening is different. I'm dreading it, because I'm pretty sure they're about to tell us that the FBI is sending them somewhere else for their next case. That they're leaving Taryn and me behind.

The diner is packed. A popular boy band song filters out

of speakers along the ceiling. Waitresses skim between the tables, dropping off sizzling burgers and frosty shakes. My mouth waters when a juicy cheeseburger goes by right under my nose. My stomach growls. Our waitress, my good friend, Viv, approaches with a tray full of delicious eats. Justin holds up a hand, asking her to hold our food for a minute because he has something to say. He stands.

My eyes skim across the table to where Taryn, my mirror image, is tucked against Esau's side. He's a tall, broad-shouldered emo cowboy with a love for directing. And my sister, of course. They're so cute together it makes my teeth ache sometimes.

When she meets my eyes, wondering if I know what Justin's on about, I shrug. *No clue*, I mouth.

Viv snaps up one of Esau's fries and eats it under his indignant glare.

Taryn smirks and I huff a laugh into the back of my hand.

Standing and running a hand down his button-up, Justin starts telling the story of the first case he and Karen worked together. My eyebrows rise when he says it was hate at first sight. "But even back then," Justin says, gazing down at where my guardian is sitting in the booth, "I knew she was different."

A hoot goes up behind me, and I shift enough to see a pack of teenagers, all of whom are friends from school, loudly playing the cup game in the booth next to ours. Fiona, her black hair in loose coils around her shoulders, catches my eye with a wink. Dariel, Marissa, Erin, and a couple other guys make up the group.

I squirm in my seat. What I wouldn't give to climb over the divider between booths and sink down between Fiona and Marisa. I do not want to hear whatever Justin has to say. He's been shifty the past week or so, and the other day I caught him talking in hushed whispers on the phone. When he spotted me, he hung up. Too quickly. "You didn't hear that, did you?" he'd asked, a harried look in his eyes.

When I asked Taryn if she'd noticed, she agreed Justin was acting weird. He was up to something, something my gut was screaming would change our finally mostly normal life in Hacienda.

Now, I squint up at our erstwhile man of the house, wondering why he won't just get to the point. If he and Karen have been assigned to a new case, they should spit it out already and put us out of our misery. Especially if he's about to announce that they're leaving. We're going to have to start over. Again. I don't know if I'll survive it.

My eyes pinched closed, but I pull them open. Force my gaze back to Justin.

He's grinning like a fool. An odd expression for someone about to lower the ax. My breath hitches. Maybe we're the ones being sent away. My attention shifts to my sister across the table. How will Taryn handle being separated from Esau earlier than she planned?

Noah shifts and his thigh brushes against mine. My entire body lights up with nerves. That date we talked about going on after the trial was over? It still hasn't happened. He never asked me about it again. He's probably changed his mind. In the past couple of months, he's treated me like just a friend. No more. I have no idea what happened, but it stings. I scoot away so not even an inch of our skin is touching.

Karen is sitting next to Esau at the edge of the booth the diner's staff reserved for us, a hint of a smile on her face as she watches Justin. I have never seen this woman grin, but she's as close to it as she gets. Oh, this is bad. I thought she liked living with us.

I stifle a groan as Justin goes on about how much he has enjoyed getting to know us these past few months. How great it's been working with Karen without having to hide their relationship. Despite his severe military haircut and the suits he wears, he's almost effusive. There's no trace left of the creepy stalker he seemed to be last fall. The change in the man is like night and day. Turns out, he took so many photos of my sister and me while he was tailing us because he was bored. Justin loves people. It's why he joined the FBI, to help as many people as he could. He's clearly leading up to a revelation of some kind.

"I could go on all night, but I won't. Cheers." Justin clinks his beer bottle against Karen's and takes a long drink.

Huffing a laugh, Noah taps his milkshake glass against mine. His eyes shine behind his thick black glasses. "I still say salted caramel is the superior flavor."

"In your dreams." I muster half a laugh, but even Noah can tell it's hollow. His gaze catches on mine, weighing something behind his eyes. One corner of his mouth falls, and he leans to whisper in my ear. I start to reciprocate, but I'm interrupted when Justin kneels down in front of Karen and pulls a black velvet ring box out of his pants pocket. "And that's why I've decided now is the perfect time. Karen, love of my life and partner in crime fighting, will you marry me?"

Karen's eyes widen almost imperceptibly. "Of course." They smile at each other as Justin slides the ring onto her finger.

I'm in shock.

Cheers and clapping erupt from the booths around us as Justin pulls his new fiancée into a gentle embrace. She pats him on the back before pulling away, fiddling with the ring he slid onto her finger.

"It's a little loose," she says, peering down at the white gold circlet.

"We can have it sized. Tomorrow. No problem." Justin's fingers run over Karen's as if he's never felt anything softer and more fine than her skin. Ick.

My entire body slumps against the red vinyl seat. They aren't leaving. They're getting married. That's a good thing.

Since Justin is done soliloquizing, Viv approaches the table and dishes out our orders. Another waitress swings by to congratulate the happy couple.

"So, how's waitressing?" I ask Viv, trying to get my mind off the hummingbird trapped behind my ribs. Truth is, I need a job too. I've been doing more photography, and there are a couple of lenses I'd love to buy. They cost money I don't have.

"It's good. I'm going to be able to buy so much fabric. And buttons! Buttons aren't cheap, you know?"

Through the kitchen window, one of the cooks hollers that there's an order up.

"That's my cue." Viv reaches across the table and feigns stealing another of Esau's fries. He covers his plate with his work-worn hands, making her laugh as she goes.

"Can I have a fry?" Taryn bats her lashes at Esau, who grumbles that she should have ordered fries if she wanted them even as he nudges his plate toward her. Grinning like the cat that ate the canary, she takes two. While munching, my sister leans forward on her elbows to get a better look at Karen's shiny new ring. Esau tries to get out of the way by folding in on himself, but ends up only crossing his arms.

My eyes flick to Noah, who meets the shade of a smile on my face with one of his own. Under the table, his pinky brushes mine, but retreats. An accident. My heart deflates a little. That date? I wanted it. It would be something in my life that I didn't share with Taryn. It would be just mine. And Noah's.

"That is gorgeous. How'd you pick it out, J?" Taryn gushes about the ring, talking about cut and carrots and other stuff I don't understand. Leave it to Taryn to know all about fine jewelry. My twin sparkles.

"Congratulations," I say, still sounding a little off, but Karen thanks me.

I sink in my seat, feeling like I'm the one in need of a polish. I wish someone would look at me the way Esau looks at my sister. Like Justin looks at Karen.

In some ways, I've moved far beyond the wallflower I was when a serial killer took a shine to me and decided to make me his. But in other ways? It feels like my growth has stunted, leaving me once again losing the perpetual fight I'm in with Taryn to get my share of the sunlight.

In my pocket, my phone vibrates, making my stomach drop. Probably that mouth-breather calling again just to listen to me say hello before hanging up. It happened a couple of times right after the trial, but it's been ramping up the past couple of weeks.

Pulling my phone out, I glance at the screen under the table. Not an unknown. It's an actual number. This perks me up. I'm expecting a call from a reporter who wants to hear my side of the story. Months after the Gemini Killer's death, and now that Mr. Baugh's trial is over, I'm finally ready to speak out. Tell everyone what really happened.

Maybe getting it all out in the open will absolve me of the guilt I feel for everyone who died, once and for all. Maybe after I spill my guts to this reporter, the permanent knot in my stomach will loosen.

"I have to take this," I say to no one in particular as I slide out of the booth.

13

Taryn starts to climb past Esau and Karen. I wave her off. Noah slides out too. "Want me to come?"

One of Esau's prominent brows slashes upward. *Okay?* he mouths.

"I've got this. Be right back."

"If you're sure." Taryn moves seamlessly back into conversation with Justin about ring shopping. Karen sips her drink, hiding a satisfied smile.

Cold air is like a slap to the face when I step outside. My breath sails away in white puffs. It's absolutely frigid out. Pulling my scarf tighter around my neck, I move down the sidewalk toward the side of the building. I don't want anyone hearing my conversation with the reporter. It would be too embarrassing. Everyone can read my story in the article when it comes out. When I'm safe at home where no one can stare in horror or pity. Maybe Noah will come over and binge our favorite anime show with me as a distraction. It's a solid plan.

The light in the alley behind the restaurant is wan, casting a thin flare of light over the concrete. The dumpster looms in the dark. The concrete is sticky with grime, making me turn away. Wow, it smells terrible. I stand directly under the light, facing the street. My phone vibrates, and I answer. "Hello?"

Heavy breathing fills my ear. Ugh, not this again.

"Hello?"

More gusty breathing.

My nose wrinkles as I pull the phone away from my ear. So, not the reporter, then. Just another murder fanboy who gets off from hearing my voice. Yay me. The poster girl for sickoes everywhere. Le sigh. One thing my therapist made very clear is that I do not have to listen to people like this. Thrill seekers who treat me more like an exhibit in a twisted museum than a person. It's not my fault some people get a kick out of

14

skirting so close to death. "Listen, you sicko. Stop calling me! Go crawl back into whatever sewer you came out of." I hang up, wishing it were more cathartic than simply tapping my phone's screen.

Sizzle.

Crunch.

The light goes out.

Something thuds behind the dumpster, making me whirl to look. Footsteps pound over the pavement. A tall shadow lunges toward me.

My heart scrambles up my throat. What the hell?

A hooded body slams me into the wall, knocking the air from my lungs. Shiny metal glints in their hand.

No. Not again. Please.

My body goes rigid as I wait for the knife to

sink

into

my

flesh.

Chapter 2

This is how I die. Shanked in an alley by a brute in an ironic *Baywatch* hoodie.

My hands flail, trying to keep the knife from sinking into my flesh through my coat. Better to lose a finger than my life. Panic makes my thoughts fuzzy as they whiz by. I'm braced for the sharp cut of pain.

It doesn't come. What the hell?

The stranger's hands grope all over in a frenzied search for something. My skin goes clammy under the unwanted touch, and I fight harder to get away. With a fierce yell, they shove me harder against the brick wall. A sharp point cuts into my shoulder blade, making me yelp.

My arms swish and swat, but I can't get them off me.

"Where is it? Give it to me!" The voice is harsh and garbled. It sounds robotic, like they're wearing something to modulate it.

"Get off!" I scream. Pull my arm back until it hits brick. Punch my attacker in the gut with everything I've got. One of their hands covers their stomach. The other strikes my cheek. Splayed fingers burn my skin. Agony sears along my cheekbone as my eyes water

That same hand snakes into the front pocket of my jacket and yanks out my phone.

"Hey! Give that back."

The diner's front door slams, making both of us freeze. Booted feet stomp toward where I'm gasping in the dark. Each step matches the loud thud of my heart in my chest.

"Sheriff!" I screech as the man rounds the corner. Sheriff Lamb's silhouette is distinct in the red light from the diner's neon sign.

"What the hell?" He looks from me to the hood shoving me against the wall.

My attacker's hands jerk away. They run. Loud slaps of shoes over concrete.

"They stole my phone!" My voice is high and thready.

"You okay?" At my nod, Sheriff Lamb bolts after my attacker, but already the thief's footsteps are fading. They've got a good head start, so I don't know if Lamb will be able to catch up. The sheriff roars orders into his radio as he pounds to the far end of the alley.

I sink back against the wall, taking stock to make sure I'm in one piece. My stomach's contents fester, threatening to come up. Leaning forward, I brace my weight by clutching my knees. Blood rushes to my head, making my vision swim in the dark. I'm okay. There was no knife. They weren't trying to kill me. It was a crime of convenience. Some goon was hiding out back here, saw me on the phone, and took advantage.

I sink down onto the dirty cement, not caring that my pants will be a lost cause after this. I have to catch my breath. Wrangle my innards into submission. Convince my panicking mind that I'm not about to die.

I sound like I'm wheezing after running a marathon. Justin and Karen come barreling around the corner from the diner. Taryn, Esau, Noah pile after. People gather at the alley's mouth as my group runs over to me.

"Are you okay?" Karen asks, kneeling. Her hand is solid on my shoulder.

A flash whites out my vision. Blinking, I look up.

Justin leans an elbow against the wall, shielding me from the street and whoever decided it was a good idea to start taking photos.

Taryn hunkers down on my other side. Wraps her arm around my back and holds on tight. "We heard a shout and came running. Are you okay? Do we need to take you to the hospital?"

I let out a low cough, wishing my lungs would cooperate. "I'm okay. Someone stole my phone. I think they were looking for money, but I didn't have any on me."

Karen frowns, exchanging a glance with Justin. There's something in that look I do not like.

"What? What is it?"

Sometimes I really love that Karen is a no-nonsense woman. Squaring her shoulders, she meets my eyes. "This doesn't feel right. Your name and face are still plastered all over the news. It smells like more than a coincidence."

My head shakes vehemently, but I have to stop when my stomach threatens to spill over. "No. No, it was nothing. Some deadbeat took my phone. That's all. They didn't hurt me. I'm okay." I don't mention the voice modulator. Because what low-life carries one of those around in case they get the chance to commit petty theft?

One hand on the holster at his hip, Justin extends his free hand. "Let's get you back inside, and then we can talk about it."

I bite my lip. Let him pull me to standing.

Nearby, a siren squawks. Red and blue lights flash as a patrol car pulls to a stop blocking the alley. A female deputy gets out and pushes through the gawkers toward where we're standing. Her partner pushes the bystanders back and away from the grimy hole I'm in.

I sag against the wall, grateful my audience is gone for now. "I'm fine. Seriously."

Stepping forward, Noah holds out a glass dripping with condensation. "Are you thirsty?"

"My throat feels as dry as a beached whale's," I take the glass and sip the cool liquid. Shivering, I hand it back.

Noah nods when I thank him, his expression tense.

Sheriff Lamb comes clomping back from the far side of the alley, his hat dangling from one hand. Going straight to the deputy, he starts giving orders. Something about a perimeter and a sweep of the nearby parks and walking trails. Once the deputy is gone, Lamb turns to my little group. "Sorry to say they got away. It's pretty cold out here, so let's go back inside. We need to talk."

My churning blood turns to ice.

Once we're all inside the house, I sink onto the couch and wait. Dread, my old companion, comes slithering out of whatever shadowed corner it's been hiding in the past couple of months. Tension plucks at my nerves like a talentless hack torturing a guitar. Out of pitch, my nerves make my teeth grit. I think I'm going to be sick.

I insisted everyone come here for our little chat. The stares of everyone in the diner made my ears burn. If the sheriff has more bad news, I do not want to hear it when I'm sitting in one of the red booths being scrutinized by literally everyone in town.

I'm on the couch, with Taryn and Esau on one side and Noah on the other. Noah leans to one side, retrieving his phone from his jeans pocket to take a look when it dings. His

19

jaw clenches as he puts it away. His every movement is stiff, like he doesn't want to be here.

"You can leave if you want to."

His eyes skirt to mine. "It's fine."

I am not reassured.

Sheriff Lamb removes his cowboy hat the second he steps inside, his boots clomping over the tile and muffling on the carpet as he moves into the living room.

Glancing over my shoulder to make sure the blinds are closed, I take a long drag of the hot chocolate. It scalds my throat all the way down. My knuckles strain around the ceramic mug. Suddenly, I'm livid. Hot anger courses through me like a wildfire through underbrush after a drought. I was just starting to heal from my ordeal with the Gemini Killer. Settling into life in Hacienda. Making strides with my therapist. Finally feeling safe enough to explore and take some photos without constantly feeling like I was being stalked.

One chance encounter with a sleazeball mugger and I'm back to constantly checking over my shoulder. I wish I could close my eyes and forget the last half hour. Instead, it's one more tick in the litany of traumas I've gone through in the last few months.

"Bunch of crap," I mutter under my breath.

"What?" Noah asks, his eyes round with concern behind his black plastic glasses.

"This is crap." I say it louder, making the three adults turn. My resolve hardening, I stand. "This is total and utter crap. I'm not going to be terrorized by some idiot looking for their next fix. They stole my phone. So what. A phone is replaceable. It's over and done in a day."

The air vents rattle as the heat comes on, slowly cutting the chill from the air. Taryn tried to take my coat and hang it

20

up when we got inside, but I wouldn't let her. Having the extra layer feels a little like wearing armor, and based on the sheriff's grim expression where he stands a few feet away whispering with Karen and Justin, I'm going to need the protection.

The sheriff clears his throat, his cowboy hat hanging slack from one hand. "It's either a huge coincidence, in which case you have lousy luck, or it wasn't. And my gut is telling me it wasn't."

My bravado wavers, but I fight to keep it. "Why—why not?"

Lamb holds out his hand, palm up, revealing a small device.

"A voice modulator," Justin murmurs.

There it is—the other shoe. It drops with a thud onto the creaky wooden floor.

Lamb glances at Karen, who gives a bracing nod. His attention returns to me. He makes a sound between a sigh and a groan. "I was headed to the diner tonight to let you know we received a threatening note. Well, a journalist at the paper received it. Could be nothing, but in my experience it wouldn't be smart to underestimate something like this, especially when it has to do with a witness in a high-profile serial murder case like yours."

Taryn stands, grasping my hand in both of hers and squeezing tight.

A beat goes by when I can't think. It's like my brain jutters to a stop and takes a second to rev its engine to life again.

Noah takes my other hand gently. I wish he'd hold on tight and never let go, but he won't. Still, the anchoring he and Taryn provide allows my mind to clear of everything but the pressure points in my palms. Both hubs of contact are all that keep me upright. This cannot be happening.

"What does that have to do with me?" I say, my words sharp.

The sheriff sucks his teeth, weighing me with piercing eyes. He must make a decision, because he takes a folded slip of paper out of his pocket. When he unfolds it I realize it's two sheets. "The note was attached to the article." He hands them both over.

The first one is a copy of an article stating the verdict of Mr. Baugh's trial, highlighting my testimony. I've read it already, so I shuffle it behind the photocopied note. It takes me a second to get past the medium to the actual message. But when I do, my heart stops.

The second sheet is a photocopy of what can only be described as a murder note. It's made up of letters cut from magazines. Blocky ones. Cursive ones. Symbols standing in for others. I didn't think anybody made these in real life, much less actually sent them.

Pay attention, it reads. *I'm gonna show you what bloody havoc I can wreak.*

My gaze cuts from the note to my twin—the white line bisecting her cheek.

Chapter 3

Day 247, Saturday

The wind makes the trees bluster and blow, and the few dead leaves that remain on the ground eddy and swirl. Sighing, I tear my gaze away from the car window.

Taryn shoots a grin my way. "Thinking about Noah again?"

My cheeks go hot. "No."

She laughs, adjusting her grip on the steering wheel. Her face twists into an exaggerated grin that makes her look like a brainwashed Barbie. "Yeah you are. Whenever you think about him you make this goofy smile. Everyone has noticed. It's cute."

"Ugh. I do not. Who's everyone?"

Taryn makes a left turn, glancing in her rearview. "Esau, the girls. Even Dariel asked me why you kept making that face."

I grimace. "Great. Survive a serial killer only to die from shame." And okay, it is embarrassing. But I can't stop the warm feeling that spreads through me when I realize that I have a ton of friends who noticed and actually asked my sister about it. It... feels good. Really good.

"So, what are you going to do?"

I stare at my twin. "I don't know."

She gives me an unimpressed look, one eyebrow arching. "Ask him out. We were supposed to go on a double date, but it never happened. Make it happen."

I slump a little. "It's not that easy. I've been waiting for him to show some interest. Sometimes, I think I see it in his eyes, but then it fades and I'm left second-guessing it."

"It would help if he wasn't constantly having to babysit. His parents work too much."

"They have to." I defend Mr. and Mrs. Lopez, but I agree. They work a ton, and it seems like they ask Noah to babysit nearly every day. I try not to judge, though, because they have responsibilities I don't.

"Good thing you're looking for a job. Then you'll have some money and you can take Noah out instead of waiting for him to make a move."

I don't bother to stifle my groan. "I wish he'd just tell me how he feels. That'd be so much simpler."

"He likes you. It's obvious to literally everyone. You two are darling together."

"You make us sound like puppies." I pull my hair from behind my ears to hide my face.

"If the moniker fits…"

"You're the worst."

She winks as she pulls into the grocery store parking lot. It's the largest building in the strip mall, flanked by a shoe repair shop, laundromat, mattress store, and a nail salon. "Here we are. Go on in."

"Thanks. Wish me luck."

She opens her mouth, and my hand hovers over the door latch. "Try not to worry, okay? Lamb said they'd be on the lookout for someone in a *Baywatch* hoodie." She mimes running

24

in slow motion, just like they did in the show. "Plus, the sheriff said they were going to try to trace the phone's location to find the thief. If they find them, they'll be able to figure out if they sent the note."

"All they'll have to do is check their garbage for massacred magazines." I crack a smile. "I'm so glad you weren't murdered."

Flicking her blond ponytail—Karen let her dye it back after the truth came out about there being two of us—Taryn releases her seat belt. "Thanks. Me too. I'm too pretty to die."

Coming to the grocery store on a Saturday was a mistake. There are people in every aisle. I have to dodge a bunch of carts just to reach the service desk that runs along the front wall of the building. I press myself against the counter so a woman with two overflowing carts can get past me. I ring the bell and wait for the store manager to appear.

"Hey, Audrey!"

When I turn, Viv is drawing closer pushing a full cart of bagged groceries.

I offer to help her take everything to her car.

"That would be great. I may have overshot it a little this time." Laughing, she steers the cart out of the store.

We pile the bags into the trunk of Viv's car.

"How's the job hunt going? You try the diner?" She slams the trunk shut before stuffing her hands into the pockets of her puffer coat. She rolls her eyes when I shake my head.

"They said they wanted someone with more experience."

"That's bull. They hired me, so..."

We both laugh. I lean against the car's bumper. "Your mom still acting weird?"

"Yep. She got all dressed up to go out last night, so I'm

25

pretty sure my guess was right. New boyfriend."

"Think she'll introduce you?" I scan across the lot to where Taryn is hunkered down in our car, probably texting Esau.

Viv shakes her head. "Mom's seen and read so many horror stories, working at the paper, that she's super cautious about who she introduces me to. I've only met one guy, and that was only because she thought he was going to propose. Whoever the new one is, I probably won't ever even hear his name."

"I'm glad Karen and Justin aren't like that. They've ramped up the PDA now that they're engaged and everything, which is a little weird, but the sneaking around was definitely worse. Mostly."

Viv laughs. "I'm used to it. Lemme say hi to Taryn." She meanders toward where Karen's car is parked next to one of the spindly, naked trees.

Bracing myself, I go back inside to talk to the store manager.

I'm still unemployed when I come out of the grocery store. The manager took one look at my mostly blank résumé and said, "We're not hiring right now." He didn't even let me get a word out. I'll never earn enough money for new camera equipment if no one will even give me an interview. Frustration makes my feet stomp over the gravelly pavement. Throwing the car door open, I stuff myself inside. The door slams shut.

"Any luck?"

My glare stops my twin from asking any more questions. Instead, she maneuvers the car toward home. Her hands are tight on the wheel as she steers, unwilling to shift her hand position.

"Did something happen while I was inside?"

She shakes her head, her eyes glued to the road ahead of her. "No. I saw some jackass in a hood taking photos of you and Viv, so I got out of the car and told them to stop. It was probably some gossip hound looking for photos to sell to the tabloids. The whole vibe was strange. Anyway, they ran off."

My spidey senses are tingling. It could have been some low-life gossip columnist, just like she said, but it doesn't sit right in my gut. I've ignored my instincts too much in the past to let anything slide. "Did you get a good look at them?"

"That's the weird part. They were wearing a huge black hoodie, sunglasses, and a scarf wrapped around their face. I didn't think it was that cold out, but…"

"Red light."

"I see it." She slows the car to a stop.

Chewing on my lip, I debate saying anything. "Could it have been a middle-aged guy? You know, like the third Baugh brother?" I found out from Noah a few days ago while we were hanging out, that he did some digging into Robert Baugh but didn't find much.

"No. Audrey, we talked about that. The FBI didn't find even a whiff of evidence that that guy was anywhere near any of the crime scenes. Can you please let it go?"

I huff. Everything Taryn is saying is correct. Justin and Karen looked into Robert Baugh after Albert was killed and John was arrested. There was nothing connecting him to the Gemini killings, or me, personally. But it hurt that Taryn didn't even try to understand. That Robert Baugh is still a lose end, like a bit of food caught between my teeth. An irritation I'd like to be rid of. I didn't push it because I didn't want her to shut me out like she did all those months. It hurt more than I can say.

27

"Noah was just trying to help," I say, wrangling my tone into a calm cadence. "You don't have to bite my head off for it."

"Sorry."

"About the dude taking photos of me and Viv. What if they were hiding their face on purpose?"

"What—that's absurd. It's cold out, that's all."

"You just said it wasn't that cold."

"I changed my mind. It is cold, which makes a lot more sense than whatever you're implying." Taryn shoots me a look, but I push harder.

"That someone hid their face in order to take photos of me?"

"Come on. We're old news. Why would anyone do that now?"

"Oh, I don't know, because they're obsessed and want to torment me?"

"The Gemini Killer is dead, Audrey. Albert Baugh is dead. Want me to show you where he's buried? Because I know. I made Karen take me to the gravesite."

My jaw drops. Something cold and hard expands inside me. Wariness forged into the sharpest blade. I had no idea Taryn had gone there. When Karen asked if I wanted to go, I refused. I hadn't wanted to see it, thinking that seeing his name, knowing where he was buried would make him more concrete in my mind. Not less. And I desperately needed him to be less.

Taryn yanks the wheel, making a quick right turn. The car behind us honks, but she waves them off with an apology they can't hear. She takes the main road through town toward the other side. Oh God, she's actually doing it.

The blade inside me twists, making me suck in a shallow breath. "No. Taryn, don't. I don't want to see it."

28

"Maybe you should. Maybe it'll help you move past it once and for all. See? This is why I told Noah not to tell you he'd looked into Robert Baugh. I knew it would bring up all sorts of crap you weren't ready to deal with."

My heart plummets into my favorite Converse. She's still treating me as the twin who needs to be shielded and protected. Younger. Lesser. I can't believe my own sister told Noah to hide information from me. That she thought herself superior enough that she would know what I need more than I do. That she would try to take the choice away from me. My nostrils flare.

"I am not a baby to be protected from the big bad world, Taryn."

"Oh really? Then why are you freaking out about some overzealous journalist in a parking lot?"

I pause for a deep breath. I don't want to fight about this. "I don't know. Because I was stalked and kidnapped?"

"I was stalked and kidnapped too, and it was indescribably awful, but it's over. He's dead. I'll show you." She slams on the breaks and kills the engine.

My hands clench when I realize where I am. I was so busy arguing with Taryn that I didn't see that she brought me to the exact place I didn't want to go. The cemetery. My attacker's body is buried somewhere in this expanse of green spotted with gray headstones that stick out of the ground like rows and rows of jagged teeth. Reaching over, I relock the car door. Cemeteries have always creeped me out. "I'm not going out there."

I'm surprised when Taryn doesn't argue. Instead, she sits quietly in her seat, eyes skimming over the cemetery.

She's not going to try to force me to go out there. My body starts to unwind. I look over the immaculate grounds.

From here it doesn't look so bad.

"I've been thinking," Taryn whispers.

". . . Dangerous."

"I'm serious. About the mugging. They took your phone, right? But they didn't try to hurt you at all."

I thrust up a finger. "Excuse me. Being slapped hurt a ton."

"Sure, but I mean they didn't try to stab you or kidnap you or anything, right?"

My eyes cut to where a groundsman is riding a mower over the grass in the far corner of the cemetery. I think back to this morning, when Justin offered to drive us around while I job hunted. He hadn't insisted, but I could read the undercurrent in the room. Neither he nor Karen were thrilled about Taryn and me leaving the house alone. They haven't said as much, but they're more watchful of us now than they were before the mugging.

Taryn taps her foot against the floor mat. "Are you listening?"

Oops, I zoned out for a second there. I'm not sure what I've missed Taryn say, so I just nod.

"Okay, so I know what the sheriff said, but what if it *was* a coincidence? Think about it. There have been tons of people talking to the media since this whole mess began. People who swore up and down they knew who the killer was, or why he was doing it. And most of them turned out to be liars. What if that note the journalist got is the same type of thing? Somebody decided to try to capitalize on the GK's notoriety by sending it to get some attention?"

"...It's possible."

Taryn's warming up to her subject. "Can I continue now?"

I wave with one hand for her to go on.

"If someone planned to attack you, they'd have to be following you. And wouldn't it be awfully tricky to do that without being spotted by not one, but two trained and deadly FBI agents? Not to mention the fact that everyone in town watches us like we're exotic birds now that they know who we are and why we moved here? What you said makes way more sense. Somebody desperate or greedy saw you out there alone and decided to take a shot."

"Maybe." I desperately hope she's right, but deep down, I don't think she is.

Taryn leans back against her headrest, resting her case. She pinches at her nose with one hand. Lets out a frustrated groan. "I'm sorry I yelled at you. And I'm sorry I talked to Noah about you behind your back. We're both just—we're worried about you, okay? I want you to be able to get past this. I don't want to lose you again."

Her words hit me hard. I want to be angry at her, to fuss and fume about her treating me like a child. But the truth is, I've always counted on Taryn to protect me. She has always cheered me up when I failed, or given me a pep talk when I needed that extra ounce of courage to try something new. Until she didn't. And I don't want to lose her ever again, either.

Taryn's eyes are cautious when I meet them. They brighten when I give her a wan smile. "I know you were just trying to help me. Thanks."

She blows out a big breath. Looks out at the burial yard stretched out in front of us. "So, does it help? Knowing that the third Baugh brother was in jail for most of the time Albert was stalking you? That he couldn't have been involved?"

My eyes skim over the rows and rows of tombstones. Some are brand new with crisp engravings paid for by loved ones. Others are so old moss and weather have made them illegible. "It does help."

"So will this." She unfastens her seatbelt and digs into her purse until she comes up with fuzzy pink earmuffs. Putting them on, she bats her lashes at me.

"I don't know if I can take you seriously with those ear muffs on."

"Don't hate. I look adorable in these, plus my ears would freeze off without them." She straightens the hot pink puffs covering her ears. Unlocking the car doors again, she gets out. Leans down to meet my gaze. "Come on. Trust me."

Taryn leads through the brittle, broken grave markers to a newer section. I follow behind, picking my way through the graves, looking at the dates as I pass each tombstone. I'm absolutely stalling. When I drag my attention back to Taryn, she has stopped in front of a new grave marker. With a silent finger, she points at a flat, gray stone jutting out of the ground.

I thought I would feel something—furious anger or deep, scarring pain—when I look down at Albert Baugh's tomb marker. But I don't. I feel kind of numb. Maybe that's a good thing. Maybe it's not.

Taryn stands with her hands in the pockets of her wool peacoat. She doesn't say anything. Just stands there, staring down at the small words that mark the life and death of a man who made my life hell.

I inhale, letting the crisp air flow through my lungs and into my blood, making everything clear. The nightmare is over. I'm alive, and I'm going to beat this. It won't consume me. I won't let it. And if I stumble, Taryn will kick me in the pants and make me get up. So will Noah, minus the kicking. And Karen and Justin. Esau. Our friends.

The worst is over. Now I have to go about piecing myself back together. Find the new Audrey.

My new phone buzzes in my pocket and I slide it out, unwilling to give Albert Baugh another second of attention.

I've got a new message on my photo-sharing app. Opening it up, my breath hitches. Some deviant has private messaged me under a handle so similar to the one the Gemini Killer used it makes me do a double take.

CuteAshleeXOXOXO.

What the hell? I should delete it and move on without reading it. If I've learned anything in the past few months, it's that there are people out there evil enough to support serial killers. To love them for what they do. And whoever is messaging is probably one of them. They'd have to be sick to create a copycat account to harass me.

But I just swore I wasn't going to let this rule me. So instead of doing the smart thing, I open the message. My hands tremble as I read.

If you blink, you won't see me coming.

After that, there's a photo of me and Viv in the parking lot of the grocery store. Photo-realistic skulls are superimposed over our faces and flames lick at our feet.

Chapter 4

Day 250, Tuesday

A gust of air blows through the cafeteria when someone ducks out the exit into the courtyard, making my already messy hair whoosh around my shoulders. Running a hand through my wind-gnarled hair, I try to yank out the knots. "I thought she was going to kill someone. She was that mad."

It's true. Karen was furious when I showed her the message and photo. She went quiet, her eyes blazing. A lot of people rant or rage when they're mad. Not Agent Karen Biel. She goes still, as if it takes everything she's got to formulate a plan of attack in her mind, leaving her limbs waiting in stasis. Thankfully, Justin was there to talk her down. And to prevent her from marching down to the grocery store to demand to see their security footage.

Make no mistake, she went down there after a few minutes, but Justin convinced her not to go until she'd calmed down, saying she'd catch more flies with honey than vinegar.

Justin stayed with us, keeping Taryn and me distracted by roping us into cookie-baking in the kitchen. Turns out, he can cook. Unlike our avenging guardian, whose specialty is take-out. I hadn't made cookies since Before, when Mom used to herd Taryn and me into our small kitchen back home to roll snickerdoodle dough in bowls of cinnamon sugar. Or make chocolate oatmeal no-bake cookies that we called "cow plops." Having recently seen an actual cow plop, I can say they look and smell nothing like the cookies.

"So what are they gonna do?" Fiona asks, smacking Dariel's hand away when he tries to swipe the fudgy cafeteria brownie from her tray. He's already wolfed down the two he sweet-talked the lunch lady into giving him, and is currently scoping out each of our lunches in a quest for more. Dariel's sweet tooth is ginormous, rivaling even Viv's penchant for fried Twinkies.

"Karen said they can ask the cell phone company for the user's information, but they don't have to comply unless they get a warrant. Karen isn't sure she can get one, since no one has actually threatened me bodily harm." I don't add the *yet*. "It's not illegal to take photos, even if they are freaking creepy."

"Super creepy," Marissa echoes.

Viv nods in wide-eyed agreement.

My stomach twists. It's absolutely wretched that our friends are caught up in this, whatever it is. The solidarity our friends showed by refusing to give interviews about me and Taryn was huge. Not a single one of them talked.

There were others at school who did. (We are not friends, Josie from drama club.)

I look around the cafeteria, but no one's paying us any attention. After the shock of learning that Megan Pritchard was actually two people, they got used to us. We're just two more faces in the crowd. It's nice. Well, I like it. Taryn's already making plans to run for student body council at the end of the semester, aiming to raise her profile for our senior year. She's used to the fawning. Loves it, too. Me? Not so much.

"And once they get the user's information from the app

company, they'll probably pay them a visit." Picking up the square of lukewarm cafeteria pizza, I take a big bite to occupy my mouth so I don't have to answer any more questions.

"A very stern visit," Taryn adds, making a grim face. "Somewhere along the lines of, 'Stay away from my teenagers or I'll make you.'"

Esau huffs from his spot on my sister's other side, his arm sprawled along the back of her chair. "Almost feel sorry for the creep."

"Aww, poor Mr. Grumpy Pants. Did the mean old FBI agent scare you?" Taryn pats his cheek teasingly before winding a finger around a strand of his dark locks. Sometimes, she flirts with Esau just to get a rise out of him. It works. For such a surly dude, he gets flustered when Taryn tries to be affectionate with him in front of us.

"No." Pulling his arm away, Esau throws his cascading black hair up into a man-bun while giving his empty plate a stare-down.

"Of course not." Taryn beams. His eyes lock onto her. Of course, he can't always resist. PDA incoming in three... two...

Esau plants a chaste kiss on Taryn's cheek. She grins wider.

"Oh, it's kissin' time." Dariel puts a hand on the back of Fiona's neck and pulls her toward him for an exaggerated, loud smacker to the lips. She cackles. They stopped playing and got official over Christmas break. Now they're practically an old married couple. Fiona nudges him back into his space and turns to us.

Marissa's buffed-to-perfection fingernails tap along the table's surface. "The app got a lot of flack for its lax security after the whole catfishing thing. Wouldn't they want to cooperate this time around? You know, so they don't look like

36

they're protecting a human cockroach?"

"You'd think," Noah says. "But a lot of software developers are hesitant to give out their users' information, especially on a platform like that. If their customers feel unprotected, they won't use the app. It sucks, but it's true."

"I hope they cooperate," I whisper. "I'd love it if they caught this jerk quicker rather than slower."

"They will. Don't worry about it, okay? You're safe." Noah's shoulder nudges mine.

"You're right. This is no big deal." *After everything else I've been through.*

"I didn't say that, but… Nothing's going to happen to you. We won't let it." His reassuring head tilt eases the tension in my lungs. Because no matter what happens, the certainty that Noah cares about me circles and settles like a purring cat behind my breastbone.

"So, I didn't tell you guys at first, but my mom is spooked by this whole photo thing, and I think she'd want everyone to know. For protection purposes, I guess? But, um, she's the journalist who received the murder note." Viv is solemn as she waits for our reaction.

My eyebrows shoot into my hairline. I knew Ms. Miller worked for the paper, but I had no idea she was the one who got the note.

Fiona's surprised snort is loud. She prods at Viv to get her to spill, which Viv does. I lean forward in my seat, hoping to learn something useful, but my friend doesn't really know much. The note arrived at the newspaper office, addressed by name to Anna Miller. No return address or anything else to help identify the letter. It was postmarked from a town about half an hour's drive away.

"Why would they send it to your mom?" Noah asks. He's

got his thoughtful detective face on.

"She figured it was because she wrote a couple of the articles about it when the spit hit the fan. Mom writes for the crime section sometimes when they need an extra set of hands."

We chatter about it for a few more minutes, until the buzz of new information lowers to almost nothing.

The big black and white clock on the wall reads 11:57. Three more minutes until the bell rings, so I start cleaning up the detritus spread on the table.

Esau clears his throat and stops canoodling with my sister to turn his attention on the rest of us. "I talked to Miss Crabtree about this semester's production."

Taryn and Fiona squeal and jiggle in their chairs. The debate around the next play has been rife with contention. Last semester's show slayed, thanks to all of our hard work, and our bossy director's growing online presence, so the drama club is feeling the pressure is on to kill it this semester too. Esau's pushing hard for *Othello* or something else equally dramatic and tragic. Taryn's been fluttering her eyelashes at him in a bid to change his mind. She's thinking something lighter. Since I'm not in the club this semester, I stay out of it.

"She voted for *The Importance of Being Earnest*." Esau frowns, displeased, as most of the rest of us erupt with excitement.

Viv yanks her drawing pad out of her backpack and starts sketching furiously. "I can't wait to update our department's Victorian costumes. The silhouettes, the fabrics. This is going to be so good. Oh! What are your feelings on period-appropriate wigs? Okay, maybe not." She dives back into her drawing to get away from Esau's sharp look.

"Hey, this is going to be fun, okay? Maybe you'll take a

turn on the stage with me this time?" Taryn's been doing her best to get Esau out from behind the curtain for his last high school production, but he's not biting. Frankly, he's a great director, but I have my doubts about his acting ability. He's so… laconic, yet oddly transparent. Esau wears his exacting, perfectionist emotions on his sleeve.

"Can you act?" I blurt.

The boy grumbles into his cup.

Across the table, Dariel wiggles his eyebrows. "Last time this fool was on stage he had to beat the ladies off with a stick. Which is why he hides behind the curtain now."

"Oh really? I would *love* to see that." Taryn leans both hands on his shoulder and hits him with her best heart eyes.

"Not funny." Mr. Grumpy Pants cuts an incensed look at Dariel, who smirks.

Fiona mouths "It's true."

The bell rings, and everyone starts piling their stuff up on their trays and heading for the door. Swinging my bag onto one shoulder, I catch up with Viv. "Hey. If your mom gets any more notes, will you let me know?"

"You got it, chica."

"And hey, Noah's right. Nothing's going to happen to us, K?"

As I walk to my next class, I have to wonder. Is it purely a coincidence that the newspaper started receiving ominous notes around the same time someone decided to impersonate the Gemini Killer to message me on my social app? I'd like to think so, but the photos and messages I got of me and Viv in the grocery store parking lot didn't feel like a harmless prank. The skulls over our faces made sure of that.

I can't stop thinking about something Karen told me once. Maybe she's jaded by her work for the FBI, but her stance on coincidences makes a lot of sense. It won't stop ringing through my brain, enforcing my worry.

Her opinion? Coincidences don't exist.

I hope to God she's wrong.

Chapter 5

Day 258, Tuesday

Play tryouts are insane.

Esau and Miss Crabtree are in the second row of chairs surrounding the black box stage taking notes while Fiona ushers hopefuls into the center one by one to deliver their prepared monologues. Viv is backstage with Marisa, keeping her company until it's her turn. She's hoping to land the role of Lady Gwendolyn, another lead like last semester.

I blame the sheer number of students in the auditorium on the newspaper. They printed a follow-up story about the murder note. Yesterday. With a recap of my role in the Gemini Killer's trial. And since all of Hacienda knew play auditions were today, the entire school is here.

Just when everyone in town was starting to treat Taryn and me like normal people with boring, country lives, someone just had to send an ominous note to the newspaper. Mrs. Lopez is pretty nervous about it, and Noah did his best to put her at ease by talking about the sheer number of phony threats and notes police officers have gotten in the past. It did not help.

I'm gonna show you what bloody havoc I can wreak.

It's been almost two weeks, and not a single weird incident has happened.

41

I keep waiting for something. Anything. A violent burglary. A stabbing. Prank calls that aren't obviously from Dariel and his idiot friends. Anything. But there's been nothing. Folk have started talking about it like it was some big joke, but with every day that passes like nothing is wrong, I get wound up tighter.

Coincidences don't exist.

After *CuteAshleeXOXOXO* sent me that freaky message, I responded with something along the lines of, "How sick do you have to be to impersonate a serial killer on social media? Leave me alone or I'll sick the FBI on you."

That shut them up.

I should be relieved. Should be. I'm not. I'd almost rather they keep spouting off dumb crap instead of this silence. They could be up to anything. Setting traps and lying in wait for me to put my guard down, and I'd have no idea. It's like there's a land mine buried somewhere in town, and one of these days I'm going to step on it unawares.

Tick...

Tick...

Tick...

So far, a handful of people have read for the part of the girlish, naive Cecily, the other leading female role, but none of them have stood out. I can tell because Esau slumps forward in his chair, tapping his pencil on the paper. None of the people we've seen so far have made him sit up and pay attention. Miss Crabtree keeps looking at her lap. I suspect she's taking peeks at whatever vampire novel she's currently reading.

My sister hasn't gone yet. She tortured Esau all during lunch today, trying to get him to swear that he would treat her just like any other person when he casts the show. No special treatment. Finally, after an agonizing twenty minutes, he agreed.

42

I honestly don't think he'd ever play favorites, but it was entertaining watching her cajole him. For Esau, putting on a compelling play is tantamount to the meaning of life. He'd never sacrifice quality for anyone, even his girlfriend. Taryn should have known that after the way Esau treated Marisa last semester when she was struggling to learn her lines. But Taryn wanted assurances.

Hence the random drawing for the tryout order.

"Next," Esau calls, waving to Fiona where she's standing in the aisle between chair rows.

A pretty blond girl tiptoes to center stage and starts talking. At least, I think she's talking. Her mouth is moving, anyway. I don't hear a single sound.

"Louder." The tap of Esau's eraser on his pad gets faster.

The girl tries again. Still nothing.

"Try to project, please." Miss Crabtree doesn't even look up from her e-reader.

The girl's shoulders slump. Fiona walks to where she's standing center stage and leans in to talk to her. Shaking her head, the girl tiptoes out.

Only two to go before they move on.

A brunette is next. She's not bad. Esau's pencil tapping slows.

Taryn catches my eye from backstage and points to her own chest. She's next.

"Did I miss it?" Noah plops down in the folded seat beside me, stowing his backpack underneath. He pulls two candy bars out of his jeans pocket, handing me one, before settling fully into his seat.

Thanking him, I shake my head. "Looks like she's going last. So far, six other girls have read for the role Taryn wants, but Esau isn't impressed."

43

Noah gives an amused head shake. "Is he ever?"

"Touché."

Noah unwraps his candy bar and takes a bite. Swallows carefully. "So I've been thinking… Since this whole Simeon thing. I need a new case to dive into. I've been looking into old crimes that happened here in Hacienda. There are some interesting ones. Plus, with the advances in technology, some of the really old cases are finally being solved. It's pretty awesome. Want to help me find one?"

I gnaw at the candy bar, taking a big bite of chocolate and caramel to give me a second to think. Digging into another person's suffering doesn't sound that great. Now that the Gemini Killer is dead and his brother is behind bars, I'd rather move on. Put together a life that isn't framed by secrets and bloody knives. But that's only because I've had closure. The months when I could barely breathe for the fear that hobbled my lungs—they were hell. What would it be like to live like that for years, or more? I can't begin to imagine the pain of clawing my way through something like that. But if Noah and I can help take the pressure off someone else for a little while? That would make the digging—the staring straight into the face of evil and asking why—worth it. It might be worth it.

"What did you have in mind?"

Noah grins. "You're the best. No, seriously. You are."

My cheeks color at his compliment. "I try."

"You succeed."

Warmth unfurls behind my sternum. If we're gonna find a new cold case to dive into, that will take hours of research and discussion. If helping Noah find a new pet case brings us closer together, that would be worth it too.

Noah's head bobs when I ask him how he wants to start. "I was thinking we could hit the library and look through the newspaper archives. We may find some leads there."

"When—"

"In matters of grave importance, style, not sincerity, is the vital thing." Taryn's voice rings out through the room, snatching away my attention. She's standing at center stage, her form illuminated by the sole spotlight Dariel turned on before auditions began. She looks girlish and innocent in her creamy, turtleneck sweater dress and skinny jeans. Her blond hair is up in a braid crown. She has absolutely nailed the young ingenue note she was trying to hit.

Taryn worked really hard on her monologue for today, too, but the little turd wouldn't perform it for me. She wanted it to be a surprise. She said it would be easier for me to give an honest, unbiased opinion on her chances.

Glancing around the drama room makes it obvious that Taryn has everyone's attention. The chatter and gossip have quelled, leaving all staring at her, hypnotized. Esau grips the back of the chair in front of him as if he's a breath away from leaping onto the stage. Even Miss Crabtree has her eyes up.

And why not? Taryn exudes charisma. I can't look away. A pang shoots through me, recalling a time Before, when I sat in the audience just like this, with Mom and Dad to one side, equally as spellbound as I was. Taryn had made a frightening Lady Macbeth, but she's going to make a truly perfect Cecily.

My phone vibrates. I ignore it, but it starts again. Who would be messaging me now? Everyone I talk to is in this room. Except Karen. Scrambling, I take out my phone and unlock it. If she found something about the mugger or the creep who messaged me over my social, I want to know.

It's not Karen.

CuteAshleeXOXOXO is blowing up my phone.

Hello?
You there?
I'm right here.
Your sister is a talented actress.
She's practically glowing.
Too bad her time in the spotlight is almost up.
No one will be watching her when my knife and I are done.

Chapter 6

Every muscle in my body clamps down tight as I stare at the messages.

Noah leans close, whispering in my ear. "Audrey? You okay?"

For a second, I can't move. My fingers grip my phone so tightly I'm afraid I'll never be able to pry it out of my palm. My eyes rise to Taryn, who is wrapping up her audition. In an abrupt, brutish movement, I force myself to stand up. Whirl around. Scan the crowd for anyone focused on their phone instead of the stage. Problem is, pretty much everyone is still gaping at Taryn rather than doing the endless scroll. Sharp movement near the back door snags my attention. A black hood tears open the exit and bolts. Wearing a balaclava.

Pushing past Noah, I run. Not away from the hooded figure, but toward it. No one can possibly hurt Taryn while she's in view of a hundred people. But the hood? I can catch them if I'm quick.

A flurry of activity crops up on either side of the aisle as people notice I'm running like a demon is chasing me. And, okay, I flail a little bit when I run, but all that matters is catching the hood.

"Hey! Don't interrupt auditions." Esau's sharp tone bounces off like a dart that has entirely missed the target. He'll understand. Later.

"Audrey. Wait!" Noah is on my tail.

The door slams against the wall when I throw it open. Dash through the foyer. Out into the parking lot. My heart beats from the top of my head to the soles of my feet as I skid to a stop on the sidewalk. My eyes range over the parking lot, looking for someone. Anyone. No one. No one. No— Wait.

At the far edge of the lot, a maroon car roars to life. It backs up so fast it almost nails the car parked opposite it. I cringe, but there's no crunch. Acrid burned rubber hits my nose as the car peels out.

Noah comes to a stop behind me, breathing loud. "What happened?"

"No time!" I run, tearing across the parking lot toward the exit. There's still a shot at seeing the car's license plate if I can just... My feet slam over the gravelly pavement. I can't miss it.

The car lurches out of the parking lot and makes a right turn.

I'm almost past the final line of cars. Hurry. Run. "Seven-L-U— damn it." My lungs heave as I keel over, bracing my hands on my knees. Repeat the first three characters of the license plate over and over in my head so I won't forget them.

Noah puts a hand on my back, making me leap upright. "Whoa. Whoa. Sorry."

"It's fine. Just gimme a sec." My neck cranes to stare at the hazy blue sky. Can't I just be a normal teenage girl for like, five seconds? No. Of course not. That would be ridiculous. No, instead I've somehow attracted the attention of yet another sick-minded freak with too much information. Thanks to the newspapers who shared everything they could dig up about the catfishing I went through last summer and fall. And now I've got a *CuteAshlee* doppleganger to show for it. Yay.

48

As my mind starts to clear, I turn to Noah. "It could be a coincidence, right? Those exist."

"What could be a coincidence?" Taryn jogs the last few feet toward me, her cheeks flushed. Esau's at her heels.

"Couldn't this have waited until after auditions?" His arms cross over his chest as he gives me a stern once-over. His man-bun is unraveling, so he reaches up and yanks it out, freeing his black hair.

Noah is looking at me like I'm a wild animal liable to dash off into the trees. He inches closer. One hand reaches out to take mine. When I don't pull away, his grip tightens. Noah, my best friend, draws close enough that I can feel his body heat through my thin sweater. A shiver runs through me. It's freezing out, and I left my heavy coat inside.

"You all right?" Esau asks, eyeing me warily.

I heave out a breath. "Let's go inside, and I'll explain."

"Explain what?" Taryn's eyes flick down to where Noah's hand encases mine, but she manages to keep her expression neutral.

"*CuteAshlee* part two."

This prompts a grunt, a groan, and a gasp from my companions. Guess who did what? The four of us go back inside, and in the toasty foyer, I tell them all about the messages.

Black car. White truck. Brown truck.

Cars shoot past as Taryn drives us home. My eyes scan all around as we navigate through town. Looking for any glimpse of a maroon car. I know it'll be a miracle, but I can't help but hope I'll spot it. Maybe then I can see who was behind that mask.

Noah is in the back seat, helping search. Every once in a

49

while he mutters the three digits of the car's license plate under his breath.

Esau was not thrilled that we were leaving without him, but someone had to stay behind to finish up auditions, and there was no way Esau or Taryn would leave it up to Miss Crabtree.

A flash of maroon cuts across the corner of my vision. "Wait!"

Taryn's foot slams the brake, jerking the car to a stop. A horn blares behind us.

"Nothing. Sorry."

Taryn shoots a cautious look my way before she resumes driving.

"Did you see something?" Noah's head pokes between the front seats, talking over my shoulder.

"Thought so, but—Turn left! Turn left!"

Taryn jerks the car into the left lane and banks it before the light turns red.

My fingers dig into the dashboard as I lean forward. Up ahead there's a burgundy car. Four door. Kind of dusty. License plate: 7LUT118

"Follow that car."

"You think it's the same one?" Noah's hand snakes past me, his wrist brushing my shoulder as he points. "They're turning into the bank lot."

"I see it." Taryn slows the car's progress to a crawl.

"Hurry. We're going to miss it. What are you doing?" It's all I can do not to throw my foot over the center console and step on the gas pedal.

"Haven't you ever watched cop shows? If we go blazing in there it'll scare them off. This way it doesn't look like we're tailing them." My sister glides into the lot.

"Where is—there. Pull in right there." I point to a parking spot facing away from the bank. The maroon car is parked at the curb, right by the ATMs. From this vantage point, we can spy on them from the rearview and side mirrors

My breath hitches, my eyes glued to the car's reflection. The driver's door swings open. I whirl around to look out the rear window. And groan.

"What I'm taking away from this story is that you tracked a little old lady to the bank and watched her take out cash from the ATM before driving to the beauty parlor to have her hair curled." Karen looks decidedly nonplussed as she meets my eyes across the coffee table.

Noah, Taryn, and I are lined up on the sofa, with me in the middle. As soon as we left the little old lady at the beauty parlor we drove home to tell Karen about the messages. The hooded figure. Our ill-fated attempt at following the car I'd supposedly seen leaving the school's lot.

"First of all, instead of leaving the relative safety of the school, you should have called me immediately. We cannot take these sorts of events lightly, given your history. Have you talked to that reporter yet?"

I shake my head. Truthfully, I'd been putting it off to see if the creepy messages continued. It had taken over my focus. I haven't even called that reporter back to confirm that I wanted to proceed.

"Don't. I'm advising you not to do that interview. At least not right now. It's clear that someone is watching. I also think you should start wearing your tracking bracelets again."

"Fine."

"No way."

Taryn and I speak at the same time.

51

"It's not a terrible idea," Noah puts in. "They saved all of us last time."

Noah's right. If he hadn't picked up Taryn's bracelet when she dropped it on the lawn. If he hadn't been worried and followed Esau and Taryn across town. If they hadn't found me tied up in Mr. Baugh's decrepit barn workshop. All those ifs.

If they hadn't happened, I wouldn't be here right now. That is certain. I'd either be Albert Baugh's captive, or dead. Another one of the Gemini Killer's victims. Once he realized I wasn't interested in making myself a teen bride by marrying him for real... I shudder as my insides recoil. He'd have killed me. Definitely. Painfully.

"Audrey, you still with us?" Noah bumps my shoulder with his. His brown eyes are gentle behind his black glasses frames. Black curls fall forward over his brow, and I wonder if I'll ever have permission to run my fingers through them.

I swallow loudly, forcing down the what ifs that threaten to drown me if I let them. Use my senses to ground myself in the here and now, just like my therapist encouraged me to do.

Thick, nubby tweed fabric of the couch. The weight of Taryn on my left and Noah on my right.

A light, clean scent of Noah's fabric softener.

Karen watching me with concern in her calculating eyes.

My breath whooshing as my lungs work in and out, pushing oxygen through my veins to the farthest reaches of my body.

Taryn wraps an arm around my shoulder and squeezes. "You're still here with us, Aud. We've got you."

A faint smile rises to my lips. "You're right. Thanks." It falls immediately when I realize that maybe the person who is taunting me isn't after me—they're after Taryn. She's the one the hooded figure threatened this afternoon. Not me.

Wrapping an arm around her waist, I hold on tight. Rest my head on her shoulder.

"I'll wear my bracelet, but you need to wear yours too. Promise me."

Sighing deeply, she nods. The tendons in her neck and shoulder move under my cheek. "Okay. But Agent Biel has to swear not to track me unless it's necessary. And me being out with Esau does not count as necessary. I'm seventeen, and I need at least *some* privacy. Deal?"

Pursing her mouth to one side, Karen considers for a second. Gives a definitive nod. "I can work with that."

The door rattles as someone pounds out a knock.

Taryn looks at her phone and brightens. "Esau must be done with auditions early." She springs to the door and throws it open. Her face falls. "What now?"

Sheriff Lamb steps inside, his boots crunching on the wood floor. Removing his cowboy hat, he runs a hand along the worn brim. Looks from Taryn, to Karen, to Noah and me. Heaves a sigh. I can't say that I'm thrilled to see him. Usually, when Sheriff Lamb shows up, he's closely followed by Very Bad News.

Noah shifts on the sofa, his thigh pushing against mine. I'm sure it was an accident, but I take strength from the contact. Noah doesn't have to be here with me right now, but he is. I'll take it and be thankful for it, even if it's not in the way I want.

Lamb clears his throat. "Just got a call from a nice but terrified old lady who told me an older tan sedan followed her all the way from the bank to the beauty parlor. She was afraid she was going to be carjacked and her bingo money stolen. You three know anything about that?"

"No." We all speak at once, each looking incredibly guilty.

53

The sheriff levies us with a weighty stare. "No following anyone, ever. Leave the policing to those of us trained to do it. Understand?"

When we agree, he continues, addressing Karen. "I talked to the ladies in the school office, and there weren't any unusual sign-ins on campus the day of auditions. No one reported seeing anyone who wasn't supposed to be on campus, either, but I'll keep an ear out." He steps closer. Slips a file from under his arm I hadn't even noticed he was carrying, thanks to his grim expression. "Also, I brought over a copy of the report from the mugging so you can have a look. Not much to go on, but I thought you might want it." Handing the file to Karen, he replaces his hat over his brown hair, streaked with gray. The shade reminds me of my mom, who used to tease us that we caused each of her silver hairs by stressing her out. Karen's got some new gray hairs too. Maybe Mom wasn't wrong. Seeing as how we've put Karen through her paces since we moved in with her last fall.

Karen opens the file and leafs through the pages. I edge closer to get a look, but she moves from sheet to sheet faster than I can read or process what I'm seeing.

Taryn closes the door and approaches, skirting around the sheriff to look.

Pausing on one page covered in the sheriff's hasty scrawl, Karen looks up at him. I scan the page, seeing something about a maroon or burgundy car. My eyes widen.

"Sheriff? This report from a witness, how credible do you think it was?" Closing the file, Karen taps its edge on the side of her leg.

Lamb nods "I wouldn't discount it. It's from a lady down the street. A professor at the community college."

Then it's true. Coincidences don't exist. The mugging and

CuteAshleeXOXOXO are connected. The professor down the street? She saw the car that streaked away after my phone was stolen when I was attacked behind the diner. It was a burgundy car, she said. And the license plate? It started with 7L.

Chapter 7

Day 265, Tuesday

Leaden, steel-gray clouds enclose the sky like a mantle, and the wind's bite is sharp. Withered brown leaves blow across the windshield as Noah pulls his car into the library parking lot. We sprint from the beater, bursting inside and shoving the door shut behind us. It is gelid outside, and the car's sputtering heater was not cutting it. In spite of Sheriff Lamb's warning to keep our noses out of his investigation, we've been cruising around town looking for the maroon car. It's easy to slip away when Esau and Taryn and the rest of our friends are so focused on the play.

The cast list went up yesterday, and today is their first meeting with the full cast and crew. Who knows how long they'll be there reading through the show and talking about first steps. I kind of wish I was there. There's a part of me that misses being on the crew like I was last semester. It was nice to feel part of something. Plus, joining the drama club as Megan allowed me to make kick-butt friends.

But the larger part of me is so focused on finding out about *CuteAshlee* that I don't have the mental space to devote to drama this time around. The last thing I want is to be in the way while Esau and Taryn try to pull together their magnum opus. It's Esau's last show before he graduates and goes off to college, and it's eating at Taryn. She won't admit it, but she's going to miss him like crazy.

Part of me wonders if they'll survive dating long distance while she's still in high school. Most couples who try don't make it, do they? Esau is clearly crazy in love with my sister, but he's so one-track minded that I could see him getting sucked into classes and work at college and forgetting to put the time in with Taryn. Which would piss her off.

Shaking my head, I force myself back to the here and now. After an hour of trawling town, we came to the library to look through the newspaper archives. Noah is pawing through the racks of folded newspapers, antsy to find an unsolved crime that occurred in Hacienda to dig into. His true crime loving brain needs something to puzzle over that is far removed from the real-life story we're living through.

My head falls back as I surrender my weight to the wall. I'm looking forward to helping Noah since it'll be completely and one hundred percent unrelated to the crap heap that is my life. Besides being an effective distraction, maybe we'll be able to help in some small way. Who knows, but Noah thinks it's worth a shot. Noah is so gentle, considerate and helpful. Truly empathetic. He catches me looking at him and stands a little straighter.

I sigh as Noah assembles a pile of newsprint. "You ready?" He leads through the shelves and stacks to our usual table in the middle of the A-framed space. The stack of papers slides across the table's surface when he sets it down. I run my fingers over the headlines, wondering where to start looking.

"I need a snack. You want anything?" Noah sees my head shake and walks toward the vending machines.

I sit back in my chair and survey the library. From this

table, we can see the front and back doors, the information desk, and out the building's large windows. Justin is stationed in a chair by the front door, flipping through a cooking magazine he picked up somewhere.

Yep, I have a shadow again. Only this time he's not in stealth mode. It's much better this way. I honestly thought he'd put a stop to Noah's and my tours around town, but he hasn't said anything. Either he hasn't realized why we're cruising Hacienda's streets, which is unlikely, or he's okay with it since he's right behind us for every mile.

A gleeful laugh draws my attention to where a toddler is pulling books off the shelf in the children's lit area. The tiny cherub's mom is trying to wrangle two other kids, throwing up her hands when she sees what her toddler is up to. The librarian is shelving books in the history section. Someone left a copy of yesterday's newspaper on the next table, open to the front page. I can't read it from my chair, but I don't need to. The front page story is still fresh in my mind, thanks to Karen's habit of reading the paper at breakfast.

Journalist Receives Another Copycat Message

I don't know why they're calling the message-sender a copycat, because no murders of twin parents have occurred in this entire state since the FBI neutralized Albert Baugh last October. It's been three months, and twin families up and down the state are breathing easier.

Still, the messages are creepy. If *CuteAshleeXOXOXO* is behind them, why don't they send them directly to me via the app? If it isn't *CuteAshlee*, who is it? And why are they mimicking a dead serial killer? If the messages aren't for me, who are they for? The police don't think the notes are directed at them, but they don't know for sure.

All Sheriff Lamb has on the sender is questions. The

message Viv's mom got three days ago is no exception.

No one understands your disturbed mind the way I do.

The worst part is that something about it is familiar, but I can't put my finger on what. Taryn said it's probably because the phrase is overused in romantic books and movies everywhere, but I don't think that's it.

Sliding my phone out of my pocket, I open my social app. Tap on the messages. *CuteAshlee* hasn't messaged again since auditions last week. My free hand grazes over the silver bangle on my wrist, knowing that it sends a signal to a corresponding app on Justin's phone every couple of minutes. If *CuteAshlee* wanted to scare me, they succeeded. I've been on edge all week, wondering if or when they would make a move against Taryn. So far, nothing.

Maybe their *only* goal was to scare us. If so, mission accomplished.

My finger hovers over the messages between me and the Gemini Killer. Yes, I still have them, even though I haven't read them since before the trial. My therapist encouraged me to delete them when I'm ready. I can't do it.

I click. Scroll through without really reading. The amount of stuff I told Albert Baugh makes me squirm. Private, deeply embarrassing secrets. Revealing truths. Worries, fears, the feelings of inadequacy that were my constant companion thanks to my parents fawning over my louder and more assertive sister.

I meant all of it, and he used my emotions to hurt my entire family.

My eyes snag on a familiar word, and I stop. There it is: *No one understands your mind the way I do.*

A message the Gemini Killer sent me months ago. It matches the murder note Viv's mom got, almost word for word. How?

It hits me then: the reason for the mugging. They wanted my phone so they could read all of the sordid details. A shudder rips through me. Yet another person is privy to my darkest and most private thoughts. Putting my forehead down over my folded arms, I hide my eyes against my forearm. Someone, please make it stop.

The pop of a chip bag being pried open makes me start.

"Sorry I scared you. There wasn't much in the vending machine, but I found a couple good snack options. You interested?" Noah slides into the chair across from me and pushes a wrapped cookie in my direction.

Thanking him, I unwrap it and try to eat it. But my stomach is buzzing with the realization about my phone. All I have to do to cut off *CuteAshlee 2.0* from access to Albert Baugh's messages is to delete them.

My finger hovers over the trash can button. It would be so easy. A single, quick press of my finger pad on the screen. But if I do it, I can't torture myself with the messages late at night when the guilt compresses my chest, making it difficult to breathe.

I can change my password. That should keep them out for a while. Karen is not going to be thrilled.

"Did you know that one summer in the 80s three teenage girls were killed by a fortune teller?"

"Huh?" I mumble, still focused on my phone.

"Yeah. One was killed by bees, one drowned when she crashed into the levee, and a third was buried alive."

I blink as I try to process what Noah has just said.

"I blindsided you again, haven't I? Sorry about that. It was just so strange I wanted to share it with you." Noah sucks his bottom lip into his mouth and bites it, a penitent look in his eyes.

"It's fine," I say quickly. "Don't worry about it. A fortune teller, huh? That is weird."

"Yeah. And then a fourth girl disappeared. Most people figured she'd run off to be with her boyfriend." His finger runs down the page, picking out details and reading out loud.

"I'm not surprised. It's always the boyfriend, right?"

The tips of Noah's ears go pink. He swallows. "Good thing we're not dating. Sheriff Lamb might look at me sideways."

"Yeah, good thing." I think I sounded pretty normal for a girl who just lied through my teeth. Our eyes meet as we both fall into a silence that feels pretty darn awkward.

I wish I knew how he felt. If he'd just give me a sign, I'd ask him out. But there's been nothing. And I'm not willing to blow up our friendship over a one-sided crush. Noah is too important to lose over a romantic rejection. Does it sting sitting across from him, walking to classes together, hanging out at his place, and not being able to be completely honest? Yeah, it does. But being rejected would be worse. So much worse. So I keep my mouth shut.

Justin appears at the end of our table, his hand on his gun holster. His eyes skim over me as he cases the entire library. "We need to go. Come on. Get your stuff. Noah, we'll see you soon I'm sure."

"...Okay. Is there something wrong?" Noah's palms land without a sound on the table top, bracing his upper body half out of his chair.

"Nothing to be concerned about. It's just time to go." The tight coil in Justin's muscles makes me start to shake. He's lying. Tiny tremors begin in my core and move outward until my fingers are trembling as I attempt to zip up my backpack and stand.

"You ready? Let's move." Justin's hand is still on his holster.

"I'd like to come, if it's okay. I can help." Noah stands fully, eyes locked on Justin. Chin lifted slightly.

I don't move, don't know if I can. The worried vibes Justin is giving off are freaking me out. I'd rather stay here in the library, where I'm safe. Where being overwhelmed by the words of thousands of authors woven into finely-spun stories is the worst thing I have to worry about.

"I need to get you home." Finally, Justin's eyes land on me and everything I see in them makes me want to barf. Care. Concern. Determination. Something is wrong.

Anger rises to combat the helplessness I've felt for so long. I am not helpless. I am not a child to be coddled and prodded. "I'm not leaving until you tell me what's going on." Mustering my best glare, I lob it at Justin.

"Not here. Come on." He pivots away from us.

"No." I don't move a muscle other than my mouth.

Noah rounds the table to my side. His pinky wraps around mine. He's got my back.

The muscles in Justin's throat tighten. "I'd like to get you home first, so Karen can be involved in this conversation."

"Give me an overview, then. I refuse to be controlled by fear. Not for one more day."

Justin inhales deeply, his eyes never stopping their patrol of the library. Briefly, his gaze locks on mine. Square jaw tight. "There's been another murder, in Arizona. We almost missed it because it wasn't flagged, but we caught it. Twin parents."

"A copycat." My lower lip threatens to tremble, but I bite into it savagely. I'm afraid if I look at Noah I'll see a curious gleam in his eyes, but when I force myself to peek all I see is sadness. How dare I think he'd be more interested in the copycat than the lives ended today? Shame on me. I wrap my pinky tighter around his.

Someone familiar with the Gemini Killer's sick MO murdered the parents of twins yesterday, probably for the attention. Someone saw Albert Baugh's name plastered all over the news and wanted that notoriety for themselves.

My shaking stops as my fists clench.

I'm not out. This isn't over. But this time, I'm not hiding. I'm going to stop it.

Chapter 8

Day 268, Friday

Taryn

Viv is fitting Marisa and some of the other cast members for their preliminary costumes in the hallway outside the costume closet. The gushing is audible where I'm standing, at center stage, removing some of the pieces of blocking tape Esau laid down at our last rehearsal.

When I asked him about trying the scene we're working on in a different way—okay, there might have been some unabashed, flirty nagging involved—he was willing, so I got here early to redo it.

Okay, honestly? Technically he didn't say it was okay. He just didn't say it wasn't okay, and I'm taking that as permission. If he hates it, I will personally fix the tape. But he won't hate it. My idea for the scene is going to kick it up a few notches. I can see it all clear as day in my head.

Strips of black tape make a satisfying squelch as they yield. It creates an oddly shaped blob that sticks to the seating platform when I toss it that way. Justin sits a few rows back, watching a group of the stage crew in a huddle in the corner. Fiona gives out work assignments while Dariel stands by, nodding and pretending he's co-leader of the crew. He feigns being affronted when Fiona gestures that he should be in the lighting booth, but grins and gets moving. She laughs.

My eyes swivel to my twin sister. Watching Audrey retreat into herself is the worst. I didn't know how much I was missing her until she appeared in front of me again, smiling in her favorite pair of loved Converse and a hoodie with wolf-eared anime characters on the front. But after weeks of coming out of her shell, being more open about what she wants, she's retreating again.

Right now, Audrey is tucked into one of the chairs, doing homework. Or she's supposed to be. Her eyes are glazed as she stares at the seat back in front of her. Problem is, when I bug her about what's bothering her, she refuses to say. Girl finally admits that she hates the vegan smoothies I've been making for us, but she won't tell me why she looks like a ghost half the time.

I crouch and plant a large blue tape X on the stage's worn-smooth boards.

The way she scans the headlines in Karen's paper every morning gives her away. Plus, Audrey's entire body tenses when a certain alert beeps on her phone. I stole it one day while she was in the bathroom and discovered that she's set up notifications for any news related to the Gemini Killer or the apparent copycat. That's when I realized what it was that's eviscerating Audrey from the inside out.

She's waiting for another murder. Absolutely sure there will be another. Positive that it will, in some way, be her fault. And yet, seven days have passed since the murder the media is saying was done by a Gemini Killer copycat. There hasn't been a single additional related incident.

Something twists painfully in my stomach. It feels like

we've gone back in time, only on this go around I believe my sister when she tells me that someone is taunting her. This time, we're more prepared. Instead of Justin trying to follow on the sly, he strolls along. It's a carefully-crafted facade. If danger presents itself, he'll snap into action.

I sigh, glancing over to where Karen is entering the theater with two steaming coffees. She may look at ease, but I recognize the tight line of her shoulders and the unceasing shift of her eyes as she evaluates the drama room. She looks almost as intense as when Esau tries to kiss me goodnight on our front porch after a date. I won't lie: it's a huge pain in the butt. I thought dating with a chaperone was a hundred years out of favor, but here I am—going on dates with my boyfriend and an FBI agent who files any and all PDA under "must express disapproval with a glare that threatens personal bodily harm."

Which is why I spend all of our drama club meetings flirting shamelessly with Esau. He'd call it arguing, but he loves it. He'll say something; I contradict it. He glares: I grin. He snakes a hand around my wrist to pull me backstage to argue; I turn it into an impromptu makeout session. We've only been busted by Miss Crabtree once.

WORTH. IT.

Because Esau and I both know our playful arguments aren't really about the blocking or the stage cues or the lighting.

The door swings open again and Noah and Esau come in, chatting as they walk. My boyfriend nods as Noah slides into the row of seats and plops down beside my sister. She jolts, giving the boys a tired smile. Audrey and Noah look so cute together, totally oblivious to the fact that they're totally in love. Esau made me promise not to meddle, or I would have gently and kindly shoved her into him weeks ago.

Speaking of the devil, he turns toward me and freezes, eyes

locked on the tape I'm in the middle of ripping off the stage floor. His gaze slides up to mine and watches as I finish peeling the tape off the wooden planks, grinning widely. *Oh yes, this is happening. What are you going to do about it?*

My boyfriend's nostrils flare. He stalks between the rows of chairs, entering the stage area on a prowl until he's way too close. And also way too far away. His huff is warm over my ear. "What are you doing to the tape I worked so hard on last week?"

"Nothing."

"Looks like something."

"Looks can be deceiving."

"I'm aware. Take you, for example."

My eyebrow wings upward. This I have to hear. "Me?"

Esau's eyes move over my shoulder. Probably making sure we don't have an audience. The man is a grump in public and a cinnamon roll in private. But if I ever told anyone that, he'd kill me. Not literally of course. It would probably involve tickling my sides with merciless fingers until I begged for mercy.

"You look like a beautiful, intelligent, sweet girl, but really you're an evil goddess sent to test me." I've had worse compliments. My grin widens.

"And do I? Test you?" Batting my lashes makes Esau's hands rise at his sides. Almost like he's going to touch me. One of the guys in the cast comes creeping out of the wings toward us, wearing what might be a dashing suit if it wasn't for the pins stuck around the pant hems making his movements tentative. "Ouch," he mutters, going still. "Esau?"

"Garrett?"

"Viv wanted me to ask you if this is what you had in mind. For Jack's London suit?"

"—It's fine."

67

"—Don't you think it could be flashier?"

Esau and I catch each other's gaze. His mouth twitches up at my toothy smile.

I mount my best argument that Garrett's costumes need to be bolder and more dichotomized, since he's playing a man who uses different personalities based on where he is and the company he is keeping. Esau listens indulgently, waiting until I'm finished to nod. Without taking his eyes off me, he answers Garret. "Have Viv see me at the end. We'll discuss it."

Garrett disappears behind the curtain.

Esau's hand wrapped around my bicep keeps me from skipping across the stage to tear up and reposition more blocking tape. "I'm not finished with you, Goddess."

"Unhand me you foul mortal, before I smite you. I am magical, you know."

His fingers glide down my arm to circle my wrist. "I haven't forgotten. There's no other explanation for all the arguments you win against me. But you won't win this one. I worked on that blocking for weeks. Put it back, Taryn. Please."

I frown at the firm underpinning of his tone. "I know you worked on it, and it was really good, but I think this will be better. Let me just finish this and I'll have them run through it. Once you see it, you're going to love it."

"I'm not budging on this."

I want to rise to the challenge. Call Marisa and the others from behind the curtain to have them play out my idea in a visual tableau that's sure to bring Esau around to my way of thinking. But involving the cast wouldn't be fair, to them or to Esau. So I bite my tongue.

"I'm putting the blocking tape back where it was." Esau stoops and tears a long line of blue from the floor. Moving to the next one, he does the same.

I can't bare just watching when I know my idea is good.

"Wait. Please. Let the cast walk through it. I just know it'll make the scene flow as they move across the stage. Maybe if they're in their costumes it'd be easier to see. Maybe we should…" I trail off.

There's that expression behind Esau's eyes again. A closed-off, blank look that terrifies me. At first, he only did it when I pushed him too far. And, okay, fair. But recently he's started doing it when he talks about being gone for college in the fall. Like he's picturing his future. Without me. It scares me, the way that far-off look makes me feel. Like Esau's going to leave. Which is dumb. I know he's leaving in the fall because going to film school is his dream. Directing is his dream.

But my dream is to be together, and every time he gets that closed look in his eyes, I can feel our future as a couple slipping farther away. Which is why I push him. Engage with him now. Argue with him now, about things that don't matter. Because if he's arguing with me, I know he's all, completely, one hundred percent here. With me.

"I let you talk me through your vision for the scene. Twice. I listened to all of your reasons. I prefer it the other way."

"I think that's a mistake." I hate the edge in my voice, but I don't stop.

"Not your call to make." Esau rips up another line of blue. "Where'd you put the tape?"

Grimacing, I march across the stage and hold up an empty roll of tape.

Straightening, Esau shoots me a hot look. Not a hot, let's-make-out look. More of a keep-pushing-and-we'll-really-be-fighting look. Does it stop me? Someone else be the judge.

I can feel eyes on my back, but I don't look over my

shoulder to see how many of the cast are watching our little squabble.

Fiona strides toward where I'm standing. Mouth set in a firm line. She's totally team Esau, so I know what she'll say before she even opens her mouth. "I used up the tape," I say in a sing-song voice, hoping to lighten the mood. "There isn't any more. Guess we'll have to put my tape back and make do."

Black eyebrow slashing up, Esau's attention shifts up to Dariel in the sound booth. "Toss me a roll of tape, yeah?"

Dariel tosses a black roll that my boyfriend catches in one hand. Traitor.

Fiona pauses at the edge of the stage, eyes shifting between Esau and me. I wave her off, mouthing *we're fine*. Eyes narrowed, she studies me for a second, looks to Esau, and sighs. She retreats up the stairs to the booth.

"I hate it when Mom and Dad fight. Ouch." Dariel yelps when Fiona playfully smacks him upside the head.

I don't move as Esau continues replacing my tape marks with new old ones.

"Next year," he speaks lowly while he works, "I'll be gone, and you can direct whatever play you want. However you want. But now, it's my time. Don't fight me on this." *Please.* He doesn't say it, but I can see the plea in his eyes when he looks up at me from a crouch.

"Hey, you guys want anything from the gas station? Guys? Taryn!"

I whip around, pulling my pout away from Esau long enough to meet my twin's eyes. "What?"

Audrey points between herself and Noah. "We're going across the street. Can I bring you anything?"

"I'm fine. Go ahead." I turn to Esau.

"Go with them. Take a break." He doesn't even look up.

70

I retreat a step, cheeks flushing. My boyfriend wants me to leave. He wants to work alone. I've finally pushed him over the edge where he realizes that he doesn't need me, so he's pulling away. I have no way of knowing if it's a conscious choice he's making, or some deeply seated self-preservation instinct, but it feels like a stab to the heart. I stare at him, a jumble of emotions I can't hope to parse. How do I get him to stay present with me? There has to be a way. "So you can do everything without me? I don't think so, you big, uncompromising—"

Esau cuts me off with a short kiss. There's no anger behind it. Only a sweet press of his warm mouth against mine. And then he's easing back, deep brown eyes tuned to mine.

I splutter, casting around to regain my ire. "You can't just stop every argument like that. It's cheating."

The guy shrugs, expression unreadable. Shifting closer, he whispers. "Don't have many tricks that work on a goddess, but kissing does."

"But it's cheating."

"Said that already. But seriously. Take the break. We'll be here when you get back."

Still unsure of what to do, I ask, "How about I help you put the blocking marks back, and then we both go?"

His lips twitch, pleased. My insides warm at that smile.

The thing about Esau and me is, once we stop bickering about our differing ideas for the play, we come up with some pretty kick-ass stuff.

I turn to my sister and Noah, whose eyes are on her face. His cheeks are tinged pink, but Audrey doesn't seem to notice. It's super cute. Maybe I should decline so they can go alone. No, now that I've thought about it, one of those frappés Karen calls sugar milk sounds pretty good. "Give us ten minutes, then we'll all go. Okay?"

Audrey flashes a thumbs up.

The roll of tape squeaks pitifully as Esau and I tear into it, working as a team to adhere black Xs all over the stage.

White clouds hang in the icy blue sky like pendant lights suspended from an invisible ceiling. Forget a chilled coffee. I'm getting a mocha latte with marshmallows. Icy fingers from a winter wind yank at my hair, slapping my face with the wispy ends of my ponytail. Esau must see my shiver, because he puts an arm around my shoulders and tucks me into his side. He's so warm, I snuggle closer.

My inclination is to charge across the parking lot after Audrey and Noah, but Esau's pace is slow, steady. I wouldn't leave my spot under his arm for almost anything. Even a caramel frappe. The caffeine shot is exactly what I need to help Esau finish blocking the scenes in Act 1. After the tape incident, we're both feeling a little more compromising, if our conversation about the following scene was any indication. Esau asked for my thoughts, listened, and actually incorporated some of it into his plans. Be still my beating heart.

I giggle, which brings Esau's attention to my face. "What?"

"Just picturing you giving in when I finally find your ticklish spot." My fingers tighten on his waist in warning.

"Not gonna happen."

"Yeah, I know. You're *not ticklish*."

Footfalls pound as someone, no, two someones jog up to where we are at the curb, waiting for the signal light to turn green. Fiona catches my eye. "I'm glad you two finally worked out your blocking issues. For a second there I thought it would come to fisticuffs."

72

"Fisticuffs?"

"I've been surrounded by people using fun, old words all afternoon. It seemed like it worked." She shrugs, unconcerned.

"It does." Esau meets her gaze over my head.

"My thanks, Lord Director. Oh! I hope they have that new flavor of Pringles I've been wanting to try." She starts jogging in place, waiting on the light to change.

"Nobody wants hot honey Pringles." Dariel stands beside her, mouth cocked, hands deep in his pockets.

Another shiver runs through my body. It is freezing out.

"I thought it might come to tickling." Esau whispers in my ear, dipping a finger into my armpit through my sweater.

I squeal, trying to pull away, but his firm grip on my opposite wrist stops me. "No tickle fights in public," I hiss.

Esau's grin grows. "Why? Can't have people seeing your weakness?"

"You were right. I think your blocking will be dynamic and interesting to watch."

"What—?"

His grip on my wrist loosens, and I escape. Esau's laugh follows as I dance over to where Marisa is regaling Audrey with her character's motivation in the opening scene of the play. Esau tapped her to play Gwendolyn, which she is absolutely going to nail. She's a lot more confident since her turn in last semester's play. Noah is on Audrey's other side, chatting with Dariel about a history assignment.

Audrey sneaks a peek at Noah, biting the inside of her cheek. They could be so cute together. I wish one of them would man up and make a move already. I look over my shoulder at Esau, who shakes his head. He's made me swear on my favorite dress that I won't interfere.

Killjoy.

The crosswalk light turns from Don't Walk, to Walk and I trip into the street. My momentum carries me a step before my toe catches a crack in the pavement. I go sprawling. Tiny stones cut into my knees when I push up onto them. My palms scrape under my weight. I swivel around to see Audrey rushing closer, mouth widening.

"Taryn!"

A car's engine roars as the vehicle lunges. It's burgundy or maroon.

Wait. Is that the same one… The driver—oh, no—a balaclava. My mouth drops open in shock as the car barrels toward where I'm bleeding onto the pavement.

I never could understand why animals wouldn't just get out of the way when they met cars on the road, but now.

Move, legs. MOVE!

My eyes close as a memory eviscerates my thoughts. *A figure looming toward me. The gleam of a metal blade. Sharp, coursing pain as blood flows down the side of my face.*

Forcing my eyes open, I rip my feet off the ground. Tripping in panic, my foot flies out from under me. Freaking gravity slams me down onto the black, tarry asphalt.

Someone is screaming.

Tires screech. Burning rubber makes my eyes water. I scramble to stand up, but my ankle twists painfully. My heart climbs my throat to abandon ship as I go back down.

Someone hooks their hands under my arms, lifting. Shoving. A screech tears from my throat as I go flying. Land hard on my side. My palms throb, pierced and torn. Blood from where I bit the inside of my cheek taints my mouth.

Metal meets flesh in a sickening smack.

A gun fires.

Glass shatters.

More yelling, laced with agony.

The car's engine groans as it speeds past, its wind buffeting my aching body.

I blink once. Twice. A hundred times. My vision clears.

Noah is holding Audrey back from the street, but she's fighting with everything she's got. Finally, after a long second, she goes limp. Buries her face in the front of his jacket. She's okay. My sister is okay.

Marisa and Viv are staring in horror from the opposite curb. Fiona pushes past, crouching beside me. "Are you okay? Are you hurt anywhere? You're bleeding."

Her rapid-fire questions snap me out of my panic. "I'm okay. I'm okay."

"They're getting away." Noah yells, pointing down the street.

A few feet away, Justin yells into his phone about a car trying to run over one of the Thomas twins. Backup requested. Corner of Main and 7th street.

"Here. Let's get you up." Fiona pulls me up by my armpits and doesn't let go when I wince at the pain in my ankle.

Everything goes quiet.

Fiona's grip shakes out a memory. More of an impression, really. Someone pushed me away from the car. Lightning hits my brain and I spin, heedless of the knives slicing along my calf. My focus hones in on my sister, who clutches at Noah.

"Is he okay?" Audrey's mumble is barely audible through his arms, but she might as well have a megaphone over my ear, the way that simple question reverberates through every fiber of my body.

Noah's chin rests on top of her head as he holds her tightly. "I don't know."

Esau. Where is—? No.

My beautiful grump of a boyfriend is lying in the street, not moving. His eyes are pinched shut. One arm is pinned underneath him. Too high. It has to be broken.

With a cry, I fly toward him, flinging myself down beside him. My hand slides along his temple into vines of ebony hair. "Esau, baby, are you... Can you talk? Look at me?"

A stuttering sigh, and Esau's beautiful brown eyes open, focus on my face. He tries to move, but winces. A groan escapes his parted mouth.

Justin hunches, tapping Esau's shoulder. "Stay put until the ambulance arrives, all right?" Esau blinks up at him. Nods.

Justin looks him over carefully without making contact with any of Esau's injuries. One arm is clutched against his chest, and the whole left side of one leg is torn and bloody.

My eyes want to clamp shut, but I muscle them open. Shards of glass litter the asphalt. Something hot drips down my throat, and I swipe it off. The back of my hand comes away red. Silent, angry tears track down my cheeks when I look at my boyfriend. The damage done to his body in a split second. A split second after he risked everything by pushing me. Out of the way. Of a car.

Flopping down beside him, I take his free hand in mine. My teeth clench tight. Someone is going to pay for this.

Done talking to Audrey, Justin stands between us, watching as a deputy's car pulls up to the scene. His gaze swings to me. "Karen is on her way. Everyone is going to be okay." He sighs, dragging a hand over his jaw. "It could have been a lot worse."

He's wrong. I don't know if I'm going to be okay. Not after this.

Because deep down in the darkest parts of me, I know. That driver wasn't simply trying to scare us. They were attempting to end our lives like unlucky animals caught in the middle of the street. That maniac was gunning for us. And my beautiful, insightful, cranky boyfriend almost lost his life saving mine.

Everyone I care about might be okay if okay means not dead, but no one I care about is safe.

Chapter 9

Day 270, Sunday

Audrey

One of the line cooks slides the plates onto the sill between the kitchen and dining area. "Eggs over easy, bacon, sourdough."

I pick them up with nervous hands. It's my first shift at the diner and I am determined not to drop anything. And after the hit and run two days ago, I'm grateful for the distraction working will provide. My eyes skirt to where Justin is sitting at a table near the back, eating a burger. My protection for today.

"You're doing great," Viv says as she breezes past, taking a tray full of dirty plates and cups to the sink. She got me this job. One of the waitresses left without notice, leaving the diner staff scrambling. Viv called me, and I hot-footed it over as soon as I could throw on the requisite dark jeans and a black tee. Before the manager could even glance at the résumés on his desk, I was in his doorway, looking hopeful. He caved.

When I promised not to be any trouble, he had to remind me that my sister almost got run over by a serial killer copycat less than forty-eight hours ago. He did not find it helpful when I told him we weren't sure who was behind the wheel.

The manager put Viv in charge of my training, and she

walked me through it with way too many *Star Wars* references. Erin must have made her watch the original trilogy again.

I tighten my grip on the plates as I move through the diner. This happened so fast, it didn't give Karen time to overthink it. Working a few hours a week provides a way to get out of the house. Don't get me wrong, Karen and Justin don't have my sister and me on house arrest—despite the many threats to the contrary.

In the day and a half since the attack, they haven't let us go anywhere. It's easier to protect us at home, where there are fewer variables. I get that, but we're already not allowed to step a toe out of the house without one of them chaperoning. I needed this today.

Taryn has made it very clear that the FBI's constant presence is ruining her time with Esau, who she visited at his uncle and aunt's house since he couldn't do his normal Saturday farm chores with a broken arm. There was some moaning about not being able to ride his tractor, which I chose to take literally. Because yuck.

I have to admit, seeing Esau hopped up on painkillers after he got home from the hospital was both guilt-inducing and entertaining. The stupid-wide grin he kept aiming at Taryn was adorable. He kept trying to pull her into his lap, despite an audience made up of Fiona, Dariel, Marisa, Viv, and me. The normally anti-PDA dude was downright handsy. I almost managed not to laugh.

Taryn was so mortified she chased us out and slammed the door.

"Excuse me, I ordered a Dr. Pepper. This is Coke."

"Oh, sorry." Blushing, I swap it for the right one and deliver it with a sincere apology.

After a couple of hours, I can completely understand what

Viv says when she calls waitressing "organized anarchy". When the diner is full, which it has been all afternoon, there is no time to stop.

Thankfully, Viv is here to help out whenever I have questions. "Check table three," she whispers as she buzzes up to the counter.

When I look over at table three, it's packed. I grin as I greet the new customers.

Fiona crows from between Marisa and Dariel. "Now I have two friend servants at the diner. Excellent."

"Let's order a plate of nachos as an appetizer." Marisa snatches a menu and flips it open. "The only question is, chicken or ground beef? Can we do both?"

I shake my head. I have no idea.

"It says it's an extra buck," Dariel flicks his menu, "but I'm game. Nachos sound gooooood." The guy next to him gives him a fist bump.

Taryn smiles nervously when I meet her eyes. Her chin and arm are mostly healed from the hit and run. She's back to her usual, beautiful self. I barely even notice the scar on her cheek anymore. Hopefully she doesn't let it bother her either. My head tilts at the empty space beside her. "Where's Esau? Is everything okay?"

My sister shrugs, avoiding my eyes. Okay... We'll have to talk about that later.

From the hallway, the manager cycles a hand in a wrap-it-up gesture.

"I'm glad you guys are here. Do you need a minute, or are you ready to order?"

After I put in my friends' order, Viv comes over. "Why don't you get them their food and then take your break? I'll take mine after."

I glance around the diner. Now seems like a good time for a break. "You got it."

Winking, she's off again.

Sliding into the booth beside Taryn, I steal one of her fries and dip it in a deliciously huge amount of ketchup. "Wow, that hits the spot."

"Get your own," she says with a laugh. Honestly, the piles of fries they dish out here are so huge she never finishes them. Which is how I know she doesn't really mind me stealing one or five.

"Try it with some of this." Fiona pulls a spice shaker out of her purse. Its contents are a green powder mixed with what looks like sesame seeds. "It's my newest snack-topping obsession. Za'atar. It's amazing on popcorn, so why not fries?"

"Okay…" Taryn sits still while Fiona sprinkles a little of the green stuff on a few of her fries. She tries one. Nods politely.

Dariel cracks up laughing. "That good huh?"

Fiona elbows him. "It's delicious."

"She hates it. Look at her face."

"No I don't. It's good. I like it." Taryn pops another fry into her mouth, chews like she's in an eating contest, and swallows. Then she chases it down with a giant gulp of her drink.

Fiona's eyes narrow. "You guys just don't appreciate a varied palate. More for me." She takes Taryn's tainted fries and plunks them down on her plate, blocking Dariel when he tries to steal one.

"No, no, no. Angel was Buffy's best boyfriend. Spike was gross." Marisa's voice carries through the diner to where I'm standing at the counter, delivering a breakfast platter. From what I can hear, the entire table is in the middle of a heated argument about the classic vampire slayer show.

Esau comes in, stomping his work boots on the mat at the front door. He looks… less than pleased as he sweeps up and pins Taryn with a sharp look.

"Care to explain this?" He holds out his phone with his free hand, his casted arm resting on the table top with a plunk.

"No." Leaning away from the lit-up screen, Taryn takes a sip of her soda.

"Uh, I have to go to the bathroom." Marisa bolts out of her seat. Fiona glances at Esau, then follows, tugging Dariel along with her.

Once they're gone, Esau's attention shifts to me. Holding the phone up so I can read it, he waits.

"You asked if she wanted to go for a drive tonight, and she said… No? Taryn, you told him you had to clean your room? Seriously?"

"I do need to clean my room." Her answer couldn't sound prissier.

"On Saturday night?"

"It's dirty." She crosses her arms, clearly hoping to end this conversation.

"You're avoiding me. Why?" It's so quiet I'm surprised anyone can hear Esau's question over the singing of two small kids who are treating the next booth over like their own personal stage.

My sister squirms in her seat, avoiding his eyes. "I-I just. Arguing with you the other day, it got me thinking. If I had just done what you suggested and gone across the street, you wouldn't have been with me, and you wouldn't have been hit by a car. Since we started dating, you've been held hostage, stabbed, and almost run over. That's a lot."

Esau slumps down onto his knees, leaning past me to cup Taryn's cheek. "I'm fine."

Taryn stares pointedly at the cast that swallows his entire forearm.

I consider ducking out under the table, but the floor looks like a sticky, disgusting mess. I make myself very interested in the edge of the table where the top meets the plastic trim.

Esau's nostrils flare. "Taryn. None of that was your fault. Will arguing about it make you feel better?"

"Maybe. But it won't be the same." A smile flares across my sister's face before she smothers it.

Leaning back, Esau runs a hand through his hair. Taking the chance, I scoot out of the booth so he can slide in next to my sister.

"Is it safe to come back yet?" Dariel calls from where the three of them are standing in front of the drinking fountain. Taryn nods, and Fiona, Dariel, Marisa, and I pile back into the booth from the opposite end.

Esau's eyes skim over them before sliding back to Taryn. "Anyone got a rubber band?"

Fiona takes a hair tie off her wrist and hands it to him. It snaps loudly around his skin. Then he levels a look at Taryn that is not diner appropriate. "You drive me insane. I thought you finally realized you hated me."

A small squeak escapes Taryn's mouth before she wraps her arms around her boyfriend. I don't tell them that her hair is in my orange soda.

"I absolutely do not hate you. Opposite of hate you. Remember that thing we talked about the other day? Maybe you should bring it up later." Taryn pulls back enough to give Esau a quick peck on the lips.

Viv sighs. She stands right behind them, watching. "Aww,

so cute. Audrey, your break's over. My turn."

She wiggles past me next to Marisa, leaving the space on the end for Taryn and Esau, who—wait. Where did they go? I don't want to catch them making out (once was enough), but I do need to ask her to do tonight's dinner prep. It was my turn, but Justin and I are both here at the diner. Maybe they went down the back hall? Straightening my apron, I head that way.

Nope, no Taryn or Esau. Instead, Justin is at the other end of the dimly-lit corridor past the bathrooms.

He's pacing. Phone pressed to one ear, muttering. It sounds like he's arguing with whoever is on the other end.

"What's up?" I whisper, leaning back against the wall to keep out of the way of his restless shifting.

Justin pauses, listening with a grimace. He hangs up and drops the phone into his sport coat. Turning toward me, he does a thorough examination. The calculated feel of it makes me want to squirm. "Did something happen?"

Justin's mouth flattens. "I had a disagreement with Agent Biel. Don't worry about it."

Oh boy. He's calling Karen *Agent Biel* now. That doesn't sound good. Not good at all. Did something bad happen with their wedding planning? Or worse? "Usually when one of you tells me not to worry, that means I should be worried. What is it?"

He takes a long second to rest a hand against the wall. Taps the shiny red paint with his fingers. "We'll talk about it later. After your shift, maybe. Karen and I are a team, and if she's not ready to tell you something, I'm going to respect that. Understand?"

That's just great. Now I have to wait for hours for more bad news.

Chapter 10

Hours Later

By the time I clock out and Justin drives us home, I feel like I'm about to pop. What was that whispered phone argument about? So many things could have happened today. Maybe another ominous note in the newspaper. Another sighting of the maroon car. Oh no. Another murder? That has to be it. Someone else is dead. I try to stop from thinking *because of me*, and almost succeed.

Tearing into the old house, I yell up the stairs for Taryn to come down and meet us in the kitchen.

Karen is there, stirring her millionth cup of coffee. She looks up when I rush in, eyes flicking from my face to her partner's and back. "Where's the fire?"

I stop right in front of her. "What were the two of you arguing about on the phone earlier?"

Karen shoots a look at Justin over her mug.

He shrugs. "She caught me. Didn't want to lie to her."

Outside, it's completely dark. The days are short and the sun vanishes early. We're hidden in night's ebony blanket. Just like Karen and Justin are still keeping Taryn and me in the dark when it comes to news about the newspaper messages, and their investigation into *CuteAshleeXOXOXO*. All of it. It ends tonight.

"He didn't tell me anything. He said we'd talk about it later."

"And we will. Don't worry about it." Karen turns away. I can't help but wonder if it's to hide the worry I saw flash behind her eyes. My throat tightens.

"You know you're going to tell us eventually, so just get it over with. What are we supposed to not worry about now?" Taryn puts in from the doorway.

Karen cuts a glance to Justin before sliding her attention to my twin and me. "When I keep information from you, it's because I think you're better off not knowing. I'm trying to protect you. Both of you. And this is one of those times." The finality in her tone bounces off the tile backsplash.

I hate it. I do not want to be kept in the dark anymore.

Taryn looks like she agrees, because she opens her mouth to argue. Karen holds up a hand, the snapping gesture stopping her, barely.

"I get that," I say, "but we're almost adults. I want to know. And if you don't tell me, Noah will, once he finds out. Which he will. He can be really resourceful." I stand up straighter, mentally thanking Noah for being so nosy sometimes.

Taryn's hands land on her hips. "Yeah, he'll tell us if you won't."

Justin and Karen look at each other, having a silent conversation. It's a little intense for a second. Like she's winning whatever argument they're having. Justin lifts his chin toward us. Karen relents.

Setting her mug down with a clink, Karen locks eyes with me. "I got a request from John Baugh's lawyer today. Mr. Baugh has asked to meet with you. My first inclination is that nothing good could come from it, but Justin seems to think it might be beneficial for you. Help you close this chapter and move forward, if you will."

I'm stunned. Blink a couple of times to give my brain time to absorb what she's said. Pick up an abandoned glass of water off the counter and glug down some of its contents. "Mr. Baugh wants to talk to me? What about?"

Karen shakes her head. "I have no idea. The request wasn't specific, just that he would like to see you, if you'd be willing."

"In the prison. He wants her to go to the prison." Taryn marches over to stand next to me. Her warm, steady hand brushes mine. "If she gets to go, I want to go too."

Justin frowns. "The request wasn't for both of you, just Audrey."

"That won't stop me. I make the magic happen, remember?"

"It's a process, getting approved to visit an inmate. And if Mr. Baugh doesn't want to see you, there's nothing we can do to make him." Karen lays it out in a logical, cool voice. It makes sense to me even though I have no idea why Mr. Baugh would want to see me without Taryn. The only thing I can think of is that he wants to apologize, but if that's true, why wouldn't he want to see us both? He hurt both of us. Not just me. And Esau and Noah too.

"Has he requested to see anyone else?" Surely he has. That's the only reason it would make sense.

Karen shakes her head. Takes another drink of her coffee. "Not as far as I know. Audrey, you do not have to go. We can tell him you're not interested. He can rot where you never have to see him again. I can only imagine what it would be like for you."

I can't stop the full-body flinch that goes through me. Until this second, I hadn't thought about actually seeing Mr. Baugh again. Sitting across from him and listening to him justify why he helped his brother. Even if he does apologize, do I want to hear it?

"See, I knew this was a terrible idea. Next time I tell you to keep it to yourself, will you listen?" Justin nods in answer to his fiancée's question, shooting me a worried look.

"Good. Nobody sees Mr. Baugh. Good plan." Taryn takes my hand. "Come on. Let's go watch something." She pulls at my arm, but I don't budge. I'm still processing, thinking it through.

All three of them stare at me in surprise when I speak. "I want to do it. I want to visit Mr. Baugh in prison. Hear what he has to say."

There is an immediate and intense reaction. Karen starts arguing that it's a terrible idea. Taryn emphasizes how it'll traumatize me to visit that place without her as backup. To see that man's face again. How I've been making good progress with healing and how going there will set me back.

Justin is the only one who isn't yelling. Gently, he puts a hand on Karen's shoulder. Gives a little squeeze.

I tune out the arguments Taryn's warnings about how I need her with me if I go through with this. She's wrong. I can handle this.

Maybe agreeing to see Mr. Baugh will turn out to be a horrendous mistake.

Maybe it won't.

Either way, it's something I can work through with my therapist.

I hold up my hands until both my sister and my guardian fall silent. "I've made up my mind. I'm going."

Chapter 11

Day 275, Friday

Photos of all of the murder notes that have been sent to the local newspaper flicker before my eyes. I saved them to my phone. One by one the macabre messages pass over the screen as I attempt to put the pieces together in a way that makes sense. It feels like I'm missing a single piece that will clarify the bigger picture, but I can't find it. "There has to be a connection, but I can't figure it out. What is it?"

Noah glances at me from the driver seat before his eyes resume scanning the street ahead. He's such a cautious driver, especially after the hit and run. The one and only time Noah drove my sister and me somewhere, Taryn teased him for driving like an old person. He was entirely unruffled. "That sounded like a rhetorical question."

Truthfully? Noah's unerring respect of the rules of the road are one of my favorite things about him. Well, not just with driving. He's so good. So careful with the people around him. He makes me feel cared for and safe. Now if only he'd pull over, shut off the car, and profess his undying love. Then we'd be getting somewhere.

A girl can dream.

"Read them to me again?"

Pay attention. I'm gonna show you what bloody havoc I can wreak.
No one understands your disturbed mind the way I do.
You ruined my life. Now I'm going to ruin yours.

Viv's mom got a new note that was published in the newspaper yesterday. I can't stop thinking about it.

With the first note, it sounded like a bid for attention. Someone with a twisted mind who saw all of the press the Gemini Killer got and decided they wanted the spotlight. The second and third notes feel more specific. More personal. It's almost as if the composer is writing to a single person. Someone they hate. The letters used in the latest collage look like they were ripped out instead of cut. Jagged edges pasted at uneven intervals so the letters stagger across the page. Disquiet settles low in my belly when I look at the notes. Rage emanates like steam off the latest one.

Wait.

I read all three of the notes again. Something clicks in my brain.

The first message could have been directed at the press. It makes sense. *Pay attention.* It feels showy and loud. It definitely got everyone's attention.

The second note was yanked from my conversations with the Gemini Killer, so that one must be for me. I swallow at the tightness in my throat. The sender read all of those private messages. They've seen deeper into my head than just about anyone. I haven't even let Taryn read the messages, even when she asked. "I want to understand you better," she'd said. I denied her. We're making such great progress as sisters, I don't want to blow it all to hell by letting her see the ugliness in my head.

But the third note. I don't know. Grief can do all kinds of weird things.

90

I suck in a breath. What if a surviving family member of one of the GK's victims is the one who's trying to hurt Taryn and me? It would make sense. Lots of parents, people's moms and dads, were murdered by a man with ties to my family. Ties I'm working hard to sever. It's one of the reasons I'm determined to talk to a reporter at some point.

The media knew I'd been chatting with the Gemini Killer during his killing spree, and during the trial, they blasted that fact on repeat. It was clear that some of them blamed me. I saw the clickbait headlines that proved it. Someone lost in the depths of their grief might buy into that and decide I needed to pay for my part in the bloody mess. My fists curl in my lap.

It's only five, but the sun is already descending toward the horizon. Noah makes a left turn, and the glow hits me square in the eyes. I squeeze my eyes shut against it.

We're both quiet. K-pop plays in a low hum from the speaker in Noah's phone where it's propped in the center cup holder. We were supposed to go home after the library, but neither of us were feeling it. Instead, we're cruising through town, chatting when we need to and settling into the relaxed ease of a friendly hush.

Once, Taryn tried to describe to me how driving around with Esau feels. It was like being wrapped in a warm blanket and knowing deep in your bones that you're where you're supposed to be. As soon as she said it, I knew what she meant. When I'm with Noah, it feels right. Like we were supposed to meet, somehow. Like he was meant to be part of my healing process, after the trauma my sister and I went through. Are still working through.

It's taken me until now to look that feeling full in the face. I spent the first few months in this town fighting the pull I felt toward Noah with everything I had. I was in witness protection. I couldn't tell him anything. Who I was. Why I moved here. The mounting shadows in my past.

But once the trial was underway, once I dropped my shield and let him in, there it was. That comforting sense of safety. Of stability. The care he always took with me. I will never forget listening to the tape of the night Noah showed up on the roof to check on Megan, not knowing who he was really talking to. How I wished it had been me on the other side of that window pane instead of my sister. Our conversation might have gone so differently.

I had to make sure you were okay. I need you to be okay. I couldn't sleep, thinking about how scared you might be.

If it had been me listening to those words from Noah, I would have wanted to kiss him. Might have actually done it. If it had been me.

Biting my lips, I look over at his beautiful profile. His brown skin glows in the aurelian sunset. Long, slim fingers laze over the top of the steering wheel, moving it to his whims. I release a sigh. "I have a crazy idea. If I tell you about it, will you help me?"

Noah gives me an easy smile that makes my stomach dip. "You know I will. You don't even have to ask."

Something inside me slots into place. I welcome the warm wave that sloshes over me. "Pull over. Please?"

"That's such a big favor. I don't know if I can do it." He glides the car onto the shoulder of the two-lane road. Almond orchards line the street as far as the eye can see. There's no one else on this stretch of pavement. It's peaceful. Perfect.

Well, as long as I ignore Justin parking his car behind Noah's and lifting his cell to his ear. He's been pretty flexible about us cruising town, so I'm pretty sure he'll stay put as long as we aren't in any danger.

Noah kills the engine and sits back, hands dropping to rest in his lap. Head lounging against the rest, he rolls his gaze over at me. Fading light hits one side of his face, leaving the other shaded in navy and indigo. "Why'd you want to stop? Did you think of something?"

"No. I want to do something, and I don't want to wait anymore."

The inner corners of his brows flick upward in question. He pushes ebony curls off his forehead with a languorous sweep.

Boldness overtakes me. Click goes my seatbelt as I free myself from it. Inhale deeply. Leaning over the center console, I click his open too. My heart jounces wildly in my chest. I slip into his space; inches separate us.

Noah swallows. His gaze dips from my eyes to my mouth. Lingers. There it is.

"Noah?" My breath leaves in a rush.

He nods. It's the tiniest gesture, but it's enough. I close the gap and press my mouth against his. My heart explodes into a thousand glittering crystals.

When we part, Noah sighs against my mouth. One hand caresses my hair, pushing it back from my face. "Wow."

"Yeah?"

He nods, eyes aglow behind his specs. His fingers linger, feather-light on the side of my face. "I have wanted to do that for months. You have no idea how often I've dreamed of kissing you, Audrey."

A smile breaks across my face. "You dreamed about me?"

"You're the star of all my daydreams."

If I could see myself in the mirror right now I'd probably look like that smiling emoji with giant red heart eyes. This is turning out profoundly better than I could have imagined.

Noah's chuckle cranks up the wattage zipping around my chest. Eyes catching mine, he leans in. "Can I kiss you again?"

His lips are gentle and soft and OMG now I know why Taryn and Esau spend half an hour saying goodnight on the front porch when he brings her home from a date. Kissing is FUN. I could do this for hours.

"Wow. Okay." Noah breaks away, wrapping his hands around the steering wheel. "Next time you need a favor, I'll definitely help if it's going to end like that. Not that I wouldn't help you anyway! But, you know—That was great."

"Wait." My hand stops his from turning the key to resurrect the car's engine. "That was amazing, but it wasn't the favor I mentioned earlier. It's kind of complicated."

"Complicated, huh? Lay it on me."

I do, hoping that he'll be as enthusiastic about my plan as he was about the kiss. Doubtful, considering that it's probably stupid. Dangerous. But I'm doing it anyway, and hoping Noah will come with me.

Chapter 12

Day 278, Monday

Searing pain shoots through my legs from squatting for so long. My core muscles wind tight, holding my body in its place. Perched on a closed toilet seat. Never thought I'd be hiding in a bathroom to cut first period, but desperate times.

The bathroom reeks. Seriously, it smells like someone came in here after eating a three-day-old fish sandwich. The entire gray tile-lined room is filled with the stink. Mingled together with the heavy scent of lemony chemicals, it's making me wish my nose was defective.

Words are scrawled across the stall walls in thick black marker. Naughty doodles and phone numbers mixed in a visual mush. *Rocky loves Emily. Karen is a bench. Anybody got any weed?*

My legs wobble, and my arms shoot out to brace against the walls to keep me from falling onto the slick, grimy floor. Inhaling through my mouth, I check my phone. It's been fifteen minutes. That's gotta be long enough.

The stall door emits a wince-inducing shrill as I swing it open. At the far end of the room, the hall door mirrors it. I freeze.

This cannot be happening.

Taryn halts in the doorway. Her attention sweeps over me

through narrowed eyes. My own widen. Crap, I'm caught.

A ripple of awareness flits over Taryn's expression as she studies me. I have no idea how, but she knows about my plan. Noah wouldn't have told her, so how could she have found out? Maybe, after seventeen years, the twin telepathy that everyone kept teasing about is finally manifesting? That might be pretty cool, for a while. Useful for when we want to communicate without Karen or Justin hearing. But seriously? In the long term, having Taryn in my head all the time would be too much. "I know what you're going to say, so don't bother."

Tossing an odd look my way, she runs water over her hands. They're covered in bright orange ink. "I have no idea what you're talking about. I'm just here to wash up."

". . . Your pen exploded."

"All over my desk. Yeah. Got me out of a snooze-fest on the Battle of Waterloo, though, so that's something."

I huff. Jab my thumb over my shoulder. "I should probably go...."

Taryn scrubs at her skin with a palm-full of hot pink foamy soap, hissing when she sees her hands are still the same shade as a navel orange. Going for round two, she fills both hands with pink bubbles. "Don't let me keep you. Tell Noah I said hi."

"I'm not meeting... I mean, I won't see him until lunch."

"Then why is he waiting for you out in the hallway?"

Busted. My face scrunches up as I back away from my sister. "I can explain. It's not dangerous, or anything."

Taryn eyes me in the mirror. "Noah's going with you?"

"Yes."

"Don't go far."

"You're not going to warn me off?" I ask over my

shoulder.

One of Taryn's perfectly shaped eyebrows wings upward.

"Right. Look who I'm talking to. Miss plays hookie and almost gets immolated in a corn field." Saying that out loud makes it sound so much worse. I bite my lip, knowing that the plan I've dragged Noah into is not smart. It's actually kind of stupid, but I have to do it, and I figure it'll be safer if I have Noah with me.

Wiping her hands, Taryn spins around to meet my eyes. "Have fun with your *friend*. I won't say anything. But Audrey, you know Karen will flip when the school calls to let her know you weren't in class."

It had occurred to me that our guardian will find out pretty quickly. Which is why I need to go. Now. Before she shows up at the school looking for me. I'm hoping the silver bracelet I left in my locker will give me some lead time.

"You're the best. Here's one for the road." I give my sister a quick peck on the cheek. My hand is on the knob when she speaks.

"That better not have been a goodbye kiss," Taryn shoots after me.

When I messaged the Anderson twins on social media last week and asked them if they'd be willing to meet, only Kate agreed. Now that Noah and I are here in a park, three hours from home, I'm disappointed I never heard back from Nate.

Noah, helpful soul that he is, went along with it when I came up with the idea to contact each of the Gemini Killer's survivors. Ask them if they'd agree to talk to us. See if they've received any creepy messages. Gauge their emotional response to everything that's been going on. To seeing me. Most of them have either declined or ignored my message.

After hours in the car to think about it, I've decided that maybe bringing Noah along for the ride wasn't the smartest idea. It was my fault the Gemini Killer threatened his family in the first place. And now I'm dragging him off to have a chat with some of the murderer's other surviving victims. People who might be after me in a twisted bid for revenge.

When I spent time with the Andersons at twin camp that summer, we had an absolute blast. While Taryn was off with some of the older girls doing makeovers and putting on elaborate plays in the camp's amphitheater, I was learning to play soccer with Kate and her brother Nate. It was glorious—that feeling of invincibility as I ran down the soccer field.

Opening my phone, I check my inbox yet again. Nate still hasn't responded to my message. Definitely read it, though. His silence was a surprise. In the first couple of months after that summer, he'd been the one I kept chatting with. When I messaged the other survivors, I assumed it would be obvious if they were angry, or if their grief was presenting in a different way.

On the off chance this goes sideways, how long will it take Karen and Justin to trace my cell phone and hightail it up here to yell at me? My mouth bunches to one side. Can't think about that now. This meeting isn't a risk. Nate and Kate are mourning teens, just like me. They wouldn't hurt me.

"Hey. Earth to Audrey. Where'd you go?" Noah catches my eye from up the picnic bench. I've been completely zoned out, considering possible outcomes to the next half hour. Some of them are fine. Some end in blood and screaming.

Giving him a weak smile, I push my hair back over my shoulders. This is fine. We're fine.

"I think they're here. See?" I follow the direction Noah is pointing toward the parking lot, and gulp.

Kate has arrived, and it looks like Nate came too. The Anderson twins climb out of a car and approach over the slippery grass. The closer they get, the worse I feel. Kate and Nate lost their parents at the hand of a man I'm connected to. A man whose sick fantasies I unknowingly fed into. I suck in a deep breath, fighting to breach the surface of my own grief. I need to apologize for my part in the events that ruined their lives.

A horrifying thought strikes, making me go rigid.

If Nate and Kate have been paying any attention to the news around the Gemini Killer and John Baugh's trial, they likely have heard the comments that hint at my culpability. Nate and Kate might actually blame me for their parents' deaths. They could be the ones sending threatening messages.

Plus, three hours is pretty far from Hacienda, but not inconceivable. Noah and I drove it before lunch time on a school day. If they wanted to, it wouldn't be impossible for Kate and Nate to drive to Hacienda to terrorize me. Thanks to the numerous articles about the case, and me, my sister, Karen and Justin, I wouldn't be hard to find.

The twins could have conspired to try to flatten Taryn outside the school. If they're responsible for all that, of course they'd agree to meet me. Then they'd probably pull a knife or a gun. Kill me where I sit. Noah, too.

In the middle of the park. On a picnic bench covered in bird crap. How long would it be before some poor stay-at-home parent and their kid stumbled on our bodies?

For a survivor of a serial killer, my self-preservation instincts are far lower than they should be. Trees along the park's edge draw my attention away from the twins. This park is heavily wooded. Tall oak and eucalyptus trees form a green and brown barrier most of the way around the park's edge, blocking the view from the street. We're practically in the middle of a forest. Didn't Noah say once that it's difficult to find a body in the woods because of the underbrush?

Our phones are off, so no one knows to look for Noah and me here. My pulse kicks up. Kate picked the park as our rendezvous spot. Maybe she knew it would be the perfect place to end me without witnesses. No one would see it if they were driving past, minding their business.

Why is hindsight so much sharper than foresight?

Noah touches my hand where it's clenched in my lap, snagging my attention. "Hey. What's going through your head right now?"

Exhaling, I push my spiraling thoughts down. I'm being ridiculous. The Anderson twins were my friends, once upon a summer. They won't blame me for violence that wasn't my fault. I'm here to apologize and check in on two people who used to be good friends.

"Nothing. I'm okay." So far I've had no indication that Kate or her brother want to see me bleed. As my mom used to say, I'm borrowing trouble. The wooden bench seat jiggles under my weight as I relax. I'm here to talk. I can do that. If there's any hint of deceit, then we run.

I scrub a hand over my forehead as Nate and Kate get closer. My heart constricts at the broken looks on their faces.

Kate slides onto the bench on the opposite side of the picnic table. She attempts a smile and quits halfway.

Under the table, Noah puts a hand over mine and squeezes, just a little. It's enough.

"Thanks for coming."

Nate shrugs, standing a few feet away. Kate gestures for him to sit, but he shakes his head roughly, eyes downturned, like he can't even bear to look at me.

My ribs suddenly feel too tight around my lungs.

Push through it, Audrey. He's hurting. "I bet you were surprised to hear from me, huh?"

"You could say that, yeah." Kate looks to her brother, but he doesn't respond. Simply stares past us into nothing, shoulders curled inward. Clearly he's thrilled to be here.

Biting her lip, Kate looks at me. "Nate and I, we were both surprised to hear from you. We weren't sure you even remembered us. Twin camp was a long time ago, and with everything that's happened lately…" One of her fingers follows the grooves in the table top.

"I remember you. When I found out…" My voice gives out. Swallowing, I try again. "When I heard about your parents, I was devastated for you. At the time, it felt like all of it was my fault."

"Because of the messages." Kate's focus lifts to my face. It fuels my courage to continue.

"Right. Because of the messages. But the truth is, I should have reached out when I found out. Should have told you how sorry I was that you lost your parents, too. And I hope it's not too late to tell you that. I'm so sorry. I wish there was something I could have done. To stop him from… from taking them from you. From taking anyone else."

Nate huffs. Arms crossed. Eyebrows slashed downward. Anger radiates from every muscle. I don't blame him. If our roles were switched, I'd probably be mad at me too.

"Nate, I'm so—"

"Don't. It doesn't change anything." Kicking up a cloud of dirt, he turns away. Paces toward the nearest stand of trees. Swipes at his face. Is he crying?

Noah's eyebrows twitch upward.

My frown droops farther.

"Nate, come sit, okay?" Kate's words go unacknowledged, so she swings around to face Noah and me. Her eyes are definitely wet, which makes mine start. I'm a sympathy crier. Always have been. My mom used to joke that if anyone in my class got hurt, I felt it right along with them.

"Uh, here. Sorry it's not a tissue." Noah holds a dried out wet wipe in front of my face.

The crinkled fabric pulled from one of his pockets, looks so pathetic a tiny laugh escapes.

I use it and shove it into my pocket. "Thanks. Kate, I'm glad you came, if only so I could apologize again."

Her teeth peek through a weak smile. "Thanks. That means a lot. We should probably go. We snuck off campus to meet you."

"Take your time. I'm not in a hurry to get back to that fish bowl." Nate calls from where he's still standing with his back toward us.

Noah gets off the bench and ambles to where Nate is standing. He doesn't say anything, just stands there, offering what comfort he can to a stranger.

When Kate turns from looking at both boys, she leans in. "I'm doing okay, I guess, but Nate is... Well. You understand."

I do. I understand him probably more than anyone else on this planet. Except Taryn. Because the walls he has up around himself? The defensive attitude? It reminds me so much of Taryn during the time when she wasn't speaking to me. After our parents were murdered.

"Um, can I ask... Have you gotten any weird messages? Like, on social media?"

Kate's eyes roll. "Ugh, yes. Some people are so desperate for attention they think I'll bond with them over... what happened to our parents."

"Right, but... no threats, or anything?"

Kate's brows scrunch. "Threats? No, why would anyone threaten me? I haven't done anything."

It's clear by her tone that she doesn't mean it as a slight, but it stings, nonetheless. "No, of course." My eyes cut to Noah. He's listening, head cocked, as Nate grumbles something I can't make out. "It's just, I've gotten some pretty creepy messages, so be careful, okay?"

She nods. "Sure, of course. You too."

My eyes pin the back of Nate's shirt, just for a second, before I focus on Kate. I speak loud enough that Nate can hear every word. "I've been going to a therapist once a week to talk about things. It's helped a lot. If you aren't seeing anyone, think about it. Okay?"

She nods gratefully. "We will."

Noah doesn't say anything else until we're both in the car, seat belts on. "I got Nate talking about cars. Neither his nor Kate's matches the one we're looking for. You still want to go to their house while they're out?"

I don't, actually. Based on our conversation in the park just now, I know I was wrong in thinking Kate and Nate could have anything to do with the crap that's been going on in my life. "Not really, but we should anyway. Look, they're turning, and we can't lose them."

Noah follows the twins at a distance until their vehicle pulls into what must be their high school parking lot. When we're sure they've gone inside, I pull up the address I found on the internet. The Anderson place, which is sitting empty and untouched since the police finished combing through it for evidence. Hopefully their parents' cars are still there.

A piece of caution tape clings to the door frame, tattered from months of exposure.

Telling Noah to keep the car running, I go around to the side of the abandoned house, hoping there's a window into the garage. Bingo.

Lifting onto my toes, I peer inside. And strike out.

The garage is empty.

Even so, I take Nate and Kate off my suspect list. From what I saw this morning, neither of them blames me. Nate was withdrawn, but I can't blame him for that after everything he's likely experienced in recent months.

I'm quiet all the way back to Hacienda. Despite my belief that they're innocent, there's still a twinge of unease in my gut. My conversation with the twins plays over and over in my head. Every second is dissected and analyzed in my brain, in the hopes that I'll find some clue that points to them as suspects, or innocents. I'd love to believe they're completely guiltless, but I can't. I thought Mr. Baugh was a good man and teacher, and look how that turned out.

As if sensing I need the time to think, Noah doesn't say much. Instead, he sings quietly along with the radio, which at some point switched from J-pop to Disney classics. Listening to Noah sing every word of the *Princess and the Frog* soundtrack makes my heart squeeze in my chest.

"Sorry," he says when he catches me looking at him under lowered lashes. "It's Anza's favorite movie, so I've seen it about a hundred times."

"Don't apologize. It's cute. I mean you're cute. I mean… I'm going to go back to not talking now."

He laughs. "Thanks. You're cute too. Hey, maybe we should—" The car goes over a rough patch in the road and I jolt. Noah pulls the car over along the same stretch of road where we shared our kiss. My cheeks heat. Maybe he wants a repeat. I do, too.

When I look, he's watching. Adjusting his glasses, he reaches for me. "Audrey."

"Yeah?" That sounded way more excited than I was trying for.

"Can you open the glove box?"

"I—What?" That's when I clock the red and blue lights flashing in the rearview mirror.

An unmistakable tan Bronco parks behind us. The door swings open and Sheriff Lamb gets out.

"Were you speeding?" My question is barely audible.

"No, I don't think so."

"You don't know?"

"I was kind of distracted." Raking a hand through his hair, Noah lowers the front windows. Wraps both hands around the steering wheel and holds on.

I sit as still as I can and look innocent. Think of baby sheep. Tiny baby piglets. Owlets with large, wide eyes and a blankly sweet expression. We weren't doing anything wrong. Well, except playing hookie. And having clandestine meetings.

Baby owlets, baby owlets, baby owlets.

I jump when Sheriff Lamb appears on my side of the car. "Mr. Chavez, Miss Thomas."

"How can we help you, Sheriff?" Noah's tone is deferential.

Lamb gives Noah a harsh look before zeroing in on me. "Do you have a death wish, Miss Thomas?"

"Um, no?"

A beat passes in which I am certain the sheriff is boring a hole into the center of my forehead. Heat prickles along my skin. "You sure about that? Because I just got off the phone with an irate FBI agent who says you snuck out of school without telling anyone where you were going."

I open my mouth, but he cuts me off with a raised palm. "You know, for someone who has experienced the evil will of certain individuals first hand, you make some poor decisions. Agents Biel and Chambers have put their lives on the line and you thank them by sneaking around with boys when you're supposed to be in school. You cause me almost as much trouble as my own daughter. It's unbelievable."

Huh. I had no idea Lamb had a daughter. I spend a few seconds trying and failing to think of him as anything other than a surly sheriff and fail spectacularly. He's still talking, and I realize I've missed everything he's said.

"...That's what I ought to do, but that would technically be illegal, so I won't. But if you keep pushing me, I will make it happen. Do you understand?"

Turning to Noah, who is wide-eyed but calm, I nod vigorously. "Yes, sir. I totally understand. Please don't do that." Whatever that is.

Sighing, Lamb runs a hand along the brim of his hat. Pulling his radio off his belt, he talks into it. He lets whoever's on the other end know that he's found "Twin A" and "her boyfriend." That's who we are to him. My cheeks flush in embarrassment.

"Follow my car. I'll escort you home. No detours, understood?"

Chapter 13

Day 279, Tuesday

"She was pretty mad, huh?" Viv's mouth is full of pins as she works on the costumes for the play. Gleefully, she rips out seams. When she said she was excited about reconstructing some of the drama department's costumes for *The Importance of Being Earnest*, she wasn't kidding. A clothing rack full of costume pieces of various textures and colors draws my attention. I can't make heads or tails of the remnants.

Just like I can't make sense of anything else that's going on in my life right now.

"Pass me that silver thread, will you?" Viv's hand is outstretched and wiggling in my face as she points at a spool that must have attempted an escape, because it's feet away from where the rest sit in a neat row on the black-painted floor.

Swiping it, I hand it over. After I ditched school to do something admittedly stupid, Karen and Justin forced me to sign up to help with the stage crew for the play. They're probably hoping that Taryn will help keep an eye on me during practice. As if. They clearly have never paid attention during play rehearsals, because Taryn spends all of her time either practicing with the other actors, or arguing with Esau about everything. If I didn't know for sure that they both think of the arguing as some sort of weird flirting, I'd have to conclude that they still hate each other. The stiff, defeated way Taryn holds herself when she came back from their most recent date lends weight to my assumption.

Marisa comes sock-skating across the wood floor and almost loses her footing on the slick boards. "You guys have to see this. Martino has mono and has to drop out of the play, so Esau is stepping in as Jack. The chemistry between him and Taryn's Gwendolyn is so delicious, I'm craving chocolate."

In seconds, everyone backstage crowds around the curtains to take in the black box in the center of the room. The drama club does all of their plays in a four-way stage in a method called "acting in the round". It makes everything three dimensional and dynamic. And more challenging to set and block. Just ask Esau after an argument with Taryn. Stifling a snicker, I squeeze in next to Fiona and Dariel to watch.

Esau and Taryn are alone onstage. The other actors have stepped out of the round and stand transfixed. Mr. Director's eyes are locked on Taryn's as his character entreats her with a question. Would she still love him by another name? Taryn insists she wouldn't love a man by any other name than Ernest. Esau's answering expression is heartbreaking. They move through the scene so fluidly together that I wouldn't be surprised to see a physical tether grounding them, closing their orbit around one another until there's no space between them.

Sighing, Fiona leans a head on Dariel's shoulder. He slings an arm around her waist.

Esau/Jack goes down on one knee, eyes pleading with Taryn/Gwendolyn. He proposes, heart in his eyes. Gwendolyn accepts.

Marisa grunts when Viv hushes her squeal with an elbow to the side.

Taryn daintily holds Esau's hand as he rises, and everyone erupts in cheers. Actors and crew spill onto the stage, laughing and teasing. Marisa gushes about how amazing the play is going to be. "OMG Esau. Too bad for Martino, but you can't recast his part. You have to do it. That was freaking amazing."

Esau mumbles a thank you.

"No seriously, that was really good. Martino's fine, but you two are fire." Fiona points between the two of them. Dariel makes an exploding noise.

Smiling, I turn to Taryn, but she's—Where did she go? Pushing through the crowd, I wander backstage looking for my twin. Unusual for her to bow out when there is adulation to be had. A knot thickens in my stomach.

A soft sound makes me pause. Is that a sob? Jogging down the hall, I step into the costume closet. It's more a small room crammed full of clothing racks. It is seriously dark without the overhead light on.

Fabric shifts. Another sob comes.

"Taryn?"

Clothes rustle at the back of the room, so I push my way through the odd assortment of period clothing. Powder blue polyester suit. Renaissance corset and skirt. Orange prison jumpsuit.

Taryn is pressed against the back wall, face in her hands. One hand gives way when I take it in my own. Throwing her arms around me, my sister sobs quietly into my shoulder. "I don't think we're going to make it, Audrey. When I was doing that scene, it was so beautiful. We go together so well. But he's leaving in the fall. He'll be three hundred and fifty freaking miles away, and I can tell he has big plans for his future, but it feels like I'm not in them. I can't help but wonder if he'll be too busy to spend time with me. We'll start fighting—"

"—You argue all the time."

"—And it won't be fun anymore."

"—Fun arguing is overrated."

"—And then we'll both be miserable, and he'll break up with me. He won't want to, but he won't really have a choice. I don't know if I can live through that. I love him so much, Audrey. Maybe I should just do it now. Get it over with? You know?"

My head is spinning. Taryn used the L word. She loves Esau. I mean, I knew they were pretty hooked on each other, but love? My brain can't comprehend that concept, so I move on.

"You want to preemptively break up with Esau so it sucks now instead of later? Don't you think that would be a bad idea? Seeing as how you have to work with him on the play you pushed for and adore, that goes for the next four months?"

Wiping her face and then rubbing her palms on her jeans, she straightens. Sniffs one more time. "You're right. That would be stupid. I'll wait until the play is over, and then I'll do it."

"You don't have to decide right now, T. It's February. You have so much time."

The dead-eyed stare she lays on me shuts me up. She whispers in my ear. "I'm so far gone, I don't know if I'll be able to survive this any other way. Losing him will kill me, so I'd rather it be self-inflicted. Better to stab my own heart than to wait for him to do it."

Something inside me pinches as Taryn transforms from my heartbroken sister back into a serene, confident actress. She shoves through the costume racks and pauses in the door. Looks over her shoulder. "You coming?"

A deep sigh washes over me as I follow. I've seen enough

stab wounds and shattered hearts to last the rest of my life. However short that ends up being.

Chapter 14

Day 289, Friday

Rain. Rain. Lightning. More rain.

Rows and rows of grapevines shimmer and sag under the sheets of water pouring down on the earth. Despite the warmth inside the vineyard's cozy bed and breakfast, I pull my puffer coat tighter around me. Good thing we were close to the three-story stone building, or we'd be in the middle of the vineyard in a torrential downpour.

Taryn edges closer to the window pane, eyes upturned. She's always loved thunderstorms, even though they were a rare occurrence where we used to live. One time, the thunder was so loud it sounded like the roof of our house was going to cave in. Lightning flashed so bright it lit up our room like the middle of the day. Just like now, my sister pressed against the glass, taking it all in with wide eyes and a breathless grin. Weirdo.

I only like thunder a normal amount. From a distance. While inside a safe, secure, and warm house. Preferably with a blanket and a new manga to read.

In the next window, Justin shifts. I don't need to see his hand to know its wrapped around Karen's. The way he handles her so reverently is really sweet. His excitement when she agreed to scout out the vineyard as a possible wedding location made me smile. Karen is gruff and no-nonsense, but I caught the smile she hid behind her collar. Underneath her crusty exterior, she's looking forward to this too. And why not? After having to hide their relationship from Taryn and me for months, planning a wedding must be wonderful.

"It's perfect, don't you think? Imagine us standing under the arch, covered in roses—" Justin says.

"Lilies," Karen interjects.

"—lilies, sorry. And you're in a full-length—"

"—knee length—"

"Right. Knee-length gown, and all of our friends are there to watch us get married."

"You mean the director and our fellow agents. Whoever can come between assignments. It won't be very many people."

Justin's grin is catching. "You've thought a lot about this."

His fiancée shrugs casually. "I'm a planner."

"You are. It's one of the things I love about you." He presses a kiss to her temple.

"My parents will come, of course."

Karen swallows. Her focus moves the storm outside to Justin's downturned face. "They still don't like me."

Justin chuckles. Gives a gentle tug on their entwined hands. "It's not you. They were hoping I'd meet a nice kindergarten teacher or a veterinarian and retire from the service. Don't take it personally."

"I won't."

"So, we're doing this? Getting married in this beautiful vineyard?"

"Well, it doesn't look great at the moment, but assuming tonight goes well... I suppose. Yes." We're staying at the vineyard B & B tonight so Karen can assess their facilities to know if she can recommend the wedding guests stay here or not. Since it's off-season, Taryn and I each requested our own rooms, and I'm looking forward to staying in a fancy room by myself.

Lightning crackles across the storm-gray sky at the exact moment he points out the window. Justin beams at Karen and at us. "We're getting married right out there. Hopefully in better weather."

The vineyard director comes in with hot drinks for us, and she and Justin hammer out the wedding day details. Our guardians are getting married in 123 days.

Thunder booms overhead and the skies dump their heavy load. Purple lightning streaks across the clouds' fanning underskirt. Karen takes a long pull of her latte.

I focus on the warmth seeping into my palms cupped around my hot cocoa. I'm glad Taryn and I are involved in planning for the wedding. It makes it feel much more real: the idea that we're a family. I've tried not to think about it a lot, since Justin and Karen could request a new assignment at any time and move Taryn and me into a different guardian's care, but our agents have become like parents over the past few months. They could never replace my mom and dad, but having the agents watching over us makes me feel safer than I have in a while.

Taryn's phone buzzes and she starts texting, body angled toward the window. I still catch the sly smile she's trying to hide. So, texting Esau.

It's been a week since her meltdown in the costume room, and she hasn't mentioned breaking up again. I'm hoping she's decided not to do it, because their relationship gives me hope. If she and Esau can start in high school but last into college, maybe I can, too.

It's so dark outside. I shiver, glad we're not driving in the storm raging beyond the glass. Leaning back on the couch, I transfer my cocoa to a side table and shoot a text to Noah asking how it's going.

Baking soda volcanoes with food coloring = not a good idea. Three changes of probably stained clothes later, and I just found another puddle of lava with my sock.

My lips lift, imagining Noah with a bright red stain on the front of his t-shirt. Glasses fogged up from laughing. Wild curls spilling over his eyebrows.

How's the vineyard?

It was great until the thunderstorm hit.

The little dots appear to let me know he's typing, stopping, typing again.

A notification flashes red at the top of my screen. I swipe to clear it. Wait. Scrambling to find it again, I read it. *CuteAshleeXOXOXO has sent you a message.*

My hand shakes as I open my social app and zero in on the mail icon. *CuteAshlee 2.0* has been eerily silent since the hit and run. What could have brought her out of hiding?

Pressing my eyes closed, I take a breath. Click on the tiny round 1 that indicates a new message. Dread pours through my veins like molten lava.

Come out, come out, wherever you are.

Karen must notice my shift in posture, because she moves closer, eyeing me. "What's wrong?"

Wordlessly, I hand over my phone.

Karen reads it, Justin tucking his chin over her shoulder so he can see it too. Letting out a little huff, her eyes move to mine. "We're still working on tracing the IP address attached to that account, but whoever it is clearly doesn't know you're here."

Justin adds, "Try not to worry about it. We'll keep you

115

safe."

Karen nods in agreement. "Looks like it's a good thing we're staying here tonight."

"A preview of our wedding night, eh?" Justin's eyebrows lift flirtatiously as he tries to lighten the mood.

Clearing her throat, Karen steps out of his embrace. "Girls, I know this past year has been incredibly difficult on you. Both of you. But I promise you: we're going to find this person, and we're going to put them away. They aren't going to get away with any of this. Okay?"

"If you say so," Taryn mumbles at the same time as I say simply, "Okay."

My gaze falls to the phone Karen is holding out for me to take. Jabbing at it with a finger, I open it and re-read the message from *CuteAshlee 2.0.*

Come out, come out, wherever you are.

Chapter 15

Later That Night

The B & B guest room where they put me is pitch dark when something startles me awake. Rain plinks against the window, drowning out all other sound. Heart rate picking up a tick, I ease my body to sit up. Eyes roaming over the room from the floor by the bed, to the dresser, the plush reading chair in the corner, and the closet doors shut tight. As I watch, the closet door starts to ease open, shadows swirling out from inside.

Somehow, our attacker got inside the house after we went to sleep, and lurks only feet away from where I was dozing. Maybe the closet door creaked. Woke me up. Or maybe somewhere buried deep inside is an alarm bell ringing against the evil hiding in the empty closet.

The storm has abated while I slept, its fury finally spent, but I don't dare look away from the closet. Maybe if I'm watching, the ghoul hiding there won't come out. Which is ridiculous, I know. Although most evil flourishes when it goes uncaught, the person who is after me doesn't appear to care. Their attacks have gotten increasingly visible and dangerous. My pulse races at the number of deaths they could have caused with each attempt.

The closet door opens the tiniest bit more.

No. Although evil flourishes in the dark, I have the power to turn on the light.

I yank on the cord and the lamp on the nightstand comes blazing to life. The warm glow illuminates an empty room. The closet doors are completely closed. Plucking up my courage, I run across the room and fling them open. It's empty.

But now that my blood is pumping too quickly in my veins, I have to go to the bathroom. It's cold inside the B&B, and the low fire in the room's fireplace has died to a pale amber glow among the coals. In a rush, I pull on the gift shop clothing the host gave us when they took our clothes to be laundered. I'm now the proud owner of an oversized vineyard tee, sweatpants, and hoodie. Tightening the cord so the hood is snug around my face, I creep down the hall toward the bathroom. Eerie shadows loom between the dimmed wall sconces hanging every few feet. The fear licking up my spine reminds me of when I was a kid who ran to the bathroom and back in the night because it made me impervious to the monsters that lurked.

If only.

Shutting the bathroom door as quietly as I can, I lock it. The version of me I see in the mirror is tired and drawn. Messy hair falls around my shoulders and purple half-moons perch under my eyes. *I promise you: we're going to find this person, and we're going to put them away.* Leaning my palms on the counter, I hang my head. I hope with every cell in my body that Karen was telling the truth.

I'm almost back to my room when I pass Taryn's door. Curling my bare toes into the rug, I stop. Glance up and down the hall, finding nothing. My sister's door is standing open, which, okay, could be nothing. But I could have sworn her door was closed when I passed by a couple minutes ago. A

118

shiver travels through me as I peer into the dark of Taryn's room. It's empty.

A clipped beat of panic starts up in my brain when I scan the room: the window is wide open.

My yelling brings Karen barreling out of her room. A speedy thudding up the stairs reveals Justin, also dressed in vineyard swag, but holding his gun. A small handful of other guests pool out of their rooms to stare. Karen wraps an arm around me while Justin makes the rest go back into their rooms. Flashing his badge does the trick.

Taryn is missing. She's not where she's supposed to be. I open my mouth, but no sound comes out after an initial squeak. Wordlessly, I point.

"Stay here." Karen flips on the light in my twin's room, and I gasp. A wide, crimson stain slashes across the hotel's rumpled white sheets. Congealing blood on a pristine backdrop. My hands rise to grip my own throat. If Taryn… if she… If she's…

Karen steps inside, sniffing the air. "Do you smell that?" she asks over her shoulder.

Unbidden, my nose takes a deep whiff of the air in the room. The fresh, cool scent of newly fallen rain. The musk of a dying fire. And the tang of wine. There's no hint of the sour bite of metal that comes with that much blood. But then— "Is that wine?"

Karen runs a single finger along the stain and brings it to her nose. When satisfied, she turns to me. "It's wine. But that doesn't explain where your sister is."

A gust of wind blows in through the window, pushing a sheet of paper off the nightstand. It swoops through the air and sticks to my legs, pinned by the chilly current. Stooping, I pick it up. My fingers tighten on the paper as I read.

Twenty years ago, you ruined four girls' lives. Now I'm going to ruin yours. This is for Y, D, T, and L.

My forehead wrinkles in confusion. Twenty years ago I wasn't even alive. Who are Y, D, T, and L? "This doesn't make any sense."

Taking the sheet, Karen looks it over.

Taryn strolls into the room, completely unharmed. "Where's the fire? And what the heck happened to my bed?"

I throw myself at her and hold on tight. "I thought you were dead. I saw all that red and... Where'd you go?"

Taryn takes a deep breath, eyes skimming over the puddle of wine on her bed. "Needed a glass of water." Her eyes pass to the window before landing on me. "Please tell me you're the one who spilled an entire bottle of red wine on my bed."

When I shake my head, she growls. "Ever-loving daughter of scum."

As soon as we get home, I toe off my damp shoes and jog up the stairs. Trying to look unhurried. Casual. Like I said earlier tonight, it's just another day. Bloody sheets and an indecipherable but threatening note? No big deal. I'm used to being surrounded by bloody chaos.

Lies. Every single one.

"Where are you going?" The pall of Karen's concern trails after me up the stairs.

"To get some sleep," I lob over my shoulder. No matter that it's almost five and there's no way I'll be shutting my eyes again tonight.

The stark pool of red on Taryn's bed swims to the front of my vision, but I send it away. Wipe a hand down my face. That was wine. I've seen so much worse. Still, no one else is going to bleed. Not if I can help it.

Closing my bedroom door, I shuck off my clothes and toss them at the hamper. Burrow under the pile of quilts on my bed in my underwear.

A creak sounds in the hallway.

Breathe in. Breathe out. Listen.

"Hey, can we talk?" Taryn pokes her head in, cheeks sallow. Sliding in, she closes the door. Leans back against the paneled surface. "I can't believe that just happened. That note. I thought being run down was bad, but this? Why are they doing this to us? And how did they know where we'd be?"

I've thought about that last question. It occurred to me the second my eyes landed on the silver circlet at my wrist as I stood in the B&B waiting to be escorted out to one of the deputy's cars.

My sister tracks my line of sight. "No way. You think they hacked into the FBI's tracking app?"

Honestly? I don't know. At this point I'm so jaded from everything we've been through that it wouldn't surprise me if an evil supervillain was hunting us for sport. ". . .No. But I did wonder if they found out from someone in town. Justin's been pretty excited about all the wedding planning stuff. What if he told the wrong person?"

"He's an extrovert, not an idiot." Taryn's fingers rap on her arms.

I shrug half-heartedly, out of ideas.

"So what are we gonna do?"

"Stay close. Stay safe. Maybe have Esau come over here to hang out for a while instead of going for those long drives you seem to enjoy so much."

Taryn's body slumps. "Nothing like quality time with your boyfriend when there are two FBI agents watching your every move."

"Think you'll die from not enough making out?"

A smile hooks her mouth upward. "Hey now. I'm not the only one who's been lip locking in motor vehicles. When are you guys finally going on a date?"

"He's been super busy with babysitting lately, but we're working on it."

Chewing on her lip, Taryn straightens. "Don't take too long, okay? You never know how much time you'll have with him before... well, you know."

When I call her name, she looks over her shoulder, already halfway out the door. "You and Esau are great together. Take your own advice and try to enjoy it, yeah?"

With a mostly solid chin lift, she's gone.

Something clangs in the kitchen downstairs. Probably Karen making a cup of coffee.

I open my phone. Pull up the message thread with *CuteAshleeXOXOXO*.

Come out, come out, wherever you are.

The Gemini Killer took our parents from my sister and me. Took our normal and turned it into a twisted game of blood and pain.

I've lost enough. I won't allow the copycat to have any more power over me. Or anyone else in my life. I refuse to put anyone else in danger.

A text comes in from Noah. He must be up super early helping his dad at the dairy. *How was the vineyard? Pretty cool?*

Huddled under my blankets, shivering with spent adrenaline, my thumbs hover over the illuminated screen. I'll respond to Noah in a minute. But first.

I'm alone when I send a message I can't take back.

Chapter 16

Day 313, Friday

Wiping my clammy hands on my jeans, I turn to face the mirror. The subtle green eyeshadow Marisa brushed over my eyelids makes my brown eyes pop. Soft, loopy waves bring my brown hair to life under Taryn's curling wand.

"Ta-da." My twin steps back with a flourish. "Your hair is beachy wave perfection."

"Wow, thanks! I look fancy."

"Wow is right. Noah is going to howl like a dog when he sees you. Just you wait and see." Marisa winks at me in the mirror.

"Dariel only did that as a joke." Fiona uncrosses her legs and slides off my bed, coming in for a closer look. "But girl, she might be right. You look stunning."

A pleased flush spreads over my cheeks. Eyeing my reflection one more time, I can't help but be grateful to Marisa for the perfect makeup. Hello, brown-eyed girl. Viv helped pair my Converse and dark wash jeans with a nice blouse that I had previously written off as too much and stuffed into the back of my closet. Fiona cheered me on between bites of her latest snack obsession, popcorn with fizzing candy.

"You guys are awesome."

"It's amazing what a little girl power can do." Plucking a bite of popcorn out of the cellophane wrapper in Fiona's greedy hands, Taryn tosses it into the air above her mouth. Fiona snatches it out of the air and eats it.

"Hey!"

"My popcorn. You didn't ask."

". . . Can I please have a bite of your popcorn?" Taryn exaggerates fluttering her lashes.

"No. JK, you totally can." Fiona's body jiggles with laughter as she holds the bag out.

"So M, how's the line-learning coming?" Taryn plops down on the bed next to Fiona.

Grinning, Marisa delivers one of the most famous lines her character gives near the end of the play.

The four of us clap and whistle. She absolutely nailed it.

Marisa curtseys in her jeans, beaming.

"This play is going to be the best one our school has ever done," Taryn declares. "Wait until you see what Esau and I are working on for the final act. Oh, it's going to be so good."

"That evil grin you're sporting is making me a little nervous." Marisa points at her, who does indeed look like she's plotting something diabolical.

A ring of the doorbell stops all of our Ooooing and Awwing dead.

"Audrey, Noah is here," Karen calls from downstairs. Justin's boisterous voice floats up from the foyer as he asks Noah about how his mom's work at the nursing home is going.

Four sets of eyes hone in on me, and I freeze up. Anxious feelings push every other thought out of my brain. What am I doing? What if this was a terrible idea? Maybe Noah and I are better off as friends. But that kiss. Blinking, I focus on Taryn.

"Here." Handing over her gorgeous wool peacoat, she

124

steers me toward my bedroom door. "Have a great time tonight. Don't do anything I wouldn't do."

"So sneaking around and almost being torched in a corn field are fair play." Fiona chortles, and I try to go along with it. The sneaking out is something Karen and Justin gave us a Very Stern lecture on the other day after the vineyard. I can honestly say I don't ever intend to sneak out, and I don't think Taryn will, either. She's gotten increasingly withdrawn lately. I know she's thinking of breaking up with him because of how dangerous it is being around us. Whenever she sees his broken arm in that cast, her teeth clench.

Three days ago, Taryn's pendulum had swung into Camp Seize the Day, which is when she talked me into jumping off the high dive and asking Noah out. We've been texting back and forth a lot, so I did. Over text. We squealed incessantly when he replied right away with an enthusiastic *Yes!* That togetherness fizzed through my blood like the champagne Justin let us sample at the vineyard. Having my twin sister on my side again is priceless. There's not much I wouldn't do to keep her with me.

Including sending a message to *CuteAshlee 2.0*.

Pick a time and place. I'll meet you.

They still haven't gotten back to me.

I thought the monster on the other side of the screen would jump at the chance to talk face-to-face, but there's been nothing. No messages. No murder notes. The silence has taken up like a scratchy tumbleweed of unease low in my abdomen.

Noah is standing at the foot of the stairs chatting with Justin and Karen, but he stops abruptly when he catches sight of me. A self-conscious flush warms my chest, but thankfully it's hidden under a silky collar. A few careful steps later, I'm standing right in front of him, beaming a smile to match the

125

one splitting across Noah's face.

"Wow, you look... You look really pretty, Audrey." Noah tries to run a hand through his curls, but his fingers get stuck. "Ack. Hair gel. Um."

Giggling, I take in his forest green button up, neat slim-fit jeans and shiny shoes. "You look really nice too." There is a lot of looking going on between the two of us, and it makes my breath go shallow. A goldfish is swimming in easy loops in my stomach. One of Noah's pianist hands runs up his buttons and rests below his collar. His throat bobs. When I meet his eyes, he sends me a look that says, *I'm so glad we're finally doing this.* I shoot back an *I'm excited too.*

A glance at the top of the stairs reveals Taryn, Marisa, Viv, and Fiona all leaning on the railing watching us with giddy grins on their faces. Marisa's eyes have gone completely moony. When I wave, Taryn gestures for me to go on.

Karen puts a firm hand on my shoulder, a wily gleam in her eye. "Have fun tonight, and remember what we talked about, okay?"

"I solemnly swear I won't try to lose Justin. Can we go now?"

"Ready when you are." Shrugging into his coat, Noah opens the door and holds it wide.

Twinkle lights strung across the ceiling give the entire restaurant a soft, cozy glow. A trio of fat, white candles glimmer in the center of the table next to a single rose in a vase. The red and white checked tablecloth reminds me of that scene in Lady and the Tramp when the two dogs share a plate of spaghetti and end up kissing.

Noah grins at me from across the table, and my cheeks go rosy pink. So far, dinner has been nice. The mom-and-pop

126

Italian place Noah picked for our first date is perfect. The old Italian music humming quietly through the room sets the mood. Plus, the food is delicious. My pesto and shrimp ravioli is delicious.

I take my time eating, relieved that after the awkwardness of being picked up at the house in front of an audience, this is Noah I'm out with. My best friend.

The waitress comes by to check on us and see if we're interested in dessert. Obviously, we are, so Noah orders a piece of tiramisu and some cannolis to share. The waitress stops two tables down to check on Justin, who has all but demolished an entire margherita pizza.

Underneath the nerves about this being a date, my body relaxes with each minute that passes. Noah and I have spent a ton of time together. We get along so well. Have similar interests and an ease to us that comes naturally.

"I'm so glad it's you I'm with tonight."

"I am so happy we're finally doing this."

We talk at the same time, laughing when we realize that we've said essentially the same thing.

"Go ahead." Noah takes a sip of water, eyes sparkling.

A few strands of my hair have shifted from behind my ears, so I sweep them back. Pull all of my courage into a simmering ball in my chest. "I feel like I need to explain a little, all right? In the fall, when Taryn and I were pretending to be Megan, there were so many times I wanted to tell you who I really was. Because being with you is so effortless. More than that. I always felt like you knew who I really was, deep down. And the closer we got, as friends, the more I wanted to tell you. It hurt to hear you call me by another name, even though I couldn't tell you mine. Because the circumstances were so, so bad."

Noah huffs at my understatement.

"And it took some time for me to realize that it was because I liked you. I like you, Noah, a lot. With everything that's happened to me in the past year, it shouldn't scare me to admit that, but it does. Anyway, I am so glad that you stuck with me. And it makes me so happy when you say my name. Is that stupid?"

"Audrey. Can I?" Noah's hand glides over the table and rests open, palm up.

Grinning at him, I mingle our fingers together.

Taking a deep breath, Noah forges ahead. "I don't think anything you just said is stupid. I think it's the best thing you've ever said to me. From the second I met you, I was interested. And not just because you were new, like Marisa said. I know you can't see it, but even though you've been through so much darkness, you are a light. You're a bright, pretty light, and I am so glad we're finally doing this. I've wanted to be with you like this forever. And after the trial, it was such a mess…"

"It really was."

Our waitress sidles up to the table and delivers our desserts with a wink. "Enjoy, you two."

Neither of us is willing to sever our new connection, so we eat our dessert with our free hands. It's a little tricky because I am hopelessly right handed, but I wouldn't take my hand from Noah's warm one for anything right now. Not even tiramisu that is so dang amazing I can't even stand it.

I catch Noah's eye between bites. "Did you know this is my first date?"

His fork clatters to the plate. "How is that possible?"

I shrug.

Dark eyebrows reach up to touch his curls. "But I wasn't your first kiss."

"Actually…" My teeth pull my bottom lip into my mouth as I give Noah what I hope is a flirty look.

Noah laughs, incredulous. "You really went for it. That kiss—Audrey, it was, wow."

I chortle in pleasure. "You say that a lot."

"Only when I'm around you."

When our eyes lock, I feel the intensity in Noah's gaze all the way down to the soles of my feet. I am totally, one hundred percent certain that if we weren't sitting across from each other with a table between us, we'd be enjoying our second kiss right now.

It's suddenly pretty warm in the restaurant.

Noah gives my hand a squeeze. "You still with me?"

I laugh, taking a drink. "Uh huh. Actually, I'll be right back." Springing out of my chair, I go into the bathroom. Once I'm ensconced in the black and red tiled room, I take my phone out of my pocket and call Taryn.

An ear-drum-rupturing squeal makes me yank my phone away from my ear. "Audrey! Why are you calling me? Is it going badly?"

"Is it awkward?" Marisa shouts into the phone.

"Have you seen them together? Of course it's awkward, but in the best way," Fiona chimes in.

"They're adorable." This from Viv.

"Guys! I'm in the bathroom, but it's going so well. Like, *so* well. I'm pretty sure he was just about to kiss me."

"Then why are you calling us?" Fiona snarks.

Cackling fills my ears. Hyenas. I'm talking to hyenas.

"I'm freaking out. Do first dates usually feel like this?"

The door swings open and a woman skirts around me to get to the stalls.

"Oops, sorry." I lean against the sinks, trying to take up

less space but not really caring. I'm practically high with giddiness at how well my very first date is going. *It's going so well because it's Noah.* Sweet, super smart, compassionate, quietly strong Noah.

"Audrey, dates are supposed to be fun—"

"If they're with the right person!" Viv again.

"Try to enjoy it, okay?" Taryn prompts.

Thanking them, I hang up. A few sweeping breaths help bring my pulse down from a gallop to a trot. So, manageable. I had no idea that horse's gaits had specific names until Esau told Taryn and me about them a couple weeks ago. The things I've learned since moving to Hacienda, I have to say.

The woman exits the stall as a loud flushing fills the room. Avoiding my eyes, she washes her hands. Turns to the paper towel dispenser to dry.

I'm straightening my hair in the mirror when my phone goes off in my pocket. Oops. Forgot to silence it. Taryn probably thought of something else she wanted to say. I pull it out and read the notification.

It's not from Taryn.

Bird Cage Park. 30 minutes. No FBI.

CuteAshleeXOXOXO.

I hiss through my teeth. I don't know if I can make it there in time. Don't even know exactly where Bird Cage Park is, though I've heard of it. Noah would know. Dollars to donuts he's taken the twins to every park in this town at least a few times.

My breath stutters on the last bit. I literally just promised Karen and Justin I wouldn't ditch them since, you know, someone followed us to the vineyard and threatened us only two weeks ago. No FBI. Shaking my head, my resolve solidifies.

They'll forgive me. I can't miss this chance to unmask the copycat.

Silently, I slip the silver bracelet off my wrist. It drops without a sound into the woman's purse as she brushes past to leave the bathroom. A peek out the door reveals Noah waiting at our table, reading something on his phone.

Justin's attention is on the restaurant's front door.

My thumbs fly over my phone's keyboard, and Noah's phone chimes. His eyes widen and his head snaps up to mine. A silent conversation passes between us. He'll understand. He has to, because this boy with the big heart and breathtaking smile is my only chance. Without a sound, Noah slides out of the booth and leaves the restaurant. Stops to say something to Justin, thumbing over his shoulder in my direction. Then Noah is gone. He doesn't look back.

My body sags as I close myself in the restaurant's bathroom. Alone.

Chapter 17

Somebody should have told me that climbing out of restaurant bathroom windows is not as easy as it looks on TV. For starters, it's so high up on the wall I have no idea how I'm going to reach it. Sending mental apologies to whoever is responsible for keeping this bathroom clean, I clamber onto the toilet lid. It flexes under my shoes, throwing off my balance. My arms pinwheel, grasping for something to hold onto. My palms hit the stall wall with a smack. Please, please don't break, toilet lid.

The window is shut tight, but mercifully it unlocks and opens without so much as a low groan. Man, this is a small window. I don't know if I'll fit. Don't have a choice, though. The copycat said I wasn't allowed to bring my FBI friends to our meeting, and I can't mess this up.

Praying it will take my weight, I gingerly rest one foot on top of the toilet paper dispenser. It jiggles, but holds. If I weren't trying to hurry, this whole situation might be funny. Hilarious, even. I'm standing straddling a toilet in a restaurant bathroom, eyeing the window like an animal trying to escape from its enclosure in the zoo.

Okay, I'm really doing this. Hoisting myself up, I drop my purse out the window. It plops onto the concrete below.

The next question is, how am I going to climb out without

landing on my head and doing the killer's job for them? I pull my body up, trying to find leverage with my shoes against the wall. The rubber soles don't find traction and I slip, banging my knees against the stucco. Ouch.

Stars spark over my vision, and when I blink them free, Noah is under the window. He positions an overturned milk crate under the opening and steps onto it. A half smile cocks his lips upward as he meets my eyes. I'm keenly aware of how close our faces are when he speaks. "Need a hand?"

"Desperately."

Huffing a laugh, he reaches up and braces me under the arms. My own fingers curl around his shoulders, holding on tight. "Okay, here we go."

Someone knocks on the bathroom door, making the sliding bolt rattle in its catch. "Audrey, you've been in there a while. Is everything all right?"

When I don't respond, the knocking gets louder. "Making out in bathrooms is unsanitary, guys. Come on out."

Disgust mixed with a tinge of fear forces my eyes wide. "Hurry!"

Noah pulls; I push. My jeans slide over the metal sill and we land in a heap on the asphalt. There's no time to nurse our bumps and bruises, because Justin's hollering ramps up in volume. It's only going to take a few seconds for him to come after us.

I push Noah toward the mouth of the alley running behind the restaurant. "Run. Run!"

Our feet pound over the pavement. My heart thrashes in my chest, drowning everything out as we sprint around the corner to where Noah's car is parked in the small lot. Glowing twinkle lights illuminate the sidewalk as we run past. If Justin sees us...

133

Our car doors slam. Noah ignites the engine and guns it, driving over the low curb, making our bodies bounce off the seat when the car's back tires hit the road. Twisting around in the seat, I crane my neck to look back at the restaurant. A man's black silhouette is outlined by the hanging twinkle lights. Justin's running gait gives him away. I can't see it, but I picture the anger and worry that likely contort his visage as he bolts toward the door. He bursts outside just as Noah's car turns the corner, out of sight.

Sinking into my seat, I attempt to wrangle my breathing. Get my lungs under control. It's no use. Fearful energy ripples through my body like static electricity, leaving my heart working too fast and my lungs too thin. That was too close.

My phone starts vibrating in my pocket. Justin calling. Karen calling. Then again. Next Taryn calls. I jab at it, turning it off so they can't track me. When I turn it back on, I know what I'll find. A bunch of voicemails. Probably containing a lot of yelling.

Noah shifts, sliding his cell out of his pocket and handing it to me. It goes off before I kill it, too. He breathes heavily as he navigates the car down the street. Driving carefully, he grafts our car into the evening traffic. It's dark out, but there are quite a few cars on the road. It'll be a challenge for Justin to catch up, even though he'll use every trick in the FBI handbook. Hopefully we have enough of a head start to make a clean getaway.

Justin and Karen are going to be pissed when they discover that my tracking bracelet is in a random lady's purse. I grit my teeth. I didn't have a choice. I had only a handful of minutes to act. Taryn would be proud. I hope.

A green glow illuminates the digital clock in the dashboard. Only fifteen minutes left before the meeting time

CuteAshlee named. Will we make it? "You know where Bird Cage Park is, right?"

Noah's chin lifts. "It's that big park next to where they're building that resort. There used to be a giant bird cage on the playground you could climb inside. It was my favorite as a kid."

I jump when a horn blasts behind us. Turn to look. It's not Justin. He hasn't found us. We drive in uneasy silence.

A couple of red lights later, Noah lets go of the steering wheel long enough to buckle his seatbelt. Realizing mine isn't on either, I click it into place. Run my tongue over chapped lips. "Thanks for doing this with me. I know it's a big ask."

In the dark interior of the car, Noah's eyes flick to mine before returning to the road. "You're welcome."

Closing my eyes, I picture Noah in the moment I texted him. Back at the restaurant. The way his brow furrowed as he read the words I'd sent. The slow rise of his eyes to mine. The tinge of doubt behind those pretty brown eyes. "I know it's a lot. For a second there, I wasn't sure you were coming."

A beat passes. "Me either."

"I'm glad you did."

Noah looks at me for a long second. "Should we be doing this without Justin or Karen? Couldn't they come along and hide or something?"

I chew the inside of my cheek, not voicing the fact that I was just thinking the same thing. Maybe… No. No FBI. "They'd never agree, but what if, when we get there, I call Karen? I can leave the call going in my pocket, and that way she'll be able to hear us. They can track us that way too. Does that work?"

He nods slowly.

My hands wring in my lap. Eight minutes left. Tearing my focus away from the digital clock, I skim over the buildings as

135

we pass. 7-Eleven. Grocery Store. Houses. Hotel. "How much farther is it?"

"We're almost—"

"Stop. Stop!"

Noah slams on the brakes, throwing me forward into my seatbelt. The driver behind us honks loud and long before swerving around us, yelling something unpleasant. I cringe away.

Noah calls out an apology and looks at me. "What happened? Did they message you again?"

Shaking my head, I point. "Pull over, quick."

Brow wrinkled in confusion, he does. Kills the engine. "Why are we stopped?"

I climb out and he meets me on the curb, hunching to meet my eyes. "I thought I saw something. Come look with me, please?"

"Lead the way."

"How about we do it together?" Feeling brave, or maybe desperate, I take his hand. Noah's fingers tighten around mine, and he lets me lead him up the sidewalk and into the hotel parking lot. Crouching to avoid being seen, I tiptoe between two cars. My eyes skim the lot, looking for— There it is. I point. "Look. Right up front. There."

Noah's mouth drops in surprise. "The maroon car."

Mouthing the license plate on a whisper, I have Noah snap a quick photo. Whose car is it? Which room are they in? Most of the windows are lit, blinds drawn. No point in sneaking closer to peer in windows.

A peek at Noah's phone makes me stop in indecision. Three minutes until I'm supposed to meet *CuteAshlee* at the park. I have a choice to make. Wait here and see if the owner of the car shows themselves, or hurry to the park.

A door on the motel's second story opens and light floods out.

Thinking quick, Noah pulls me down so nobody sees us. I peer through a window, watching. A guy backs out of the open portal, talking to someone inside. My eyes narrow as I take in the tall, athletic frame. Short, dark hair. There's something familiar about that back, the way he rolls his shoulders.

A woman's voice answers in a murmur. Her blond silhouette appears in the doorway, pulling the man in for a kiss that turns heated quickly. I duck down, face hot. Noah does too. I avoid looking at him, feeling super awkward.

A door shuts and the lot darkens. I peek, and gasp.

The guy coming down the stairs is Nate Anderson. What is he doing here in Hacienda? Dumb question. I give myself a mental shake. It's obvious what he's doing here.

Nate climbs into a gray pickup and drives away.

Noah and I wait for another twenty minutes, but no one goes anywhere near the maroon car. Finally, he puts a hand on my elbow. "Maybe we should go to the park? See if anyone's there?"

I don't want to leave without seeing who owns that car, but he's probably right. This might be my only shot at meeting *CuteAshlee*. I have to take it. Trepidation takes shape in my core, building until it looms large enough to drown out everything else.

Noah pulls into the parking lot next to the park and shuts off the car. His attention focuses on the tenebrous expanse in front of us. Lamp posts line the sidewalk around the perimeter of the park, but the center of the green space might as well be a black hole. "Think anyone will be here?"

It's ten minutes after the meeting time the copycat specified. I squint, trying to see something, anything moving in

137

the pitch black. Shadows flicker and ripple, but it could just be the night playing tricks. I can't decide how to feel. Twisted hope that I'm about to put a face to the person who's been tormenting me in the Gemini Killer's stead, or dread?

Fifteen missed calls. Three voicemails. Strings of unread texts from my family. My screen shuts off as I shove the phone into my pocket. I'll deal with all of that later.

We get out, lighting our phones to guide our way along the path to the middle of the park. There's not a soul here aside from Noah and me. Lowering my butt onto a chilly concrete bench, I motion for Noah to take the spot next to me. "Let's wait for a bit, see if anyone shows up."

Minutes drag on in the stillness. Crickets sing eerie songs. An owl screeches. Somewhere nearby, sirens cut through the night. Within a couple of minutes, Justin's truck pulls into the parking lot. Karen yanks her car to a stop next to it. The sheriff's Bronco halts in the only entrance, blocking it off.

Three flashlights slice through the black, heading straight for the spot where Noah and I are sitting. His breath catches when a woman in blue scrubs gets out of a fourth car and jogs to catch up to the sheriff. Mrs. Lopez. Taking my hand, Noah holds on tight. We are in deep, deep crap.

Chapter 18

Day 321, Saturday

Taryn

Karen was very close to murdering Audrey after the park. Scratch that. Justin was the one close to committing murder. Normally, he reins Karen in when she gets mad at us for doing stupid crap, but seeing how livid he was when he brought my sister home that night, the low granite of his voice as he laid into her for sneaking out like that. The hurt that flashed in his eyes. Our guardian's gregarious, people-loving fiancé was barely keeping his baser impulses in check.

I knew how he felt. I wanted to strangle her, myself, when I heard what she'd done.

Apparently, when Karen and Justin took this assignment, nobody warned them about teenagers. How we can be such a P. A. I. N. Clap clap. My palms hit together silently.

I don't want to wake Karen, who's asleep in the tent right next to ours. Or bother Justin, who sits at alert in a lounge chair next to the fire pit. Probably because he was well aware of my sister's and my penchant for sneaking off.

The great oak trees along the edge of the farm's property sway and groan in the night breeze. Justin adjusts in his seat, his eyes skimming past the fire toward the woods. Pale fingers wrap around my shoulder, and Audrey's face appears next to mine in our tent's flap opening.

When we told Karen and Justin about the maroon car at the motel, they looked into it. Cruised by the motel a few times. Spoke to the stoner who works in the office. From what Audrey and I have overheard, they haven't found any leads on the identity of the car's owner. Another dead end.

A few days ago, my sister mentioned the comet that was supposed to appear tonight, I encouraged her to present the idea to our guardians. Audrey's been wanting to try some night photography, and I saw it for the welcome distraction it was. With some wheedling, we convinced Justin and Karen to accompany us on a camping trip for better visibility. More wheedling produced permission to invite Noah and Esau, whom we hadn't seen outside school since the grounding. J and K stated they hoped the mutual punishment would deter us both from misbehaving. So far, it has worked.

Esau's uncle agreed to let us make camp on a fallow spot on the farm, since it's outside of town and more conducive to night photography. Our agents were fine with the whole thing, as long as they were in the canvas pop-up right next to us. See our history of sneaking out for reasons why.

My breath exhales long and low when Audrey mouths, "They're here. You ready?"

I nod, flourishing my hands to show off my black on black on black ensemble. Going on a night photography trip calls for a specific look. My sleek black leggings, black sweater dress, and black Uggs (which I'll put on outside the tent to keep from dragging dirt inside. I'm not a monster) won't bother me if we end up sitting in Esau's truck all night, waiting for the comet to show. Audrey's choice of black joggers and her favorite hoodie

140

were likely chosen with the same goal in mind.

"Did you bring it?" I whisper.

Audrey retrieves a canvas bag from the corner of the tent. Its contents crinkle with the movement, making her wince and glance over her shoulder. "Sorry," she hisses at Justin. "Do you think she heard that?" Silhouetted by the fire, Justin shakes his head.

Karen's getting some sleep, since she's taking the early morning watch.

She tiptoes to where I'm standing in the tent's opening, gazing beyond the house toward the street. The headlights of Esau's truck shine bright as the vehicle bumps over the ground toward our campsite. I am so ready for this night. It's peaceful out in the country, away from town.

Go.

Fight.

Win!

Shaking my head at myself, I place my fuzzy pink earmuffs over my ears.

Justin stands, watching as the truck rolls closer.

Cold air slices through my sweater, straight to my skin as I step out of the tent. Goosebumps rise up and down my arms, as if warning me to go back. Stay inside the tent where my sleeping bag is looking pretty cozy.

Not a chance. From what Audrey's said about this comet, it sounds pretty cool.

Esau's truck comes to a stop opposite the fire, and Audrey and I deposit her photo equipment in the bed before clambering inside. I'm already shivering from how unbelievably cold it is tonight. In the back seat, Audrey and Noah catch up a bit since they talked last. Noah's parents have been leaning on him pretty hard since the park.

141

"Sorry we're late," Noah says. "My mom had a rough day at work, so she decided it was the perfect night to stay up late binging Netflix and forcing me to help do some baking. It took forever for her to finally agree to let me come. But, I brought muffins for sustenance. I hope everyone likes chocolate chip, and lemon poppy seed."

"You're not late." The brown paper bag Noah's got in his lap rustles as he digs in and pulls out a massive muffin for Audrey. The scent of melted chocolate fills the cab, and my stomach rumbles.

Esau's eyes cut to mine. "Your stomach sounds like one of those orcs from *Lord of the Rings*." He must see me shivering, because he turns the engine and cranks the heater.

"Shut up. Lemon poppy seed, please." I twist to take a muffin from Noah and hum while I open it. I happen to love lemon desserts, and Esau's right. My stomach is loud. The lentil curry I had for dinner was delicious, but it wore off hours ago, and I'm starved.

Esau asks for a muffin, and I unwrap it for him. All of us fall quiet, each eating our late night snack. When Esau bites into his, he groans. "Delicious."

Audrey agrees. "So good. From here on out, these are must-have hangout food."

Noah chuckles around his muffin. "I'll tell my mom you guys enjoyed them."

"Another please," I ask, holding out a hand.

Noah plops another citrusy-smelling round of manna into my palm.

"Our tummies thank you." There's a smile in Audrey's voice.

Leaning my head against the headrest, I force my muscles to go lax, from my forehead to my jaw, neck, arms, fingers, calves, feet. I've been wound tight for weeks, since Esau got plowed by whichever vicious person was behind the wheel of that car. But tonight, I'm warm, my stomach is full, and my favorite people are within arms' reach. Justin is on guard duty, which should be a lot easier since Audrey and I are staying put this time. Here's hoping tonight is equally uneventful. Still, my eyes scan the farm for any movement. There's nothing.

Esau asks for and gets another muffin. Which he eats in two big bites.

I swing around to meet my sister's eyes. "You need help with anything?"

She shakes her head.

"Everything's in the back." Noah juts a thumb toward the truck bed.

"Great. Let's go." The two of them climb out. The truck bed dips under their weight as they unpack the equipment Audrey brought specifically for tonight. One camera gets positioned on the truck's roof, pointed in the direction whence the comet is supposed to come. Her backup camera is pointed straight up so she can take a time lapse of the night sky. My sister has her camera programmed to take photos every few seconds. She's pretty excited about that, too.

"They good to go back there?" Esau's eyes catch the corner of my vision, pulling my attention to his face. He looks chiseled from marble under the moon's soft caress. His eyes shine in the dark. His ebony hair is braided in two french braids that trace the back of his skull before falling down his chest.

"Your hair is getting so long." I trace a finger over one of the braids, still amazed that this artistically brilliant boy is mine.

"Yeah. My aunt keeps harping on me to cut it."

"Don't. Not ever."

He chuckles at my fervency. "You like it, huh?"

143

Wrapping one braid around my hand, I give a gentle tug. Bring his face nearer to mine. My lips ghost over his warmer ones. His hand slides to my nape, holding me impossibly close. Our mouths linger for a beat before both of our hands relinquish their grip.

"I missed you," he whispers against my cheek.

"Me too. Being grounded is the worst."

"It sucks." I can't stop my grin when he leans in again.

The truck door opens, and Audrey pops her head inside. "We're all set. Did you guys see that shooting star just now?"

My eyes meet Esau's in a silent apology for my sister's terrible timing before I sink back in my seat and watch the bats swoop across the indigo sky. "We must have missed it."

"Yeah, missed it." Esau's focus is still on my mouth.

Noah and my sister climb into the cab to enjoy the heat while we wait for the comet to show. Somewhere far off, coyotes sing their song to the moon. The branches of hundreds of almond trees sway along to the tune.

In the back seat, my twin yawns loudly, and then titters. Probably embarrassed. "I should have brought some coffee. Unlike someone else I know, I'm not used to being out so late." Her hand sneaks between the seats and swats at my shoulder.

"You snooze, you lose." I smirk when Esau laughs softly.

"Damn right," he murmurs. His large, warm hand lands on my knee, giving a gentle squeeze. He's probably remembering the first night I snuck out to meet him. How dark it was in that almond orchard. How we argued about the play we were doing last semester. How we almost kissed under the crescent moon. And how a car trawled along the front of the orchard, scaring the spit out of us. Clenching my jaw, I square my eyes on the sky.

au says. "Hence the donuts."

purses, and she glances back toward

probably sleeping. "Fine, go ahead, but

feed on my phone the entire time, and

es the donut place, you can forget

house for the foreseeable future.

its and back. That's it."

the truck, not bothering to wake

leaving the farm. Almond orchards

on the left. The road is wrapped up in

ike plastic army men as far as I can see

om. Old houses dot the breaks

y giving way to newer, suburban

stare out the window in a morning

king about Esau's cast, and how the

e was a dead end. How there's been no

ery time the sheriff has someone drive

on the frosty window, I turn to my

glory, let's go to A & A donuts

glance to me before returning his

"That's all the way on the other side of

Oh."

d if she figures it out."

onuts than Joe's. She knows that. I'll

sends back a quick thumbs up.

s driving. Town goes by in a blink,

Chapter 19

Early the Next Morning

Taryn

The nearing screech of a police siren rips my eyes open. Something happened. They're coming for us. Maybe Justin and Karen saw someone sneaking around the farm, so they called the cavalry. I can picture it: Karen barking at Sheriff Lamb over the phone. Demanding he climb out of his bed, tug on his boots, and round up a posse.

Peering out the windshield, I spot Karen wide awake in one of the camp chairs. Her attention is pointed toward the street, but her body is loose. Not wound and alert. Not like a woman whose alarm bells are going off. Her phone is tucked against her shoulder, and she speaks into it, unfussed.

A patrol car approaches the farm, its siren splitting the dim nighttime sounds. I watch as it grows larger. Holding my breath, I send vibes out through the dark. Don't be coming here. Don't be a harbinger of bad news. Blow right past where we're camping and keep on going. Keep driving, Deputy Whoever You Are. Keep going…

The tan and white car wizzes past. A fire truck follows, its long body peeling around the road's curve. Then both vehicles are gone.

I sag against the seat, my breaths short and shallow in my chest. Closing my eyes, I sing along with my favorite song in my head to try to calm myself down. Achingly slowly, my pulse slows to an acceptable tap in my veins. It's still dark outside, the world tucked under a weighted blanket. Sighing in relief that we're not about to be burdened with more bad news, I close my eyes.

My stomach rumbles, and I groan my eyes open again, looking at the three idiots in the truck who just slept through that whole thing. Audrey is slumped to the side in her seat, head resting on Noah's shoulder. His head is on hers, his glasses falling down his nose. I stifle a giggle with a hand to my mouth. She's totally drooling on his sweater. Just a tiny bit, but yeah. Oh, she's going to be mortified. Slipping my phone out of my pocket, I snap a photo.

We were up super late waiting for the comet to show, and when it did, when Audrey started screeching that it was happening, we piled out of the car to watch. My sister snapped a flurry of photos from her position in the truck bed, Noah beside her. Esau and I stood against the side, tracing the sparkling comet with our eyes. It lit up the sky for a long breath before burning out below the horizon. Then we climbed back into the truck's cab and all fell asleep.

"What're you looking at?" Esau's huffed words on my neck make me yelp in surprise, yanking forward to meet his gaze. He's in the driver seat, legs splayed. A warm, amused smile showcases white teeth against brown skin. Lifting a finger to my lips, I point to Tweedle Dee and Tweedle Clueless in the back seat. Esau's head bobs.

Esau's left arm shifts on the window sill, and the stark black cast snags my attention. Makes a flare of anger rise in my

chest. Whe
run vehicle
to trace th
me, who a
out there s
my Esau.

My s
fuming.

Esau
your orc s

I fak

Shru
around to
can.

"Co
Esau swi
early, bu
edges. U
chuckles
fire to w
knit cap

"M
"You're

Esa
okay if y

Ka
on me.

I n
"Yep, d

"D
canvas
"Those

"They're gone,"

The agent's mou
the tent where Justin
I'll be watching the C
if you go anywhere b
seeing the outside of
Agreed?"

"Totally. Yes. D
Karen nods.

We climb back ir
Audrey and Noah bef
unfurl on my right, th
groves of trees lined u
in the early-morning g
between the fields, slo
housing developments
haze, unable to stop th
maroon car's license p
trace of it at the hotel
by there.

Knocking a knuck
boyfriend. "Hey morni
instead of Joe's."

He cuts a confuse
focus to the road ahea
town, across from the.

"Oh, is right."

"Karen will be pis
"A & A has better
text her." I do, and Kar
"See? We're fine."
Nodding, Esau kee

motionless and sleepy except for the diner. Open 24 hours, a hot-pink neon sign glows in the window.

There aren't many other cars on the road until we approach the freeway, and even then it's only a handful. Red tail lights gleam where they cut through the night like the eyes of giant, mechanical animals that see more than they let on.

Shuddering, I push the ridiculous thought away. No one is observing us. Justin and Karen are at the campsite. The sheriff is probably asleep, and whatever deputies are on duty are either at the station, or driving around in their patrol cars, answering emergency calls.

Esau and I aren't hampered by the rules and regulations of law enforcement. If we want to drive across town to get donuts at the place that is coincidentally right across the way from a certain motel, we can. If we're lucky enough to see the driver of the maroon car that tried to run us down, and succeeded in breaking Esau's arm, well then. No one will be able to stop us from calling Lamb and bringing down the hammer of the law.

No one pays any attention as Esau pulls into the lot of the donut shop and backs into a spot so we've got a view of the two-story motel through the windshield. Cutting the engine, he unbuckles his belt, eyes sweeping over the street. Not a single light is on at the motel aside from the one over the office. A vacancy sign blinks in the glass window.

No sign of the maroon car.

My shoulders slump forward into the seat belt. Disappointment flashes through my chest, catching me by surprise. I'm just now realizing that, during the entire drive over here, I assumed the maroon car would be there. That despite the sheriff and his deputies having no luck tracking the car, we'd be lucky—or unlucky—enough to find it.

I was secretly counting on it. Because I'm finally coming

around to Audrey's way of thinking. For the past couple of months, I've been trying to move on from the horror of our past by pretending everything was fine. That the unnerving and ominous messages were a hoax designed to freak us out without actually causing damage. But after the hit and run, the B & B, and the message commanding Audrey to appear in the park, I can't pretend anymore. The threat, the danger is real. And it won't go away until someone puts a stop to it.

I can't afford to ignore the signs for another day. With that realization comes a resolve that crystalizes into diamond low in my gut. I'm going to do everything I can to catch the dirtbag who is terrorizing my family in a twisted imitation of the Gemini Killer. I'm going to stop them. I refuse to lose another person I love.

Esau and I are careful as we step out of the donut shop ten minutes later. His arms are full of a large pink box, and mine are laden with to-go trays of hot drinks.

I check the motel lot, and again come up empty. No maroon car anywhere to be seen. Barking out an annoyed snort, I'm still grappling with my realization regarding the Gemini Killer's copycat. "Wow, that cashier. He was clearly not aiming for customer service rep of the year. He was on his phone the whole time. He didn't even look me in the eye. Did you see that?"

Esau jostles the donut box to one hand, plucks his drink from one of the trays I'm carrying, and takes a long, savoring sip of his coffee. His rich eyes meet mine over its rim. "He stared at you the entire time we were in there."

I stomp a bit, walking faster toward the truck. "I almost forget I have a scar and look like a weirdo, but then people have to be awesome and remind me. I wish they would just. Not. Hey, why did you stop?"

Chapter 19

Early the Next Morning

Taryn

The nearing screech of a police siren rips my eyes open. Something happened. They're coming for us. Maybe Justin and Karen saw someone sneaking around the farm, so they called the cavalry. I can picture it: Karen barking at Sheriff Lamb over the phone. Demanding he climb out of his bed, tug on his boots, and round up a posse.

Peering out the windshield, I spot Karen wide awake in one of the camp chairs. Her attention is pointed toward the street, but her body is loose. Not wound and alert. Not like a woman whose alarm bells are going off. Her phone is tucked against her shoulder, and she speaks into it, unfussed.

A patrol car approaches the farm, its siren splitting the dim nighttime sounds. I watch as it grows larger. Holding my breath, I send vibes out through the dark. Don't be coming here. Don't be a harbinger of bad news. Blow right past where we're camping and keep on going. Keep driving, Deputy Whoever You Are. Keep going...

The tan and white car wizzes past. A fire truck follows, its long body peeling around the road's curve. Then both vehicles are gone.

I sag against the seat, my breaths short and shallow in my chest. Closing my eyes, I sing along with my favorite song in my head to try to calm myself down. Achingly slowly, my pulse slows to an acceptable tap in my veins. It's still dark outside, the world tucked under a weighted blanket. Sighing in relief that we're not about to be burdened with more bad news, I close my eyes.

My stomach rumbles, and I groan my eyes open again, looking at the three idiots in the truck who just slept through that whole thing. Audrey is slumped to the side in her seat, head resting on Noah's shoulder. His head is on hers, his glasses falling down his nose. I stifle a giggle with a hand to my mouth. She's totally drooling on his sweater. Just a tiny bit, but yeah. Oh, she's going to be mortified. Slipping my phone out of my pocket, I snap a photo.

We were up super late waiting for the comet to show, and when it did, when Audrey started screeching that it was happening, we piled out of the car to watch. My sister snapped a flurry of photos from her position in the truck bed, Noah beside her. Esau and I stood against the side, tracing the sparkling comet with our eyes. It lit up the sky for a long breath before burning out below the horizon. Then we climbed back into the truck's cab and all fell asleep.

"What're you looking at?" Esau's huffed words on my neck make me yelp in surprise, yanking forward to meet his gaze. He's in the driver seat, legs splayed. A warm, amused smile showcases white teeth against brown skin. Lifting a finger to my lips, I point to Tweedle Dee and Tweedle Clueless in the back seat. Esau's head bobs.

Esau's left arm shifts on the window sill, and the stark black cast snags my attention. Makes a flare of anger rise in my

146

chest. When Justin and Karen ran the plates from the hit and run vehicle, it turned out they were stolen. Giving them no way to trace the car or its driver. The person who tried to murder me, who almost succeeded in maiming the boy I love, is still out there somewhere. Escaping judgment for violence against my Esau.

My stomach growls a second time, interrupting my fuming.

Esau's eyes meet mine. "Did your two muffins not fill up your orc stomach?"

I fake a huff. "Guess not."

Shrugging on his coat, he leaves the truck and comes around to my side. I slide out, shutting the door as quietly as I can.

"Come on." Taking my hand in his, twining our fingers, Esau swings our arms between us. I've never seen him this early, but he's bright and crisp, not fuzzy and mussed at the edges. Ugh, he's a morning person. At my grimace, Esau chuckles, walking us around the faint glow of the simmering fire to where Karen is sitting, wrapped in a camping blanket. A knit cap is pulled down over her head, almost to her wary eyes.

"Morning," she says, voice hoarse from the cold night air. "You're up early."

Esau clears his throat. "Craving donuts. You think it'd be okay if we went to get some real quick?"

Karen studies him for a beat before turning her scrutiny on me. "Donuts, huh?"

I nod, surprised she's not shooting him down outright. "Yep, donuts. They sound amazing, right?"

"Did you polish off Noah's muffins?" Karen asks, the canvas chair chafing when she leans forward onto her elbows. "Those were pretty good."

147

"They're gone," Esau says. "Hence the donuts."

The agent's mouth purses, and she glances back toward the tent where Justin is probably sleeping. "Fine, go ahead, but I'll be watching the GPS feed on my phone the entire time, and if you go anywhere besides the donut place, you can forget seeing the outside of the house for the foreseeable future. Agreed?"

"Totally. Yes. Donuts and back. That's it."

Karen nods.

We climb back into the truck, not bothering to wake Audrey and Noah before leaving the farm. Almond orchards unfurl on my right, then on the left. The road is wrapped up in groves of trees lined up like plastic army men as far as I can see in the early-morning gloom. Old houses dot the breaks between the fields, slowly giving way to newer, suburban housing developments. I stare out the window in a morning haze, unable to stop thinking about Esau's cast, and how the maroon car's license plate was a dead end. How there's been no trace of it at the hotel every time the sheriff has someone drive by there.

Knocking a knuckle on the frosty window, I turn to my boyfriend. "Hey morning glory, let's go to A & A donuts instead of Joe's."

He cuts a confused glance to me before returning his focus to the road ahead. "That's all the way on the other side of town, across from the... Oh."

"Oh, is right."

"Karen will be pissed if she figures it out."

"A & A has better donuts than Joe's. She knows that. I'll text her." I do, and Karen sends back a quick thumbs up.

"See? We're fine."

Nodding, Esau keeps driving. Town goes by in a blink,

Esau stands still a couple steps behind me, brow furrowed over a stormy-eyed frown. Swallowing, he locks his gaze on mine. Something deep inside me slots into place at that look. The conviction, the depth of caring behind it. "You still feel like that scar makes you less beautiful?"

"No. Maybe." I look away, trying not to let him see the vulnerability I know shows in my eyes.

In a blink, Esau stands toe to toe with me, the pink donut box abandoned on the truck's roof. His fingers skim over my jaw, up the side of my nose to where the faint white line bisects my cheek from nostril to temple. His lips are a warm breeze over my skin, pressing gently on the white line that sometimes feels more like a giant, scarlet A. "You're beautiful, Taryn. Don't ever stop believing that."

I wish I could drop these coffees and step into his arms. A ragged exhale deflates my ribcage. "What am I going to do next year when you're gone and you can't remind me?"

Taking the drink trays from me, he nudges me around the truck with his shoulder. I wait, knowing Esau will answer. When he does, my heart coils in my chest. Not knowing if what he says will be enough.

He stops when we reach my door, focuses on me. "We'll talk on the phone every day. No matter what. And then when you graduate, you'll move down there. I'll become an award-winning director, and you'll be a famous actress. Emma Stone won't know what to do with herself."

I sigh wistfully, warmed by the picture Esau paints. Proof that he really has factored me into his plans for his bright future. Neither of us knows what will happen a year from now, much less a few months, but I choose to believe his plan will work for us. I open my door, taking the proffered drink trays once I'm situated and buckled.

"Smells good," Noah whispers. He's awake but hasn't moved, Audrey tucked against his side with her head lolling on his shoulder. His cheeks pink when he catches my eyes.

Audrey stammers an apology, her cheeks flushing when Noah nudges her awake and she notices the small puddle on his sweater. Being the unflappable, steady guy he is, Noah plays it off like it's no big deal, saying something about being fully familiar with bodily fluids thanks to his kid siblings.

"Where are we?" she asks, rubbing her eyes.

"A & A," Noah murmurs. "Want a donut?"

"We got you your favorite." Wrapping a chocolate sprinkle in a napkin, I pass it back to her.

Audrey's fingers wrap around it, her eyes catching mine. "Thanks." She takes a bite and chews sleepily, eyes attempting to blink the sleep away.

I take out my phone, about to text Karen we're on our way back, not noticing for a few seconds that the other three people in the truck's cab have fallen eerily silent. When I look up, Esau's hands grip the steering wheel in an unyielding grip.

"What?" I ask, looking from Esau to Audrey. My twin's visage is tight, pale, like a ghost.

Eyes wide, she points toward the motel. "Look."

Chapter 20

Dread towers in my stomach, and when my eyes land on the dated edifice, I see it. A maroon sedan. The license plate is different, the driver having ditched the stolen ones. I squint, trying to pick out any details that jog my memory. "You think that's it?"

Audrey nods, not shifting her focus away from where the car parks, brake lights blood red. "See that sticker in the back window? I recognize it. From that day."

Noah snaps a photo of it with his phone.

My fists clench. She means the day somebody tried to make a hood ornament out of me and ended up almost maiming my boyfriend.

A hooded figure gets out of the car and jogs for the stairs.

Behind us, Noah shouts, asking where I'm going. I don't respond, laser focused on the hood climbing to the second story and traversing the open-air hallway. I narrow my eyes, hoping for a glimpse of the face under that hood, but whoever it is has it pulled so low I'd have to be standing dead-on to see any of their features.

A break in the morning flow of cars allows me to trot across the street, three sets of shoes at my heels. Crouching low, I slide between the outermost row of cars in the motel's lot. I inch forward, knowing Audrey and the boys are right behind me. The faint simmer of body heat gives them away.

"Who is that?" Esau's question rumbles in my ear.

"I don't know, but I'm going to find out."

He tucks his chin over my shoulder and waits.

The hood goes into room 7. A light flicks on.

I slump. "Not even a glimpse."

"That's the same room I saw Nate coming out of, that day I saw him here meeting a girl. Coincidence, or could it be the same person?" Audrey asks, spinning to look at the boys over her shoulder.

Esau shakes his head. "I doubt it. This place is mostly for travelers who need someplace to stay the night. It's not like there's much bringing tourists to town, especially this time of year. What? As an employee of the business that puts on the only annual tourist event in this town, I know things."

"Smarty pants," I tease, but there's no joy in it.

"Mr. Smarty Pants to you," he rumbles back, gaze darting to mine.

"Should we call Karen and tell her the car is back here?" Audrey's hair is bronzed by the golden streaks of the rising sun. Shit. We're running out of time. It's probably already gone. We've been near the donut shop for so long I'm surprised Karen hasn't texted to see what's keeping us.

I bite the inside of my cheek. "You want to find out if she means it when she threatens to lock us in the garage?"

"No." Her brows scrunch together.

"Okay, then. Come on. You two stay here. Audrey and I will be right back." Standing, I point at the asphalt between us.

Esau crosses his arms, gives a rough shake of his head. *Not a chance*, that firm line of his mouth says. Noah crosses his arms too, looking decidedly less gruff, but no less adamant. Rolling my eyes, I wave for them to follow. Hood may be locked in their motel room, but their blinds are open. This donut run might actually turn a profit.

We manage to get all the way upstairs before a little old man comes out of his room. When he sees us, his face turns down in a scowl.

"Morning," I say.

The old man grunts, lifting his cane and shaking it in Noah's face. "Your music was way too loud last night. Not everybody wants to hear that racket. Didn't your parents teach you to be more considerate?"

"Sorry, sir. We'll keep it down." Noah lowers his head in a polite half-bow.

The old man grunts again, in obvious displeasure as he passes, gripping his cane and muttering something that sounds a lot like *kids these days*.

I feel like a special agent or a super spy as I sink onto hands and knees and crawl the last few feet to sit under the window we're aiming for. I'm just about to take a peek when—

SNAP

The window blinds jerk closed.

Of course.

"Anyone else got any ideas?"

We're a murmured chorus of "Nos," so Noah leads the way down the stairs. At the bottom, he looks from me to Audrey. Dark curls have fallen over his eyes and he pushes them back. Scrubs the back of his neck. "I think I saw something. Audrey, you don't think... The person who mugged you, could it have been a woman?"

"I don't know. Maybe. With the voice modulator it sounded more like a robot than a person."

I almost slam into my sister when she stops abruptly, then hunches to peer in the passenger window of the suspicious car.

155

Looking up, seeking my eyes, she points through the window. "That's my phone case."

I dial Sheriff Lamb without even thinking about it.

"Yeah?" he answers after a single ring.

"We're at the motel, and the maroon car is here. Audrey's phone is on the seat."

There's a heavy silence over the line, the only sound an exhale from Lamb's end that sounds decidedly annoyed. Then, "What are you doing at the motel?"

"We were getting donuts, and Audrey saw the car. We came over to have a look."

The sheriff is definitely annoyed when he speaks. "Go back to A & A, and do not leave there until someone arrives to escort you. If you aren't sitting at one of their tables when I get there, I will personally drive you home and lock you inside. And stay on the line until you're there. Got it?"

I grumble a response, motioning for my friends to start toward the street.

We're all tucked into a booth at the donut shop, eating in silence and staring across the street when the hood comes out of their hotel room. I perk up, leaning toward the window. Lamb hasn't arrived yet. No sirens indicate his approach, although I guess he wouldn't use them if he was hoping to surprise the driver of that car.

He picks up as soon as the call goes through. "You better be in the donut shop."

"I am! Where are you? The driver's getting in the maroon car, carrying a duffle bag. It looks like they're leaving."

As if he knows I'm inching toward the shop door, he orders me to stay put. "I'm almost there."

My heart makes a racket in my chest as the maroon car pulls up to the lot's entrance. The driver has a balaclava on, making it impossible to see their face through the glass.

"They're leaving!" I yell into the phone.

Lamb's engine guns in my ear.

The car glides into the traffic streaming toward the freeway. I watch until the car disappears out of my line of sight. "They went south on 99," I say flatly into the phone.

Sheriff Lamb's Bronco streaks past the donut shop and wheels onto the onramp's shoulder as he navigates past commuters and onto the freeway. But I'm pretty sure he won't catch whoever it is he's chasing.

Chapter 21

Day 328, Sunday

Audrey

Taryn moans. "So this is what freedom tastes like. It's so delicious." Stabbing the slice of cake on the plate nearest her, she scoops up another huge bite and eats it with relish. That one's lemon poppy seed. Or orange cardamom. I think.

Eyeing her response with interest, Justin snags the plate. The ceramic shrieks as he drags it over the tabletop to rest in front of him. "If it's so good, I have to try it. It is MY wedding we're planning, after all. Can't skimp on cake for the groom. Mmm, this is good." He finishes off that slice and studies the remaining six flavor samples the baker gave us to try.

It's wedding cake tasting day, and is easily my favorite part of helping plan Karen and Justin's wedding so far. It even beats choosing the floral arrangements, which was a highlight because Karen let me pick the flowers for her bouquet. When she looked at me so expectantly, warmth seeped through me. She trusted me to decide for her, because of my green thumb. It was pretty cool.

My eyes fall on the empty chair where Karen should be, and I frown. The bride-to-be, who never gets sick that I can tell, is home with a wicked case of food poisoning. Something she ate at the diner last night did not sit well with her stomach, and it hasn't been pretty. I don't think she slept at all, if the almost constant toilet flushing is a reliable indicator.

With the corner of my eye, I glimpse Esau clomping by the storefront, his focus flickering inside the bakery and away. My mouth tilts up. He's done that three times in the last half hour, and if I've noticed, Justin has too. But Justin is team Karen. She banned us from any activities besides school and drama club, including dates or outings with our boyfriend and potential boyfriend, when she found out we used the donut trip to snoop at the motel. Taryn's been going stir-crazy. Hence the almost euphoric way she's savoring the cake sample she's got in front of her. You'd think Karen fed us bread and water for the past week, the way my sister is grinning.

I try to hide my snicker by taking a drink, and only succeed in choking when the cool milk goes down the wrong tube.

Someone outside holds a newspaper up to read while they walk. It's yesterday's paper, based on the headline:

Reporter Receives New in Line of Threatening Messages
Your time is running out.

I wipe at my face with a napkin, hoping I don't have a milk beard. My next bite of cake tastes like nothing but bitterness in my mouth. Your time is running out. I've gone back over the previous murder notes a hundred times. One day I'm convinced they're all directed at me. The next, someone else entirely. There's no way to know for sure. It seems like they're for me if I go by the string of attacks we've endured. And yet. The wording of some of them doesn't ring true. The warnings don't pluck at my instincts, urging me to run. Hide. Fight back. I don't know what to make of them.

Your time is running out.

If it's about me, I don't know what to believe anymore.

Justin pats my back with one hand, taking another bite of red velvet cake. "I don't know. That mocha toffee one was good, but this might be my favorite."

"It's the color of blood," Taryn sneers. "Plus, it's boring. Everyone has red velvet at their wedding. I think Karen would appreciate a more unique flavor. Something memorable. Like the white chocolate pistachio."

I wrinkle my nose. I did not like that one.

"Oh come on, Audrey. It's perfect. Plus, the white and green will go beautifully with the colors Karen picked." She points her licked-clean fork at me.

"You picked the colors, and I'm sorry. I hate that flavor. You know my stance on nuts in desserts."

"Desserts with nuts are from the devil. How could I forget?" Taryn rolls her eyes playfully. "You're so dramatic."

This time it's Justin's turn to choke on his milk. Sputtering, he stands up. "Sure, Audrey's the dramatic one in our family."

Our family.

The word reverberates through my body, burrowing through my skin and muscles and organs into the marrow of my bones. Our family. Something warm seeps out of the paths made by Justin's words, from bone through blood and flesh. We are becoming a family. What started as a temporary protection measure has become something so much greater. We're not legally bound to each other, but I know that Karen and Justin care for us, just the same. They proved it the day, shortly after that sicko was killed, they rejected the offer of another job in another place so they could stay with Taryn and me in Hacienda. In the creepy old house that had somewhere along the way become a home.

Family.

It's something I never thought I'd have again. Never considered. Justin's eyes sparkle when I beam up at him. Without saying anything, I sense he knows how grateful I am for him and Karen. For the way they care for us. Every day. Even when we're complete idiots.

"You sure you don't want this divine piece of heaven?" Taryn gestures toward the marble cake she's ogling like it's one of her cheerleading trophies.

"I can't eat anymore, or I'll be as sick as Karen." Pushing back from the table, I pull my phone out of my pocket and light it up. Immediately my eyes home in on one of the notifications. A new message from *CuteAshleeXOXOXO*.

"This cake is so good, I could die right now and be happy." My sister's eyes are closed. What a drama llama. She throws her head toward the door when Justin points an elbow toward the shop's large, bright front windows.

"Might as well invite him in. He's been outside the entire time we've been here." Justin takes another bite, not quite hiding a smile.

A chuckle slides between my lips. I had the exact same idea about inviting Noah to "accidentally" bump into us while we were here at the bakery, but he couldn't make it. Babysitting duty, he said. What he didn't say, but what I could detect every time we talked on the phone and were interrupted by his mom, was that she doesn't want him spending time around me. His flimsy excuses for ending our conversations made my heart hurt. She liked me until I dragged Noah into the mess that is my life. Honestly, I can't blame her. Guilt over the hurt I've caused the people I care about follows me like a ghost these days.

I glance at Taryn. Maybe I should talk to her about it, sometime. Maybe she can relate.

"You mean it? Thank you, thank you, thank you!" Justin chuckles when Taryn rises from her seat and is off like a shot, throwing open the bakery's glass door and practically yanking Esau inside. Pulling him toward our table, she shoves him into the seat and hands him her fork. "You have to try this: it's white chocolate pistachio."

My finger hovers over the screen, hesitating. *CuteAshlee* has been silent lately. A relief. I had almost convinced myself that they were done haunting us. We've gone weeks without any violence. Looking at that notification, my hope dies. The cease-fire was temporary.

Esau eyes the cake before taking a bite. Closing his eyes, he nods. It's as effusive as I've ever seen the big guy. Taryn beams. "See? He loves it!"

Clicking on the message, I read.

10

Ten? What is that supposed to mean?

Almost immediately, *CuteAshlee* starts typing.

9

8

My eyes zoom over the numbers as they count down.

7

6

Blood rushes from my cheeks, leaving me cold.

5

4

What is this? What are they counting down to?

3

Almost frantic, I look around the bakery. A dad is sharing a huge, fudgy brownie with his toddler daughter in the corner. A few people from school are at the table in the back eating cookies and slurping down ice-cold milk.

2

Outside, pedestrians walk past on both sides of the street, doing their Saturday shopping. Cars pass in a steady stream. There's no sign of danger anywhere.

1

The world erupts.

Chapter 22

The floor-to-ceiling window at the front of the bakery shatters. Piercing glass fragments spiral through the air like tiny, sparkling, heat-seeking missiles. Dozens of microscopic shards cut into my hands where they're covering my face.

A sliver between my fingers reveals the baker and her assistant dropping behind the glass cases. A viscous clenching in my stomach makes bile scale my throat. There wasn't any blood, but that doesn't mean they aren't hurt. And the glass cases, minutes ago were filled with beautifully decorated sugar masterpieces. Now they're scratched and cracked. Utterly ruined.

I throw my head down on the table and cover it with shaking arms.

"Get down!" Justin yells. A vice grip pulls me out of my chair and pushes me to the cold tile.

Another bouquet of shots makes my ears ring. All other noise is drowned out in a shrieking chorus of screams and gunfire.

Justin crouches between me and the mayhem, watching the street outside. He hasn't fired. He can't. People run terrified along the sidewalks. Traffic is at a dead stop as people abandon their cars and flee into the shops. He doesn't have a chance to get off a single round before another bursts through the space left open wide by the shattered window. Bullets embed in the floor, throwing up poufs of dust. Pulling my hood over my head, I pull the strings tight.

Justin scans, window tracking his vision, but he doesn't take a shot. He must not be able to get a look at the shooter.

Taryn is sprawled on the ground a few feet away. "Audrey!" She shrieks. Her hand shoots out, scraping against the detritus of broken glass and shattered cake plates. Lines of red appear on her fingertips, beading with blood.

Heart pounding, I'm up and streaking across the bakery before I can overthink it.

"Get down!" Justin shouts, putting his body between mine and the gaping storefront.

My entire body shakes as I reach my sister. Tight, shallow breaths are all the air I'm able to squeeze out of my compressed ribcage. Panic crowds my brain, pushing out all else. "Are you shot?" I wheeze.

She shakes her head, panic flooding her expression.

My eyes leap from my sister to Esau. Thankful he's right beside her in this havoc.

Several more bullets careen through the bakery, and I throw myself at the floor. Glass shards cut into my thighs, but I don't dare shift away.

Justin takes a single shot, cursing under his breath.

Esau has Taryn shielded under his arm, protecting her as best he can against the onslaught. Lifting his chin, his deep eyes meet mine. He lifts his free arm, making room for me. "Come on, Audrey." His words rumble under the cacophony assailing my ears.

With a fevered look toward the window, I scurry. Crawl to Esau's other side and huddled on the cold floor. Esau tugs me into his side and wraps an arm around my waist. Firm and warm. Not letting go.

Bang.

Justin's body starts to fold in on itself as he cries out. Sheer stubbornness keeps him upright, but I don't miss the way his entire body tightens, going compact with the effort. He fires off a couple more shots before his muscles give out and he lists to one side.

Oh God. He's been shot.

Panic courses through me. Justin can't die right now. Not like this. He has to be here to cheer us up when Karen is surly in the mornings. To ferry me around town. To sit in the library for hours with Noah and me while he researches his new favorite unsolved mystery and I try not to kiss him in the middle of the library. *Go for it,* Justin had said when I asked him what guys thought about girls asking them out.

Metal clatters when he loses his grip on his gun and it drops. Justin's shoulder smacks against the debris-strewn ground. He shifts. Collapses to his stomach. One arm tucked against his chest. He tries to push himself up, but falls face-first onto the dirty floor. His groan shatters my galloping heart to smithereens.

My knees shake uncontrollably, barely holding up my body as I shove Esau's arm away and go for the gun. My fingers wrap around the cold metal exactly like Justin taught me. Hours of lessons and practice at the local gun range have left me with knowledge I never thought I'd use. I need it now. Lowering to my haunches, I breathe. In. Out. Justin was watching the roofline across the street, so that's where I focus. Waiting for my shot.

Familiar sirens howl. Getting closer. A surge of relief flies through me, but I don't move. If the shooter shows their face, I have the gun, and I'm going to use it.

Justin groans again, cutting through the deadly barrage of sound. "Taryn. Call... Agent Biel."

He's hurt. Maybe dying. And somewhere outside, unspeakably close, is a lunatic trying to end us. If they choose to show themselves now... My focus wants to jerk to my sister and Esau, but I strong-arm it. Trying to remain focused. If the shooter steps into this room while I'm distracted, all four of us are done.

My hands tremble as I realize what that would mean. Either they shoot us, or I shoot them. I shut down my panic. I can do this. I will do this.

Behind me, Taryn whimpers into her phone. "Justin, he's... I don't know." She nods. Karen is coming. Esau speaks low into his own phone. Says we need an ambulance. Gives our address.

At my back, a door opens. Heavy footsteps crunch over the broken glass. I swing around, gun aiming straight at Sheriff Lamb. His eyes latch onto mine as he approaches. "I've got you, Audrey. Put that down."

Slowly, I lower my gun as Lamb steps past my sister and Esau, toward me. Toward where Justin is curled in a fetal position on the floor. He's not moving. His groans have gone silent. I pray he's only passed out. A mercy his body gifted him to keep the pain at bay. I can't know for sure. Oh lord, there's so much blood.

Sheriff Lamb hunches, gun drawn. Attention on the roofline on the opposite side of the street. "Audrey, gently roll Justin onto his back, and put pressure on the wound. Use your sweatshirt."

Esau yelps, bringing my attention around. He's trying to hold Taryn in place against him, but she twists and shoves out of his hold. Dives for Justin. Kneeling beside his body on the concrete, she inches her palm to rest in the center of his back. Shakes his unresponsive form gently, then harder. "Help! Audrey!"

Following my twin, I squat on Justin's other side. Set the cold gun down amidst the shards. Blood, hot and viscous, squelches under the soles of my Converse. My eyes broaden in terror and visceral disgust. It's blood. So. Much. Blood.

But we do what Lamb said, balling up my sweatshirt and pressing it to the wound in Justin's shoulder. He doesn't even flinch. Taryn puts a trembling finger under his nose, eyes lifting to mine when she finds breath. He's alive.

Three deputies come in the back door and move to flank Sheriff Lamb. Their bodies are a wall of tan sheltering us from the maniac outside. It's silent inside the bakery, the only sound in my ears my own ragged breathing.

Chapter 23

Hours Later

Hospital waiting rooms are just as dreary and depressing as they are on television. Pale green walls. Stiff green vinyl chairs. Linoleum floors that squeak under my socked feet. I took my shoes off after I noticed I was tracking rust-red over the floor. My pants are crusted with red-brown. Nothing I can do about that now.

Karen paces, her thick-soled shoes smacking with every angry step. No, not angry, I realize. Worried. She's trying to hide it, but I've finally learned to read her. The gruff exterior she presents is a disguise for the softer emotions she conceals underneath.

A nurse just took Taryn to be patched up. She insisted Esau and I be looked at first, even though she was the one clutching her ribs and wincing whenever her weight shifted. Her damaged hand had clung to mine so tightly it was painful. I didn't let go until the absolute last moment, when the nurse insisted.

Esau slumps in the chair beside mine, eyes trained on the hallway. Butterfly bandages hold together a gash on his temple. The nurse told us we were lucky to get out with scrapes and bruises. She's right. We were lucky. Any or all of us could have been killed. Shot where we sat, our breath severed before we knew psychotic hatred was gunning for us.

Lamb comes in, drawing my attention away from my twiddling thumbs. He takes our measure as Karen pivots and meets him in the middle of the room. "Well?"

The man rubs a thumb along his crisp collar. He glances over a shoulder at us then down the hall. Grimacing, he continues. "They got out of the downtown area before we could put up blockades, but we found where they were firing from. There were bullet casings and a second gun on the roof of the post office. We should be able to trace the gun's ownership. We're also looking through security footage from the shops up and down the street. We have them on camera, wearing a ski mask. We should be able to glean some clues from the footage."

Karen's crossed arms tighten over her chest. "Maybe. But the assailant seems smart. They've cleaned up each of the other scenes. Pretty thoroughly."

Lamb taps the brim of his hat, dangling from one hand. "You know as well as I do that they eventually slip up. When they do, we'll be ready. It's a matter of time."

Karen exhales. A haunted expression veils her features. Her hands weave together in front of her stomach. "Not always."

The sheriff inclines his head.

"What else?" she asks finally.

"One of my deputies spoke to the motel manager. She got a name, but my gut says it won't lead to anything. Sounds like an alias. We'll run it anyway, of course."

"Any credit card information?"

"She paid with cash."

"So it was a dead end." She curses roughly.

"Not quite. I have techs going over the room now. I'm hoping they'll find fingerprints, or maybe some DNA we can use. Someone like who we're dealing with, chances are they're in the system already. Most criminals don't go from zero to shooting at people without at least some minor infractions in between."

"There's usually a progression."

"Right."

Lamb clears his throat. "We found Audrey's stolen phone, too. The sim card had been taken out, which explains why we couldn't track it, but we'll re-insert it. Dig around and see what we can find."

I try to cover my jolt by shifting in my chair, but both adults turn to look at me. They must have caught it. Karen studies me for a second, speaking to Lamb without moving her eyes from my face. "Maybe we should take this discussion elsewhere."

They step into the hall.

I wait a second, debating. Then I slink across the room. Pressing my body against the wall, I strain to hear what they're murmuring down the corridor. From this vantage point I'll be able to see Taryn when she emerges from the exam room, too.

Nurses and doctors move between the rooms. A low tide of worry starts to ascend from low in my belly. I refocus on Karen and Sheriff Lamb.

"You think they're stalking the girls, like before?" My guardian asks.

"Must be, to know where she'd be this afternoon."

They pause, a loud alarm over the intercom drawing their attention. Someone yells for assistance. Something about a code blue. That's bad, isn't it? Footsteps pound over the floor. I hope whoever needs it gets help.

Raking a hand through my hair to push it behind my ears, I wait. Wondering what tragedy is unfolding.

Karen shifting her weight and planting her hand on her hip draws my attention back to her and Lamb. "What about the license plates? Have you figured out where they're coming from?"

The sheriff hums. "I have my suspicions."

"Anything else?"

Lamb goes quiet, so I dare peek around the corner. The sheriff is running the brim of his hat through the palm of one hand. "Come with me." They move around the corner out of sight.

I sag against the wall. Lamb is right. *CuteAshlee* must be following us. I had already known that, deep down, but hadn't let myself truly accept it. After today, I'd be stupid to deny it.

When my eyes lift, Esau is watching me. His arms rest on his lap. Shoulders rising and falling on his breath. "Want to talk about it?"

I sit in the chair next to his. "Not really, but thanks."

His head bobs once, firmly.

Karen and the sheriff are gone for long minutes. My mind starts to race. What didn't he want me to hear? It can't be anything good. And what is keeping Taryn? It shouldn't take so long to clean up a few cuts and bruises. My mind replays her wincing and holding her side. What if she was more seriously injured than I suspected? I give myself a reprimanding shake. I'm not even going to entertain that thought. My jaw clenches.

Esau's hand taps his armrest, drawing me out of my thoughts. "Want to hear about this year's corn maze? We're already mapping it for planting."

I know what he's doing: trying to distract me, and I'm grateful for it. He launches into a detailed response at the nod

172

of my head.

After what seems like forever, Sheriff Lamb returns with Karen. The look in her eyes makes me shoot out of my chair. It's a composition of sadness, worry, and maybe even regret. A cold sweat breaks out over my skin. "What happened? Where's my sister?"

Karen puts an arm around me. "We have an update on Justin, and a plan. Let's go to Taryn's room, and we'll explain it to you both at once."

Esau strides over to join us. "I'm coming."

Karen doesn't argue as she leads us to my sister.

Anxious steps and familiar voices emanate from down the hallway half an hour later, once Esau and I are back in the waiting room. The swish of clothing chafing underpins the approaching cloud of movement.

I tense even though I can clearly see the deputy stationed in the hallway.

"Where is it? Didn't she say to make a left?"

"That's definitely what she said."

"Wouldn't we have found it by now? Maybe we should ask someone."

Deputy Kelley stops Fiona, Marisa, and Viv from entering the waiting room, checking their ID before moving out of the doorway. They goggle at us over his shoulder, looking around for Taryn and the FBI agents.

Our friends burst in through the double-wide doorway, hastening straight for us. The girls are on Esau and me before we can stand. They take turns hugging both of us in tight, relieved arms. Words of apology and encouragement wash over me. Our friends are here. For this moment, it's almost enough to quiet the worry rushing through me like a river running

173

toward the mouth of the sea.

Fiona lowers herself into the seat beside mine, a big plastic bag in her hands. Catching my eyes, she leans in. "Have you heard anything? Or is he still in surgery?"

I give a small lift of my chin. "The bullet nicked his carotid, but missed all of his organs. They managed to patch it up. Karen's in with him now. She told me she'd let me know when he wakes up. He's going to be fine."

Her body sinks back against the chair, her fingers tightening around the bag's handles. "That sucks. Totally and completely and royally sucks."

I nod.

She looks around. "Where's Taryn?"

I open my mouth, not sure where to start.

"Audrey! Taryn!" The plaintive voice makes my heart slow, then speed. I jump up.

After being checked by the deputy, Noah barrels in, chest heaving. Messy black curls ring his face. His eyes are wild behind the black plastic frames that make my insides go soft. His mouth hangs on a jagged breath as he looks me over from head to toe. Then his attention circles the room, looking for something—or someone—before returning to me. "You okay?"

My legs run for him almost before I can decide to move. Colliding with his warm, familiar form, I wrap my arms around his waist and hold on tight. Eyes shut, his clean, fresh scent is like a balm for my decimated emotions. His arms wrap around me without hesitation, his chin coming down on the crown of my head. "I got here as fast as I could. Had to wait for Abuela to get to the house to watch Anza and Mattie."

I nod against his chest.

"Any updates on Justin?"

174

"He's gonna be okay."

My gaze shifts to Karen, who has entered the room but is texting furiously. Sheriff Lamb stands near the double doors, talking quietly on his cell.

Noah's arms tighten around me. "I'm sorry I wasn't there. I should have been. I could've helped. Done something. I'm sorry."

My body pushes back just enough to meet Noah's eyes. "If you'd been there, you would have been hurt, just like the rest of us. You could've," I swallow, "could've been killed."

There's a tightness around his eyes, as if he disagrees but won't say it.

Someone taps on my shoulder. Fiona. Her worried eyes search mine. "Audrey, where is Taryn?"

Viv and Marisa stand behind her, watching me.

My attention moves to Esau, whose hands are white-knuckled on the arms of his chair.

My lips tremble. Tears build behind my eyes until the pressure is so great I don't know if I can hold it back. My chest rises and falls rapidly as I battle for control. I cut a glance to Karen, whose nod is so subtle I might have imagined it.

Fiona's face falls when she sees the tears spilling down my cheeks. "Oh, oh no. No." She shakes her head, disbelieving.

The color drains from Marisa's face. Viv's mouth falls open.

My tongue doesn't cooperate when I attempt to speak. No sound comes out. Swallowing, I try again. "Taryn is fine," I whisper, "but I have a lot to tell you guys. There's a plan. Can you keep a secret?"

Clutching Noah's shirt in one hand for an anchor, I beckon them closer, and start talking.

<< Breaking << Breaking << Breaking >>

The scrolling weather update cuts to a local news anchor in the studio. Hair perfectly coiffed in waves that fall to her shoulders. Graphic black and white dress half hidden behind a desk. A somber expression behind bright eyes. Looking directly into the camera, she speaks.

"A calculated assault on a local bakery ended in tragedy today when a seventeen-year-old girl was killed. Our reporter is in downtown Hacienda, waiting for law enforcement to make a statement. Elise?"

The view switches to a blustery day outside a long, low tan building with a sheriff's shield painted on the side. A wooden podium has been set up and is littered with microphones.

"Thank you, Margo. I'm standing outside the Sheriff's Department waiting for Sheriff Lamb to provide information on a shooting that occurred today in this normally quiet town. A shooting that has everyone shaken. We have no word yet on whether there were any casualties. As you can see from our footage, the usually bustling streets are now empty. A well-loved bakery, in chaos. The question on everyone's mind is, 'Who did this? And will they strike again?' The shooting comes after a string of threatening messages which have dominated local headlines for the last three weeks. Could the cryptic words be connected to today's violence? Speculation is rampant here outside the sheriff's office as we—Here is Sheriff Lamb now."

A middle-aged man with a slight paunch underneath his tan uniform shirt steps up to the microphones. A worn brown cowboy hat perched over a furrowed brow. Rough palms land on the edges of the podium, as if the man about to give the answers to the waiting crowd of reporters and onlookers needs the support of the solid wood. Sheriff Lamb's piercing blue eyes survey the gathering. Clearing his throat, he speaks.

"I'm here to address the shooting that occurred on Main Street earlier this afternoon. Unfortunately, the lives of one of our bright local youths was lost. Taryn Miranda Thomas was injured at the scene, and was transported via ambulance to the hospital, where she later went into cardiac arrest. She was pronounced dead four hours after arriving at the hospital. Her next of kin have been notified.

"Transported along with her was her twin sister, who was also critically wounded in the attack. Although she is expected to make a full recovery, she remains in the ICU for the time being."

Sheriff Lamb's hands tighten on the podium as he meets the eyes of someone in the crowd. "I can assure the people of Hacienda that, at this time, the department does not believe this was a random attack. Hallmarks of the crime have lead us to believe that it was calculated to focus on the Thomas twins, specifically. With that in mind, I can assure you that we do not believe more attacks are imminent. However, caution is advised. Avoid downtown for the rest of the day if you are able.

"I won't be taking any questions at this time."

Shouts and comments erupt from the swarming reporters as the sheriff spins on his boot heel and stomps inside the building. The camera cuts back to Bustamante. "You heard it here first. One person died in the attack this afternoon, and we've been told that further attacks seem unlikely. But as I stand in an almost deserted downtown area, I have to wonder. Will today's attack prove to be the only one? Stay safe, folks."

Chapter 24

Day 331, Wednesday

Audrey

Jabbing at the TV remote, I turn it off. It's been three days since the attack in the bakery, and the local channels have run Sheriff Lamb's statement at least fifty times. I practically have the entire thing memorized by now. The sheriff is a natural liar. It must come with the territory. When dealing with criminals every day, he somehow learned to spin tales like one.

I shift on the hospital bed where I'm sitting cross-legged in a pair of leggings and my favorite hoodie. After Justin woke up from surgery and Karen had berated him about getting shot (and kissed him when she didn't think anyone was watching), he convinced her to go home and get some sleep. He didn't argue when she came back half an hour later with a duffle bag full of clean clothes and a toothbrush.

"You doing okay in here?" Karen stands in the doorway to my hospital room, one palm gripping the frame. Dark circles under her eyes make it obvious she's not getting much more sleep in this place than I am. I don't blame her. I've seen the cot she made them put in Justin's room. It's so short it probably wouldn't be comfortable for a ten year old.

"I'm critically ill. Haven't you heard?" I shoot her a wry look. "I believe I was promised ice cream?"

Her attention cuts from me to the empty bed beside mine. I shrug.

Clicking her tongue, Karen tosses a brown paper bag onto the foot of the bed. "Here. One of the deputies just brought it in."

"Thanks." Opening the bag, I scoop out a pint of chocolate peanut butter crunch ice cream and a bright pink spoon. "If Twinkle's Emporium ever goes out of business, this entire town will probably collapse in on itself."

"It could be worse. They could be dead." Taryn waltzes past Karen and plops down on the empty bed. "This dying stuff is so boring. It's literally killing me."

"You aren't supposed to leave this room."

"I had to go to the bathroom."

Karen's gaze moves pointedly from Taryn's face to the private bathroom angled in the corner.

My sister matches Karen's glare with one of her own. "There's nothing to do in here."

"Play cards."

"Audrey has already beat me at Uno way too many times."

"Watch TV."

"Sheriff Lamb's statement is not exactly must-see programming."

"Take a nap."

"And miss all the machines beeping?"

They bicker back and forth for a couple more minutes before Karen throws up her hands. "I don't know what to tell you. It is what it is, so you'll just have to make the best of it."

Taryn chews on her lip. "I want to go home." As if on cue, her phone pings in her hand. She takes a peek before shoving it under her pillow. It's probably another fake heartbroken message from one of our friends. For some reason, they think it's hilarious to make up fake obituaries for us. I have to admit, some of them have gotten Taryn and I laughing when we really needed it.

Esau, on the other hand, has continued texting Taryn like normal, although Viv reports he's playing the bereaved boyfriend well when he does venture into town. Mostly, he's been holed up at his uncle's farm for the past three days. I don't blame him. If he's getting any of the scrutiny Taryn and I do sometimes, I get it.

I chafe under the restlessness making my skin itch. When Karen and the sheriff told us the plan, I agreed immediately, because if it draws our tormentor out into the open so they can catch the psycho, I'm all for it. Anything to put an end to this hell. But it's been three days, and not a single suspicious thing has happened at or around the hospital. I'm starting to hope that the shooter was hurt in the shootout and crawled in a hole somewhere to die.

Taryn frowns, watching me dig in my pint for a big chunk of peanut butter. Sliding off her bed, she climbs onto mine. "I want some too. Got another spoon?"

"Here." Karen hands my sister a bag neither of us noticed.

Taryn squeals when she opens it. "You're the best! Finally something good to eat around here." Pulling out a pint of half brownie batter and half cinnamon swirl, she digs in.

"Glad to help. I'm going back down the hall. Stay inside, okay?"

Taryn swallows her bite before looking up at our agent. "This is getting old."

"I agree. How much longer do we have to do this?"

"Give it a couple more days," she says.

When we're both silent, Karen takes that as our consent, and goes.

I chew on a chunk of frozen peanut butter, savoring the sweet and salty ripple on my tongue. Sneak a look at my sister. Take another slow bite.

"What?" Taryn's eyes are locked on me. "If you want to ask me something, just do it."

"Where were you really?"

My twin's eyes tighten, and she's suddenly fascinated by the swirls of brownie in the pint in her hand. She casts around for a big bite of fudge for so long that I don't think she's going to answer. "Did you know there's a growing pile of stuff outside the hospital? People are leaving candles, flowers, teddy bears, that kind of thing. There are even signs, which of course I can't read from the sky walk up on the third floor."

My first instinct is to scold her. Remind my more reckless sister that we aren't supposed to go anywhere near the public areas of the hospital, in case someone sees us and leaks the truth behind the ruse we're perpetrating over the entire town. Over the entire world, really. But I don't. I don't want to hide like a threatened animal anymore, either. Every second we wait in the hospital is one more our aggressor steals from us, never to be gotten back.

In the hours after the attack, Lamb cooked up this scheme. We needed a way to draw out the killer, he'd said. Instead of waiting for them to strike again, we'd find a way to make them come to us. Karen backed him up, the zeal apparent in her eyes. I understood—the man she loved had to have surgery to remove a bullet from his shoulder, where it had nicked one of his major arteries. If the ambulance hadn't arrived so quickly, that day would have turned out very differently.

182

I agreed to the plan right away, but was surprised when Taryn did too. Then it occurred to me that since Esau was at the bakery that day, he could have been killed just as easily as the rest of us. Looking at my sister in that moment, with my mouth open in shock at Lamb's idea, I knew what she was doing. She might have been able to pretend away the danger up to that point, but once Esau got put in the line of fire, she couldn't hide from it anymore. Couldn't use her acting skills to assert that everything was fine. The expression she was making—the one I thought was annoyance—was fury. It was resolve hardening into something so firm, so solid, that only catching the sicko who's torturing us would be able to soften it.

Taryn has finally abandoned denial. She wants to catch them as much as I do. Maybe even more.

So do many, many others. The crush of headlines about Taryn's supposed death over the last three days has been overwhelming, but in a good way. There are people all over this green earth rooting for us. Rooting for me. Mourning another tragic death. It's been encouraging, despite the fact that it's all based on a lie. The reporter I was going to give an exclusive interview to has reached out, too. Yesterday. Just to see how I'm doing. She didn't even mention the interview. It felt… nice. I haven't responded since I'm supposed to be in intensive care, but I will. I want to tell my story, share it with others. Maybe all of the awful crap I've gone through will help someone else keep fighting.

Taryn is watching when I refocus my glazed eyes on her. Looking into my sister's face, into eyes that match mine stroke for stroke, relief that she is safe floods me. "What if someone visiting the hospital saw you?"

"They'll think I'm you," she whispers. Sticking the lid on her pint, she tosses it and the spoon into the bag. Gestures toward where my ice cream is slowly melting in my hand. "You done? I'll take it down to the nurse's station and sweet talk them into putting it in the fridge in their break room."

Shaking my head, I hold out my hands. "I'll go. You're dead, remember?"

Taryn's arms shoot toward me. "Brains. Must. Eat. Brains."

Laughing, I push her off and stroll in the direction of the nurse's station. At the far end of the hall, one of Lamb's deputies is posted at the door to the ICU. No one gets in without approval. They're hiding us on this floor because visiting hours are so strictly enforced. It's easier to keep track of everyone who walks these halls, unlike some of the busier wards.

I'm returning from chatting with a very kind older nurse when a flurry of alarm bells goes off in one of the rooms. The nurses go running, leaving the counter unattended. I could say this is the first alarm in the three days we've been sequestered in the ICU, but I'd be lying. I haven't had the heart to ask how many people have died while we've been sheltering here. It's kind of morbid, hiding here and pretending to be critically ill, when people are actually losing their lives rooms away.

It could so easily have been Taryn. Or Justin. Esau. Me.

A doctor steps out of the staff elevator and into a patient room, masked and gloved up. I hope he's able to give the necessary help and care.

My fists clench as I pivot into our room. I hope the son of a bitch who's been stalking us does show their face, so we can end this. Spring the trap we've laid.

Once when Taryn and I were little, our mom and dad took us to a cabin in the mountains for a family getaway. The cabin was small, and there wasn't much to do. The ancient TV didn't even work. When we bugged Dad about being bored, he gave us the makings for a crude snare and the instructions to put it together. We spent the rest of that weekend catching squirrels, chipmunks, and blue jays by luring them into a box to get peanuts, and snapping the twine tied to the stick to drop the box and trap our prey inside. Watching the animals chitter angrily at us when we lifted the box and let them go made us giggle endlessly. That weekend, we were the hunters.

Every day for the past year I've felt like one of those squirrels. Frightened. Angry. Trapped in a dark corner with no way out. Prey waiting for the trap to be sprung.

In the past three days, we've become the hunters once again. Our snare is baited and set. We wait, grasping that long piece of twine in our hands, waiting for our quarry to show themselves. To creep into the box and grab a juicy metaphorical peanut.

Taryn and I are the hunters.

We're also the bait.

"What's going on out there? It's pretty quiet." Taryn looks up from her phone, quickly pushing it face down into the scratchy hospital blanket when I try to look.

"Anything from Esau?"

Smiling, she holds out the phone. A photo of a furrowed field fills the screen, green shoots barely breaking the surface of the moist soil. A second shows Esau, grinning in front of the field. "They planted the corn for the maze a couple weeks ago, and it's started to sprout. His uncle is pretty excited about their design for this year. He's being stubborn and won't tell me what it is."

"He tried to tell me, you know, that day."

"He what?" She screeches, laughing. "So not fair. There I was, dying, and he was telling *you* about the corn maze." She

185

flops back onto her bed, hand thrown dramatically across her brow.

"He tried to tell me. I had a lot going on."

She quiets. "I hate this. I just want it to be over, so we can finally move on. This year has been ridiculous."

I swallow, tracing the quilt's lines. "I'm glad we're finally talking... about this. I thought you'd never stop pretending everything was fine. I felt alone, Taryn. You weren't shunning me anymore, but..."

Taryn's eyes are wet when they find mine. My eyes immediately start to water. "I'm sorry I made you feel that way. It's just that—this year has been so hard. Pretending it was better, that all of this crap was over, was the only way I could keep going. But once Esau got hurt..."

"It's hard to pretend it away when someone you love is hurt. I felt that way when the Gemini Killer threatened Noah and his family."

"Yeah. Hard to ignore, isn't it?"

"But sis, last year, when I tried to tell Mom and Dad about the car I kept seeing everywhere, when I tried to tell them I was being followed, you didn't believe me either."

Taryn bites her lip. Penitence knits her brow. Sighing, she reaches out a hand. I take it. "I won't make that mistake again," she says. "I should have believed you, and I'm sorry."

We both fall silent, thinking.

After a minute, I realize something's still bothering me. I finally speak up. "Even if Esau was never hurt, you couldn't keep pretending everything was fine. Denial isn't healthy. I mean, we're going through a giant mountain of crap, Taryn, and I needed you. I need you. You can't stick your head back in the sand like a stupid ostrich, okay?"

Wiping her eyes, she nods. "Okay."

Shoving her over, I scoot onto her bed and pull her in for a hug. "Good."

Taryn chews on her lip. "Esau and I have been fighting. A lot, you know? And he's even less compromising than usual. It's like we're back at square one. The other day he tried to renege on letting me try different props for the scene we were working on, after he specifically told me I could. It's just so frustrating."

Rubbing her arm, I give her half a smile. "Hey. Esau is always frustrating. And you'll get through it. He loves you, remember? He said so."

Despite herself, Taryn can't stifle a smile of her own. "I had to tickle it out of him. You should have seen his face."

"But he did say it."

"He did."

"Hold on to that, and try not to let the rest get you down, okay?"

Taryn skims the cloudy sky outside our window, looking for something I can't see. When she turns to me, she sticks out her pinky. "Swear?"

We pinky swear on it. "Want to work on your lines?"

My offer perks Taryn up. She jumps out of bed and digs through her bag, tossing me her script. She strikes a pose in the middle of the floor, pretending to be her character in the play. I grin, watching her worry fade away as she focuses on the task I've set. I read the first couple lines of the scene, doing my best Esau impression, and Taryn barely manages to hold her serious expression. "Is that how you think he sounds? Wow, that's terrible."

I scoff. "Hey, I'm an amazing actor."

"Right."

"I had everyone fooled last semester."

"That was a team effort."

"Go team," I say, waving an imaginary pom-pom in the air.

Taryn's laughter turns serious. "It is *really* quiet out there. There haven't been any alarms in a while."

"Maybe everyone is making a miraculous recovery. What? It could happen."

"You're right. It could. After all, I'm going to rise from the dead pretty soon. Still, I think I'll just go scope it out. Be right back." Taryn waltzes over to the door, but she doesn't make it past the frame. A doctor shoves her back into the room. Following, he shuts the door. The lock snaps into place.

"What the hell? Who are—" Taryn screeches to a halt, whatever she was going to say dying on her lips.

The gun in the newcomer's hand shuts her up. The man's mouth curls in disgust. In his palm, the weapon doesn't waiver. He stands with his back against our sealed door wearing blue scrubs just like the ones the hospital's staff wear. His hair slicked back under a doctor's scrub cap. A mask covers the lower half of his face.

I can't reconcile the cruel shine of the gun's barrel with the uniform. People who wear scrubs care for people. Help them. Heal their bodies and minds. Not brandish a gun in their faces. I push my gaze upward. To a face I recognize. Shock pulses through my body, making my muscles seize. My breath snags in my chest.

Chapter 25

It's Nate. He's got a gun, and it's aimed straight at Taryn's heart.

"Nate? What—what are you doing?" I shake my head, hoping to clear my vision. Change the face of the guy holding my sister and me at gunpoint. Blinking hard, I look again. Dark brunette hair and tan skin. Just like my friend. The same determined expression he used to make when he played soccer against Kate and me at summer camp. Nate is here, right now, pointing a gun at my sister.

Floating outside my body, I go back to that day in the park. Nate barely looked at me. Imbuing his reticence to meet me was easy. He was grieving, depressed. Desperately in need of someone to talk to, even if it wasn't me. But now, looking at the guy standing in front of Taryn and me, it's painfully obvious that he isn't only depressed. He's livid. At us.

Nate's eyes jump back and forth between me and my mirror image. The gun jerks in his hand as he gestures a stubbly chin at Taryn. "You. You're supposed to be dead. All of the headlines the past few days... I watched your sheriff's statement over and over, just to be sure. I thought I had finally killed one of you. Why aren't you dead?"

Taryn gulps. Her eyes are locked on the barrel of the gun. "Sorry?"

The boy's eyes narrow. He takes a step forward.

I fling an arm in front of Taryn. Her fingers close painfully around my wrist, my skin red under her fingertips.

"You have no idea how sorry you're going to be," Nate snarls. "Kneel down."

My eyes go wide. I've seen enough movies to know that when an insane person with a gun aimed at your heart commands you to kneel down, it's bad. Very, very bad.

Okay, no kneeling.

Whipping my gaze over Nate confirms it—he definitely looks unhinged. There's a wildness behind his eyes. As if he's barely containing himself. His impulse to hurt us, whatever is causing it, is riding him mercilessly. Sweat trickles down his temple, and his foot taps on the linoleum floor in an absent way.

I have to keep him talking while I figure out what to do. "Why are you doing this?" I ask, wrestling my voice to remain steady. "Maybe if you tell us, we can help."

"Kneel!" He sneers, scowl deepening.

Taryn's knuckles are white as she gently pushes my arm down. "Hold on a second. Nate, you know us. We were friends that summer at camp. We used to watch clips of old TV shows online and mock them. Your favorites were from that lifeguard show... What was it called? We thought it was hilarious. Remember?"

Nate clenches his jaw. "*Baywatch*," he spits. "Of course I remember. The second I heard your names on the news, I knew what I had to do. The Gemini Killer took my parents, and he's dead. He didn't have to pay for his crimes. But you two, you two can pay. I can make you. So I started sending those stupid notes to the newspaper, just to make you scared. It took me hours scouring magazines for all the letters I needed,

190

but I figured they'd be harder to trace. And you know what? I was right. Your incompetent sheriff has no idea."

The cruelty in his voice makes my entire body tense like too-tight strings on a violin. Screaming echoes in my ears. Taryn's screaming from the day of our parents' funeral. She wasn't speaking to me then. I'll never forget that primal, anguished sound. Her wail had sucked everything good and right out of the world. All that remained was emptiness and pain.

We've come so far from that day. We've come so far, and we can't go back. We won't.

Taryn resists when I try to push her behind me, but I'm determined. No one else is going to bleed for me. Especially not her. My only sister.

"Nate. Put the gun down. Please. We can talk about this. We lost our parents, too, but it wasn't our fault. It wasn't my fault. I had no control over the Gemini Killer."

"You did! He was your sick boyfriend, or something. All of this is your fault." It's every fear, every ounce of guilt I've carried since the day my parents were slain, thrown at my feet by a boy gripped in the unyielding fist of anger.

I swallow. "I couldn't stop him. He would have killed me. But you, you have the control in this room. You're in charge. You can stop this. No one else needs to die, Nate."

Deep-set eyes narrow as his head shakes. One hand releases the gun to swipe across his sweat-dampened forehead before enclosing the grip. "You're wrong. Someone has to pay. I have to do this."

"It's never too late to let go," Taryn says, arms wrapping around my waist from behind. Her chin slots into place over my shoulder. We're a unit, she and I. Now more than ever. "Please let us go."

191

"I can't do that." He adjusts his grip on the gun and edges closer.

The symbols debossed on the barrel of the weapon stand out starkly against the smooth metal. My eyes snap to the hole in the muzzle that at any second could unleash lightning-fast hell on Taryn and me. A shudder overtakes my body at the thought of it tearing through our flesh. Blood. Pain.

No more.

I can keep him talking. Someone is bound to notice something is wrong. Right?

As slowly as possible, I lift one hand to cover one of Taryn's where they're banded around my stomach. The pad of my pointer presses into her skin. *One. Two. Three.*

Her chin digs into my shoulder. It's all the assent I need.

I stare at Nate, locking eyes as a matador with a raging bull ready to charge. Pour every bit of pain and determination into that look. The weight of it nearly steals my breath, but I don't waver.

Nate's finger eases toward the trigger, but his attention dips to Taryn's hands. Something Justin said to us weeks ago at the gun range crystallizes in my head. *It's much more difficult to hit a moving target. Most people aren't good enough shots to do it.*

Another press on Taryn's hand. *One.*

Two.

Three.

Taryn yanks away and bolts to the side, screaming for help. I rush in a wide arch toward Nate, praying Justin was right. My fists slam down on his elbow. Can I muster enough force to make him drop the gun? No.

A shot cracks the air.

Taryn's screaming cuts off abruptly. My heart stops. If Taryn is hurt… Red shades my vision. I hammer at our

192

attacker's hands, ignoring the smoking barrel. A lamp rockets past Nate's head and smashes into pieces against the wall.

Footsteps pound closer. Two sets. No, three? I can't make them out between blows on Nate Anderson's arms. A sickly, shocked gasp rises at the unexpected macabre pall of our reunion. I. Can't. Stop. Until. He…

With an anguished growl, his fingers unwrap from the metal. The gun falls, hitting the floor with a clang and skidding away. Clutching his arm against his chest, our attacker lunges for it. I hurl toward him, landing on his back with a grunt. Our arms tangle as we hit and scratch. Try to keep each other from wrapping our greedy hands around the gun. His elbow catches in my side, stealing my breath. I wind my fist in his shaggy hair and rip.

Taryn scrabbles over the floor like a crab, plucking the gun off the ground and hoisting it like Karen and Justin taught us. She holds it like an expert. All those hours of gun safety and handling pay off in a blink.

My heartbeat skids as Taryn lowers the firearm, aiming it at Nate's chest. When she speaks, it's in a cold, flat tone I've never heard before. "We've had enough. This ends now."

One corner of the guy's mouth twists. "This doesn't end until you're both dead and in the ground."

The door bursts open, the knob smashing into the wall. Deputy Kelley, Karen, and Justin stand in the brink, the women slightly in front of the recently injured agent man. Their guns raised, swiveling toward our attacker.

I don't miss the moment their eyes glow in recognition. Last fall, during the attacks, they read the files on each of the Gemini Killer's victims. Even face-down on the ground underneath me, they know the male Anderson twin.

Karen relieves Nate of his freedom of arm movement by

encasing his wrists in handcuffs. Justin takes the gun from Taryn, emptying its clip and securing it in his belt.

"What happened?" Karen asks.

Taryn and I both talk at the same time, our explanations melding together into a long-winded story about everything Nate said and how we kept him talking until our favorite FBI agents arrived. When we're done, I take deep gulps of air. It sounds unreal, when we put it all together like that.

Deputy Kelley takes custody of Nate and crab-marches him out of the room. He tosses a final glare at us over his shoulder as he goes, but even so, I can't hate him. I know the pain he's feeling. It's merely been misplaced.

Karen encloses us in her arms, squeezing tight. "I have never had to watch over two such disaster-prone people. How many times are we going to have to rescue you two? Not that I'm not honored to do it."

"Glad we got here in time. I've gotten rather fond of both of you." Justin pats our shoulders, his movements stiff around the large bandage on his shoulder. His grin is lopsided in relief.

"Back at you," I say.

"Seriously." Taryn snuggles closer, and I wrap my arms around her. She holds me tight.

"That was way too close," I whisper into my twin's neck.

"You're telling me. That crazy dude shot a hole in my sweater." I gasp when she leans back enough to hold the billowing fabric out to reveal a hole near the side seam.

We're interrupted by the sheriff and a couple of his deputies tromping into the room. He observes the scene with a practiced sweep. Rubbing at his temple with one hand, the older man eyes my sister and me. "You two all right?"

"I think so."

"We're so touched you care, Sheriff." Taryn smiles at him.

Karen sweeps the room, eyeing the bullet hole in the far wall. Shards of a shattered lamp glitter in a pile behind the door. Finally, her attention returns to my sister and me. "Pack up your stuff, and we'll go home as soon as we've given the sheriff the update."

Taryn and I are already finished unpacking our things and sitting around the kitchen table, waiting for news, when Justin's phone rings. His features tighten at whatever the person on the other end has to say. Glancing our way, he shifts. Probably debating stepping into the other room for privacy against the merits of leaving the trouble-prone Thomas twins alone for even a minute. Turning his back, he leans over the sink to peer out the kitchen window to the eucalyptus grove beyond. Whispers, "He wouldn't say anything?"

I hold my breath. Karen went to the sheriff's department an hour ago to interrogate Nate, and it sounds like he isn't cooperating. My stomach churns, the peanut butter and jelly sandwich Justin made me no longer palatable. Any hope I had for clarity dies in my chest. Nate isn't going to explain his motivation, his thought process, to Agent Biel. There will be no understanding why he blames Taryn and me for the pain he's drowning in. No reasoning for what finally made him snap.

Once I've tossed my half-eaten sandwich, I lean back against the counter, lingering. Waiting for Justin to get off the phone. He's just hung up, mouth opening to speak, when there's a frenetic knocking at the front door. "Stay here," Justin orders.

Taryn gets out of her chair, easing toward the archway to see who it is.

Noah. "I drove to the hospital, and it's swarming with police. Then I got Audrey's message that you're all back

195

here…"

"Kitchen," Justin says.

A set of footsteps comes tearing through the living room. Taryn melts into the wall, a frown fluttering over her face.

Noah skids into the doorway. "Is everyone okay? Are you—" His words die when he sees Taryn and me, looking rough. A purple bruise has already formed on my cheek where Nate landed a punch in the scramble for the gun.

Swiping his glasses off with one hand, my favorite guy cleans them on the front of his shirt. Slides them back onto his nose. "What happened? Audrey?"

My smile comes to life at the way he says my name. His cheeks are flushed pink, chest heaving as if he sprinted all the way here from the hospital. "Let's go sit on the couch, and I'll tell you everything."

Sighing, he sinks down on the sofa, leaving no space between us. One light hand runs across my shoulders before draping on the cushion behind my neck. I open my mouth on a question, but he beats me to it. "Abuela is with the twins."

Excusing herself, Taryn walks through the room for the stairs, phone already at her ear. I know without having to ask she's calling Esau. Letting him know he can stop pretending she's dead now.

"Wait a second, Taryn." Justin stands in the archway, phone lowered to his side. "That was Karen with an update on Nate."

"Nate?" Noah looks nonplussed.

Taryn spins on her heel, eyeing the agent. "Let me guess. Nate refused to cooperate?"

Justin's affirmative nod is weighted.

"Nate? As in Anderson?" Noah looks to me. "Can I ask what he has to do with any of this?"

Taryn fades away up the stairs as I tell Noah all about our morning. His eyes grow wider as I speak. It loosens the knots in my stomach, talking about it, so I tell him everything. The shock. Fear. Pain. Relief when Karen, Justin, and the deputy burst into the room. When I'm finished, my head lolls back to rest on his arm. "Thanks for listening. I'm so glad you're here."

"You're welcome, and me too." Noah's deep breath on my hair makes my heart flip in my chest like a dolphin frolicking in the ocean's waves. I turn my cheek against the cushion, close enough to see the flecks of light in his eyes. Smiling, I snake my arms around his waist and press my cheek against his soft flannel shirt. "Want a sandwich? Justin makes a mean PB and J, but I think I could replicate it."

Noah's chin rests on top of my head as his arms go around me. "Maybe later."

Nodding, my focus narrows to the warm, welcome pressure on my crown. I nestle my pleased grin against his chest. For the first time in almost three months, I can completely and fully relax. The maniac who has been torturing Taryn and me with threatening messages, stalking and shooting at us, is in custody. Given time, Sheriff Lamb will get to the bottom of Nate's motivation, and he'll likely be behind bars for quite a while. Maybe he'll even get the help he obviously needs to deal with the tidal wave of emotions he's likely feeling. Because despite everything he's done to us, I can't hate him.

I kind of wish I could, but what good would hate do anyway? None, that's what.

Nate let his grief morph into a hatred so strong he went after Taryn and me, blaming us for something we didn't do and had no control over.

On second thought, I take it back. I do hate him a little bit. It's something to bring up at my next therapy appointment.

Because unresolved anger clearly brings issues I do not want to deal with on top of my current stack.

Chapter 26

Day 334, Saturday

Audrey

I crane my neck to look up at the four-story, faded yellow building. Dim, miniscule windows run the length of the long concrete block like slots in an arcade game. I thought the twenty-foot high chain link fence with coils of barbed wire strung along the top was ominous enough, but the building takes it further. As far as I can see, it's a landscape of concrete. Not a slip of green anywhere. All bleak, cold gray.

Swallowing, I turn to Karen. She tilts her head. "Ready?"

I follow her inside, through security. They don't allow anything into the meeting room, not even my coat. So I shrug it off and hand it to a waiting officer, who tells me I can have my personal items back when I leave.

A maximum-security prison. It's not somewhere I ever thought I'd be. After Justin told me I had been cleared to visit Mr. Baugh, it was all I could think about. What could the man have to say? I don't know. Which is why I'm here, stepping into a long, wide room dotted with round tables bolted to the ground. Why I slide into the cold metal chair and wrap my hands around the edges of the seat to steady myself.

Mr. Baugh requested to see me. Taryn was antsy, wishing she could come hear what our former teacher and kidnapper has to say for himself. Her words.

A harsh buzz clangs through the room, and a door on the far side opens. A guard comes in, holding it against his back. One by one, men in vivid orange jumpsuits step into the room. A scruffy, rail-thin guy sits down at a table in the corner across from a woman who might be his wife or his daughter. A younger, bald inmate crouches in front of a toddler with beautiful, blond ringlets. Her toothy grin is wide as she flings her arms around his neck, giggling when he tickles her sides.

My throat tightens when Mr. Baugh enters. His eyes look past everyone until they land on me. Striding over, he takes a seat across the table. Looks from me to Karen, who is standing at my back. I don't have to look to know she's got a cold stare pinned on him.

The former teacher's attention slides to my face, looking me over. "I'm not used to seeing you without your scar."

My fingers rise to my unblemished cheek. "I didn't need it anymore."

He nods. Clears his throat. "I've had a lot of time to think, since I've been in here. About what I did."

He's thinner than I remember. More gray hairs thread through ashy brown. His skin is washed out, like someone sucked all the blood out of his veins and filled them with water. I wait, hoping he'll go on. Not knowing what to say. His hands wipe on his thighs. He clears his throat again.

"I just wanted to tell you personally I was sorry. For what I did. I knew helping my brother was wrong, but you have to understand. All my life, they were all I had. Our parents, they weren't good. I grew up knowing my brothers were the most important thing. I was the oldest, and it was my job to protect

at every time Albert was
tending to be Robert, it would
Killer's attacks. Every single

couldn't have. He was in the
ot mine. Robert, he was the
was free."

ght, the chair behind me
fore it clatters to the ground. I
I I believe a man who tried to
rother? I can't trust a single
. You're just trying to mess
e here."

e resignation in his voice. The
and bolt. She will follow.
me back, that he's not
one hundred percent done. I
he prepared. My mind leans
n the security guard in the
Cool air hits my flaming
ch churns and my speed
run. My vision narrows
g lot to the car. Its tail lights
the passenger door wide, I
ead back against the
. Focus on slowing down the
of me.

ilters into the stuffy cab.
re Karen's palm alights there,
firmly. "I'm here. I'm right

what does it: breaks me into

them. I would do anything to keep them safe. You understand that, right?"

I swallow past the lump in my throat. I thought a lot about what Mr. Baugh would say when I met him today, but I never thought I'd agree with any of it. But he's right. Family is the most important thing in my life, and I'd do anything to protect Taryn. To protect Karen and Justin. Noah and Esau. Fiona, Marisa, and Viv. "I do."

He nods. "So you understand why I had to help Albert. You have to know, I had no idea he'd been talking to you over the app. Had no idea he was posing as a teenage girl. I didn't know he was… When I showed him your photograph, it was purely as an excited teacher. I love…" he swallows, "loved working with teenagers. And you, Audrey, your photography is excellent. I just wanted to share it with someone. I was shocked when he told me what he'd done. That he'd been talking to you. He convinced me that you understood him. He said if I helped him meet you, everything would work out. I wanted to believe it, since the alternative was that he was *wrong* somehow. Nobody wants to believe that their younger brother is… not normal. So I agreed to help him. You understand."

My hands grip the edge of the chair tighter as I resist the urge to pop out of it. "I can understand wanting to protect your sibling, someone you love, but Albert killed people. He murdered my parents. He tried to murder my sister, my only family left. You had to know that was wrong."

Mr. Baugh's feet shuffle under the table, the toe of one shoe dragging over the floor. When his eyes meet mine again, there's something ominous in them. Something that makes my insides recoil. "There's something you don't know," he grits out.

The room darkens, a chill worsening the morose

atmosphere, making it sepulchral.

Abruptly, nerves assail me. I don't want to be here. Don't want him to say anything more. My instincts are blaring that whatever else he utters, it will not be good. It'll turn my world upside down yet again, shaking the ground underneath my soles and leaving me without a foundation to stand on. I shoot out of my chair.

"If you're ready, we can go. Just say the word." Karen's reassurances manage to slow my frantic heart. I came to find out what Mr. Baugh has to say. I have to see this through. I sink into my seat so achingly slowly.

"Audrey?"

I drag my attention back to my former teacher, trying and failing to ignore the dread screaming between my ears. I hold myself still. I don't want to hear this. I have to. I don't have a choice. If there's something he needs to say that I don't already know, I should listen. The part of me that wants to finish this needs to hear it. "Go ahead."

Mr. Baugh glances at the guard in the corner. "Ever since they were toddlers, my brothers enjoyed tricking people. They were identical, and they loved using that to their advantage. Teachers. Family friends. Uncles and aunts we didn't see often enough to be able to tell them apart. Our friends at school could tell, of course, but no one else could. They'd switch places at doctor's appointments. In classes before the teachers got to know them. It was a game, to see how long they could go before they were caught and switched back. The first time they got into trouble with the sheriff, Robert convinced Albert to switch places with him. He wanted to see if they could fool the police. It worked."

Dread expands in my gut. I have a strong feeling about where Mr. Baugh is going with this story. Part of me wants to

would stake my life on the fact t[...]
arrested last summer and fall, pr[...]
coincide with one of the Gemini [...]
one.

His head shake is slow. "He[...]
drunk tank that day. His words, [...]
one who… He was the one who[...]

My vision tunnels. I jolt up[...]
teetering. Karen catches it just b[...]
can't hear this. I can't. Why wou[...]
kidnap me and deliver me to his [...]
thing this man says. "You're lyin[...]
with me! I never should have co[...]

"Audrey, please." I ignore t[...]
pain. Whirling, I brush past Kare[...]

Mr. Baugh yells for me to c[...]
finished, but I don't comply. I'm [...]
don't care what other twisted lies[...]
off its axis as I snatch my coat fr[...]
lobby and yank it onto my arms. [...]
cheeks when I step outside. Stor[...]
picks up. I amp up to a jog, then [...]
darkly as I streak across the park[...]
flash as Karen unlocks it. Tuggin[...]
throw myself inside. Leaning my [...]
headrest, I squeeze my eyes close[...]
inadequate breaths that stutter ou[...]

My door opens, and cool air [...]
Warmth skates over my knee bef[...]
the faintest of touches. Then mo[...]
here."

The gentleness in her tone is[...]

a million pieces. A sob escapes as I collapse into her arms, soddening her jacket with tears. She wraps her arms around me and lets me cry, shushing gently until I'm able to calm down. It's comforting, maternal. Which makes me want to cry even more. But I wrangle my overwrought emotions and sit up, sniffing harshly. "Thanks."

Karen doesn't let go right away. Her hands rest firmly on my shoulders. Brown eyes steady on mine. "You're welcome. And I meant what I said. I'm here for you, if you ever need anything."

I thank her. Wipe my cheeks with the back of one hand. "I'm ready to go."

The agent's mouth is grim. "I need a minute to make a call, first. Let my boss know what Mr. Baugh said about his brother."

Riding toward home, we're both quiet. Karen slows to a stop at a red light in the middle of town, right across from the diner. Inside, the place is packed. It's Saturday, so Viv should be working. I should be working. It would have been so much better than visiting the prison and blowing up my life.

The light turns green and Karen eases forward. Her hands tighten on the steering wheel when I ask the question that's buzzing in my head. "Did you ever get information from the app people? About the IP of the original *CuteAshlee*? Do you know where the messages originated from?"

The tension in her hands gives her away.

"We did," she finally says. "The IP address indicated that the user who was messaging you was located in the same city as the prison. We didn't think a lot of it, assuming that Albert must have been visiting his brother while he was incarcerated. We looked into it, but didn't find a rental or where he might have been staying at the time. Now, after hearing what Mr.

Baugh told us, it makes sense. Albert must have been spending a lot of time in this area, causing trouble on purpose when he knew his brother was preparing to… act. The IP address connected to his account reflects that. It also sheds light on why he was spotted in the grocery store."

My brain stutters and starts again. "It does? How?"

Karen sneaks a look at me as she turns the corner into our neighborhood. "The man we thought was Robert Baugh was arrested multiple times over last spring and summer, and was released the final time two days before the man we identified as Albert Baugh was caught on the security footage in our grocery store."

I remember that day. It hadn't made sense to me that a man who had evaded law enforcement for months would suddenly parade himself on a local store's cameras. I had assumed it was because the Gemini Killer was closing in and had wanted to scare me. It had worked. I'd known from that day that he was coming for my sister and me, and that he wouldn't hesitate to hurt anyone who got in his way. But if that was Albert, and he wasn't the murderer… "Robert let Albert take the heat, even though he was the true killer."

"If what Mr. Baugh told us today was correct, it seems that way. Yes."

My chest tightens. If all of this is true, then the only crime Albert was guilty of was kidnapping. "Albert was Robert's alibi. This whole time, he took the blame. He *died* for his brother's crimes. The Gemini Killer… He's still alive."

My hands clutch at the seat belt strap holding me upright. Almond trees slide past in a blur of brown and gray. It's fitting that my eyes won't focus, since my brain isn't registering any of it. It's honing in on one terrifying truth: the Gemini Killer is still out there. Right now. Biding his time.

I'm suddenly certain of one thing. He'll come for me eventually. Knives sharpened and ready to carve out my heart. The only recourse I have is to sharpen knives of my own.

Chapter 27

Day 336, Monday

Audrey

"Table five is calling," Viv whispers as she skirts toward the drink station.

"Thanks," I say, thankful I have a normal job to do today. Because waiting around at home for Karen or Justin to update us on the manhunt for Robert Baugh was driving me out of my mind. Sunday's vigil stretched so far that it felt like an eternity had passed when I finally crawled into bed, even though Noah and Esau came over to hang out for most of the day.

"Yoohoo!" One of the little old ladies in the corner booth waves her hand in the air, trying to get my attention.

Sliding the hot plates onto another customer's table with a smile, I brush off my hands and pivot toward the booth. "Is there anything I can get you ladies while you wait for your dinners to be ready?"

All four of the blue-hairs boldly give me a once over, sending each other pointed looks. One retrieves a newspaper article from her purse and points to the headline. "Is this you?"

Tilting my head, I read it upside down.

Thomas Twins' Nightmare Isn't Over—Inside Source Claims

them. I would do anything to keep them safe. You understand that, right?"

I swallow past the lump in my throat. I thought a lot about what Mr. Baugh would say when I met him today, but I never thought I'd agree with any of it. But he's right. Family is the most important thing in my life, and I'd do anything to protect Taryn. To protect Karen and Justin. Noah and Esau. Fiona, Marisa, and Viv. "I do."

He nods. "So you understand why I had to help Albert. You have to know, I had no idea he'd been talking to you over the app. Had no idea he was posing as a teenage girl. I didn't know he was… When I showed him your photograph, it was purely as an excited teacher. I love…" he swallows, "loved working with teenagers. And you, Audrey, your photography is excellent. I just wanted to share it with someone. I was shocked when he told me what he'd done. That he'd been talking to you. He convinced me that you understood him. He said if I helped him meet you, everything would work out. I wanted to believe it, since the alternative was that he was *wrong* somehow. Nobody wants to believe that their younger brother is… not normal. So I agreed to help him. You understand."

My hands grip the edge of the chair tighter as I resist the urge to pop out of it. "I can understand wanting to protect your sibling, someone you love, but Albert killed people. He murdered my parents. He tried to murder my sister, my only family left. You had to know that was wrong."

Mr. Baugh's feet shuffle under the table, the toe of one shoe dragging over the floor. When his eyes meet mine again, there's something ominous in them. Something that makes my insides recoil. "There's something you don't know," he grits out.

The room darkens, a chill worsening the morose

atmosphere, making it sepulchral.

Abruptly, nerves assail me. I don't want to be here. Don't want him to say anything more. My instincts are blaring that whatever else he utters, it will not be good. It'll turn my world upside down yet again, shaking the ground underneath my soles and leaving me without a foundation to stand on. I shoot out of my chair.

"If you're ready, we can go. Just say the word." Karen's reassurances manage to slow my frantic heart. I came to find out what Mr. Baugh has to say. I have to see this through. I sink into my seat so achingly slowly.

"Audrey?"

I drag my attention back to my former teacher, trying and failing to ignore the dread screaming between my ears. I hold myself still. I don't want to hear this. I have to. I don't have a choice. If there's something he needs to say that I don't already know, I should listen. The part of me that wants to finish this needs to hear it. "Go ahead."

Mr. Baugh glances at the guard in the corner. "Ever since they were toddlers, my brothers enjoyed tricking people. They were identical, and they loved using that to their advantage. Teachers. Family friends. Uncles and aunts we didn't see often enough to be able to tell them apart. Our friends at school could tell, of course, but no one else could. They'd switch places at doctor's appointments. In classes before the teachers got to know them. It was a game, to see how long they could go before they were caught and switched back. The first time they got into trouble with the sheriff, Robert convinced Albert to switch places with him. He wanted to see if they could fool the police. It worked."

Dread expands in my gut. I have a strong feeling about where Mr. Baugh is going with this story. Part of me wants to tear out of my chair, out of this place and never come back. But I'm glued to the seat. Its edge digs into the backs of my thighs. My fingers grip it so tight they begin to ache.

"Earlier this year, Albert called me. He'd been arrested for public drunkenness. It wasn't serious, so I didn't worry about him. It wasn't the first time. He's been. . . he's had a hard time, since our mom died. They both did. But then he laughed, and told me that he'd been arrested as Robert. That he was locked up, and they thought they had Robert Baugh in custody. It ended up happening a handful of times. I didn't understand why he kept telling them he was Robert, or why they would have exchanged ID cards, until. . ." He stops talking, waiting for what he just said to sink in.

I blink, unable to believe what I'm hearing. Not wanting it to be true. It can't be true.

Karen looms over my shoulder. "You're saying your brother Robert wasn't arrested a single time last summer? That it was your other brother, Albert, who was in custody all those times?"

His solemn nod is like a death knell. I know. I *know* why he wanted to talk to me. He's letting me know the sick and twisted game that has entangled me is far from over. Too bad for me, his confession clobbers my peace. The sense of closure I'd begun to embrace vanishes without a trace.

"When—When was this? What were the dates? Do you remember?"

Mr. Baugh's eyes lock on mine. He doesn't say another word.

The blood drains from my face as the truth dawns. He doesn't need to say it. "It wasn't Albert who killed my parents, was it? He didn't kill any of them?" Before the man sitting across the table even opens his mouth, I have my answer. I would stake my life on the fact that every time Albert was arrested last summer and fall, pretending to be Robert, it would coincide with one of the Gemini Killer's attacks. Every single one.

His head shake is slow. "He couldn't have. He was in the drunk tank that day. His words, not mine. Robert, he was the one who... He was the one who was free."

My vision tunnels. I jolt upright, the chair behind me teetering. Karen catches it just before it clatters to the ground. I can't hear this. I can't. Why would I believe a man who tried to kidnap me and deliver me to his brother? I can't trust a single thing this man says. "You're lying. You're just trying to mess with me! I never should have come here."

"Audrey, please." I ignore the resignation in his voice. The pain. Whirling, I brush past Karen and bolt. She will follow.

Mr. Baugh yells for me to come back, that he's not finished, but I don't comply. I'm one hundred percent done. I don't care what other twisted lies he prepared. My mind leans off its axis as I snatch my coat from the security guard in the lobby and yank it onto my arms. Cool air hits my flaming cheeks when I step outside. Stomach churns and my speed picks up. I amp up to a jog, then a run. My vision narrows darkly as I streak across the parking lot to the car. Its tail lights flash as Karen unlocks it. Tugging the passenger door wide, I throw myself inside. Leaning my head back against the headrest, I squeeze my eyes closed. Focus on slowing down the inadequate breaths that stutter out of me.

My door opens, and cool air filters into the stuffy cab. Warmth skates over my knee before Karen's palm alights there, the faintest of touches. Then more firmly. "I'm here. I'm right here."

The gentleness in her tone is what does it: breaks me into

a million pieces. A sob escapes as I collapse into her arms, soddening her jacket with tears. She wraps her arms around me and lets me cry, shushing gently until I'm able to calm down. It's comforting, maternal. Which makes me want to cry even more. But I wrangle my overwrought emotions and sit up, sniffing harshly. "Thanks."

Karen doesn't let go right away. Her hands rest firmly on my shoulders. Brown eyes steady on mine. "You're welcome. And I meant what I said. I'm here for you, if you ever need anything."

I thank her. Wipe my cheeks with the back of one hand. "I'm ready to go."

The agent's mouth is grim. "I need a minute to make a call, first. Let my boss know what Mr. Baugh said about his brother."

Riding toward home, we're both quiet. Karen slows to a stop at a red light in the middle of town, right across from the diner. Inside, the place is packed. It's Saturday, so Viv should be working. I should be working. It would have been so much better than visiting the prison and blowing up my life.

The light turns green and Karen eases forward. Her hands tighten on the steering wheel when I ask the question that's buzzing in my head. "Did you ever get information from the app people? About the IP of the original *CuteAshlee*? Do you know where the messages originated from?"

The tension in her hands gives her away.

"We did," she finally says. "The IP address indicated that the user who was messaging you was located in the same city as the prison. We didn't think a lot of it, assuming that Albert must have been visiting his brother while he was incarcerated. We looked into it, but didn't find a rental or where he might have been staying at the time. Now, after hearing what Mr.

Baugh told us, it makes sense. Albert must have been spending a lot of time in this area, causing trouble on purpose when he knew his brother was preparing to… act. The IP address connected to his account reflects that. It also sheds light on why he was spotted in the grocery store."

My brain stutters and starts again. "It does? How?"

Karen sneaks a look at me as she turns the corner into our neighborhood. "The man we thought was Robert Baugh was arrested multiple times over last spring and summer, and was released the final time two days before the man we identified as Albert Baugh was caught on the security footage in our grocery store."

I remember that day. It hadn't made sense to me that a man who had evaded law enforcement for months would suddenly parade himself on a local store's cameras. I had assumed it was because the Gemini Killer was closing in and had wanted to scare me. It had worked. I'd known from that day that he was coming for my sister and me, and that he wouldn't hesitate to hurt anyone who got in his way. But if that was Albert, and he wasn't the murderer… "Robert let Albert take the heat, even though he was the true killer."

"If what Mr. Baugh told us today was correct, it seems that way. Yes."

My chest tightens. If all of this is true, then the only crime Albert was guilty of was kidnapping. "Albert was Robert's alibi. This whole time, he took the blame. He *died* for his brother's crimes. The Gemini Killer… He's still alive."

My hands clutch at the seat belt strap holding me upright. Almond trees slide past in a blur of brown and gray. It's fitting that my eyes won't focus, since my brain isn't registering any of it. It's honing in on one terrifying truth: the Gemini Killer is still out there. Right now. Biding his time.

I'm suddenly certain of one thing. He'll come for me eventually. Knives sharpened and ready to carve out my heart. The only recourse I have is to sharpen knives of my own.

Chapter 27

Day 336, Monday

Audrey

"Table five is calling," Viv whispers as she skirts toward the drink station.

"Thanks," I say, thankful I have a normal job to do today. Because waiting around at home for Karen or Justin to update us on the manhunt for Robert Baugh was driving me out of my mind. Sunday's vigil stretched so far that it felt like an eternity had passed when I finally crawled into bed, even though Noah and Esau came over to hang out for most of the day.

"Yoohoo!" One of the little old ladies in the corner booth waves her hand in the air, trying to get my attention.

Sliding the hot plates onto another customer's table with a smile, I brush off my hands and pivot toward the booth. "Is there anything I can get you ladies while you wait for your dinners to be ready?"

All four of the blue-hairs boldly give me a once over, sending each other pointed looks. One retrieves a newspaper article from her purse and points to the headline. "Is this you?"

Tilting my head, I read it upside down.

Thomas Twins' Nightmare Isn't Over—Inside Source Claims

Fisting and unclenching my hands, I manage to keep a pleasant smile plastered to my face. Looks like Mr. Baugh's lawyer spoke to the press. Probably hoping to spin his client's story to garner public sympathy. Good freaking luck with that. "Yes, that's me and my sister. Is there anything else I can help you with?"

If they get the vibe that I don't want to talk about the Gemini Killer, they blatantly ignore it. The one with the glasses skims over the article. "This says that one of the previous victims came after you. What I'm wondering is, this Nate fellow, was he in contact with Robert?"

Any answer I can give to her question would be a guess. Because Nate still hasn't said. Karen, however, doesn't think Nate had any idea Albert was innocent of the murders. When she mentioned it to him, apparently he blanched.

I don't have to put up with this, but these four ladies are mostly harmless. Annoying, but harmless. So I answer. "I don't know."

Emboldened, the woman speaks louder. "If he was the one writing the messages, what did those initials mean? What were they?" Between the four of them, they can't come up with the letters.

Twenty years ago, you ruined four girls' lives. Now I'm going to ruin yours. This is for Y, D, T, and L.

It's the same question I've been wondering. Nate wasn't even alive twenty years ago.

When Karen told Nate that the Gemini Killer was out there, he almost fainted. Then he started talking. Nate confessed there was someone else he was working with, but he swore it wasn't Robert Baugh. Agent Biel pressed, but the guy refused to tell her. Instead, he said he'd set up a meeting. Help them catch his partner.

Taryn did not react well to any of it. She insisted that we couldn't trust him and that he was only doing it to manipulate us. I tend to agree, which is why I'm sort of glad our agents didn't go into details about how Nate said he'd contact his accomplice. I do not want to be fixated on that. I didn't mention that if the messages Nate was sending were exclusively for Robert Baugh, they'd sounded awfully antagonistic. Why would he send such angry, threatening messages to a guy he was helping? And why would Nate work with the man who killed his parents? It doesn't make any sense.

I mull it over as I steer between the tables. Nate is a huge liar. What if he's lying about the messages? What if the murder notes he sent to the newspaper were a red herring, meant to throw off the authorities while he stalked and tried to kill us?

Taryn and Esau come in, my sister grinning as she picks a booth in my section. I greet them, taking their drink order. As I approach their table with cups in hand, I slow. Taryn is scrunched into the middle of the booth, whispering heatedly to her boyfriend, a single finger prodding his chest.

I try to back away, but she spots me. "Are those our drinks?"

"Uh, yeah." I slide them onto the table, and get two absent, "Thank yous," before they're focused solely on each other again. Taryn glances toward the kitchen when a clatter of breaking china rings through the diner.

"I have something to tell you," Esau says once he's taken a long, fortifying gulp of his iced tea.

Taryn's eyes narrow, her hand ringing around her own glass. "Okay?"

My heart squeezes. The two of them have been arguing about the play a lot. It's taken a toll on Taryn so much that I've considered asking if maybe she should drop out to keep the peace, but I like my head where it is, so I haven't.

Esau's eyes fall to her hand resting on the tabletop, and he takes it. "The reason I've been... a perfectionist at play practice."

"Understatement of the year," Taryn bites off.

Presenting my back to them, I tiptoe away, not wanting to make it obvious that I am totally listening to their conversation.

Esau tsks. "It's because. . . my parents are coming to visit. They're coming to see the play."

". . . Your parents. The parents you haven't seen in literal years."

I stop in my tracks, even though the guy at table nine is waving me over.

An affirmative hum. "That's them."

"Wow," is all I catch my twin say before my manager points to table nine, eyebrow raised.

I'm returning table nine's burger to the kitchen for the second time when my phone vibrates in my back pocket like a rock dropped into a motionless pond. I halt and then push forward slowly. Taryn and Esau are still in their booth, looking decidedly more chummy than they were when they came in, so it's probably not them texting me. Which means it's likely an update on the manhunt.

Like a robot, I collect the food for table five, careful to maneuver through the packed diner without whacking anyone in the back of the head with a ceramic plate. My phone is like a lead weight in my jeans, but I can't take my break yet. There's a queue at the hostess station of groups waiting to be seated. Table three needs their drinks. Table seven needs the check.

Any updates about the Gemini Killer will have to wait.

The humidity pumped into the alleyway from the industrial fans over the diner's stoves makes my hair frizz as soon as I step outside. I slump against the brick wall, positive that Justin will be out in a sec to check on me.

My hands shake as I pull out my phone. The photo sharing app I use appears on the screen. I've got so many notifications I'll never be able to get through them all. Even though I've set my profile to private, the barrage of follow requests is constant. A lot of people want access to me after they heard my name splashed across their TV.

Chewing my lip, I scroll mindlessly. What if Nate stole my phone not to freak me out, but to get access to my social media? He knew that I'd been messaging back and forth with Albert Baugh for months. Everyone did. So what if he took the phone thinking he could use it to get in touch with Robert instead? My hand tightens around my phone. Only one way to find out.

Scrolling through my inbox is like running through a field that I know has a single land mine in it. The odds of getting across safely are good; there's just the one mine. But if I step on it by accident? Boom.

Most of the messages are from weirdos begging me to tell them what it was like to chat with a serial killer. A fair few are dudes trying to get my attention with clever lines like, "What up?" A few are from survivors of other violent crimes, asking to connect. I make a note to come back to those later. There are some good online support groups that might be useful to them.

My eyes start to fog as I scroll and scroll without finding anything that grabs my attention. This was stupid. If Nate stole my phone to contact the Gemini Killer, he wouldn't have left evidence of it on an account I still had access to. Plus, Karen made me change all of my passwords the second I got a replacement phone. It would have shut the thief out almost immediately.

I let my head fall back with a disappointed huff. So much for that hunch. Plus, my break is almost over anyway.

The door eases open. Justin wears an expression that makes me soften. "You okay out here?"

We give each other matching half smiles. "I'm fine. Thanks for giving me a minute."

"You're welcome. Something on your mind?"

I pinch my mouth to one side, debating. Odds are he won't tell me if I ask, but I still have to try. "How did Nate say he could get in contact with him?"

Justin moves to one side, hand splayed over the door to keep it propped open. "Come back inside. It's cold out here."

I trudge up the hall toward the dining room, exhausted. I want my shift to be over so I can go home and finish off the pan of caramel brownies Noah and I made from a box yesterday when we were bored. My favorite boy showed me some tricks for making them extra luscious, and when I asked him how he knew what to do, he'd ducked his head, sheepish, before admitting he'd learned from his abuela.

Justin's question stops me. "You were just checking your photo app, right?"

I nod, afraid to turn around.

He gently prods me to one side so he can make eye contact. "If I tell you, you have to promise not to do anything unwise, all right?"

"I promise," I blurt.

He hesitates. Tiny wrinkles at the corners of his eyes deepen as Justin searches mine. He must be satisfied by what he sees. "If you were thinking he used the social app to contact someone, you were right. He hacked into your account before you could change the password and sent a single message, giving his accomplice a different account to contact if he wanted to talk. He deleted it before you could see it, and we just found it. It took a couple of techs hours to go through all the old data associated with your account."

My heart thuds behind my sternum, pooling in a heavy weight that makes breathing an effort. "And has he responded? Are they going to meet up?"

Justin's hands lift to rest on his belt. "Remember your promise."

I nod solemnly, and he continues. "Nate set up a meet with his partner for tomorrow night. We're ready for it, so try not to stress about it. Can you do that?"

Crossing my arms over my chest, I whisper, "I'll try. I hope you catch him."

"We will, and put them away for a long time. I'll make sure of it."

I'm about to clock back in when my guardian's hand lands on my arm. Gently, he tugs so I turn to face him. "I'm not going to tell you the when or where. I need you to leave it alone and trust us to handle it. Can you do that?" Justin's worry is plain in the curves around his mouth, the gentle pressure on my arm.

"I can do it." Just one more lie.

Chapter 28

Day 337, Tuesday

Audrey

The weather must have gotten the memo: something is happening tonight. Hence the rain. And lightning. And thunder so loud it sounds like there's a giant banging mountain-sized trash cans right outside the window. I blink, but it doesn't make it any easier to see past the front yard. Even if I could, the meet-up Nate arranged with Robert Baugh is happening in a park at the other end of town. I'm not supposed to know, but Taryn eavesdropped on Justin and Karen earlier this afternoon before they put on their gear, hugged us goodbye, and left.

We didn't actually say goodbye. None of us did. Because if this meeting goes like they've planned, the FBI will finally have the actual Gemini Killer. But with this storm raging? Something feels off. Thunder clangs like a warning bell through the house.

Taryn looks over her shoulder at me from where she's practicing her lines in the middle of the living room. She even roped the deputy assigned to keep an eye on us into helping her move the furniture so it mimics the set for the play. She wanted to go over the blocking again. Her body is tense as she rattles off lines, waiting beats in between for invisible, silent actors to deliver theirs. She hasn't said, but I think she's feeling extra pressure now that Esau's parents are attending opening night.

I'd be freaking out too. "You're going to be great, and I'm sure Mr. and Mrs. Chavez will like you when they see how much Esau does."

Taryn gives me a determined smile. "They're going to love me. I make the magic, remember? Magic." She goes back to running her lines loudly over the storm. The manic look in her eyes belies her words.

Deputy Kelley looks up from the corner before going back to whatever she was doing on her phone. The officer armed the security system the minute she walked in the door. I don't blame her. Taryn and I are proven flight risks. But yeah, the storm blowing outside is a major deterrent. Plus, I've decided that Justin and Karen are the adults here. They'll let us know whatever happens. My phone screen lights up when I press a button. The meet-up is supposed to happen in just a few minutes.

Taryn shaking out her hands in front of her chest hooks my attention. She's starting to spiral.

I climb off the sofa, skirting around the furniture and cut right in front of her. My sister lets out a huff, halting the frenzied pacing before she smacks into me. "Hey! What's the big idea?"

Grabbing Taryn's shoulders, I assess her expression. My eyes, my nose, and my mouth are reflected back at me. If it weren't for the scar, our identical looks would be uncanny. My entire life, I've had this whole other person who looks exactly like me. I mean, I don't usually think about how lucky I am to have had a sister for every minute of my life on this planet. The second I came into this world, I had a buddy. In the womb, even. A twin who became so much more than a sister. She means so much to me, and I don't tell her nearly often enough.

"You're freaking me out," Taryn says, eyes locked on mine.

"No way. You're the staring contest champion, remember?"

Her eyebrows twitch over a wobbly smile. "You're right. I forgot about that. We must have stared at each other for an hour that time."

"It was seven minutes."

"No way. It felt so long."

"No lie. I timed it."

Giving a gentle toss of hair, Taryn brings her hands up to rest on my forearms. "As much as I'm enjoying reminiscing, this isn't the time for a rematch. I have to get my lines down. Opening night is in two days."

"Your title is safe. I just have something to say."

"Wow, so serious."

"Taryn." My fingers put gentle pressure on her shoulders through her sweater.

"Okay, okay. I'm ready. Lay it on me. What does the great Audrey Thomas want to say?"

"You're such a smart aleck."

"It's part of my charm."

I roll my eyes good naturedly. "I'm not sure Esau would agree."

"He definitely would."

"Fine, but this isn't about that. I just want you to know that I love you. Okay? I'm glad you're my twin."

Taryn softens. "Wow. I think I needed to hear that. Thanks, Sis. I love you too, and I wouldn't want anyone else for a sister."

Puffing, I turn to the maelstrom outside the window. At

first, I was miffed that we weren't allowed to be anywhere near the meet-up. That we'd have to wait here for news that the hellish past year of our lives was finally, truly over. Taryn put up a fuss, wanting to know the second the Gemini Killer was in custody.

No dice. Karen insisted we stay safe at the house, far away from the action. Justin implied that she wouldn't be able to focus on the job if we were in danger, but he was probably just saying that to assuage our disappointment at being left behind. It was nice of him to try.

I didn't fight it. I want to know as soon as they've caught him and put him where he won't be able to hurt anyone else. But I don't need to be there. It's why we have cell phones. They'll let us know as soon as it's done. Clasping my arms loosely around my knees, I rest my chin on them. I'm glad we're inside where it's warm and dry. Thunder cracks the sky. Yeah, definitely glad I'm not going anywhere tonight.

Taryn's phone beeps where she left it on the plush chair she shoved into the corner. "Finally!" Marching over, she scoops it up. "Boo. He's not coming."

"Esau?"

She frowns up at me. "He's at the farm. They're worried the levee will rupture, so they're putting out sandbags. It sounds pretty serious."

"I'm sure they'll be fine. It's not the first time that's happened."

"But let's hope it doesn't."

"Totally."

"Remember that time the floods were so high they had to rescue a dog off a roof with a helicopter? What if it happens again and they have to get Esau off the barn?"

"Then they'll get him off. Hence, the helicopter."

"So not helping."

My phone buzzes this time. Probably Justin or Karen with an update. I pull it out and skim over the message. All the blood drains from my face as I read it again. Before I start to spin, I go through the exercise my therapist recommended.

Hear the rain.

Smell the hot cocoa we made an hour ago.

See the worry lines on Taryn's face.

Touch my pulse, thrumming a rapid beat in my neck.

Taste the tang of fear on my tongue.

Okay, that didn't help.

Taryn's face falls. "What is it? What happened?"

"Shh," I hiss, cutting a glance over to where Deputy Kelley stands looking out the window. A steaming cup of coffee in one hand. Gesturing for Taryn to follow, I tiptoe into the hall. "Look." Hold my phone out to her.

Unknown: I have your friend.
Unknown: If you don't show up at this address in the next half hour, she's dead.
Unknown: If you tell the cops, she's dead.
Unknown: Don't even think about bringing your tracking bracelets or phones. I'll be checking.

Taryn's expression dies as she reads. As the phone pings a final time, she gasps.

Unknown: [Image]

My gut twists at the image of Viv, her wrists and ankles duct taped so tight the binds cut into her skin. Tears stream from her puffy, bloodshot eyes. A gag pinches into her cheeks, wet with tears and drool. Blood trickles from her temple.

Lifting her phone, she types. Meets my eyes. My cell dings.

Is it real?

The image of Viv is branded behind my eyes. I type back.

Looks like it.
How would they fake something
like that?
Nobody would be that cruel.

Panic shoves at my heart until it's shivering against my jugular. I *know* that isn't true. The past year has been a crash course in the cruelty of people who choose to do evil. My stomach clenches before I even ask the question. I already know the answer. "What are we gonna do?"

Taryn's hands brush over her upper arms as if to ward off the shivers. Her eyes pinch closed.

We have to go.
Just give me a second to think.

The storm seems to mirror the unrest in my soul, thunder crashing overhead. Lightning shoots through the black sky, striking a tree across the street with a loud CRACK. Hissing, I swivel on Taryn.

Please don't tell me we're going out in that.
We don't have a choice.

"Girls?" The deputy pokes her head into the hallway, eyeing us with more than simple curiosity. Frankly, she should be suspicious. We are acting so weird right now.

"We're just grabbing our coats. It's cold in here." Taryn plays up shivering as she swings open the hall closet and pulls out our jackets.

"Right." Deputy Kelley isn't buying it. She leans against the wall, in full view of the front door, and stares us down.

I shrug on the coat Taryn hands me, before sending another message.

> *Are we going to bring our babysitter at least?*
> *You read the message.*
> *It said no cops.*

"Who are you both texting so furiously?" Kelley asks.

"My boyfriend," Taryn says. "He works at Del O'sso. They're worried about flooding. See?" She brandishes the phone, screen pointed at the deputy, who reads it quickly.

"I hope they have enough sandbags out there. It doesn't look like it's going to stop raining anytime soon."

"Me too." Taryn nods, a touch too enthusiastically.

I grimace, feeling super awkward. "Hey, Taryn, want to go upstairs and watch something on my laptop? It's usually warmer up there."

At her nod, we both smile at Deputy Kelley—not at all oddly—and make for the stairs.

> *They always say "no cops".*
> *Nobody should ever do that.*

Taryn steps in so close I can feel the heat leaching from her body.

Are you willing to risk Viv's
life by going against their
demands?
Because I'm not.

My throat closes as my tongue goes dry. There's no argument I can make against that. I'm not willing to do anything that hurts Viv. Slowly, I shake my head.

Taryn's peacoat-clad arm brushes against mine. She tilts her head toward her room. Leaning into the hallway, she calls to where our keeper is standing at the foot of the stairs. "We're going to get ready for bed before we watch. You up for a couple episodes of *Dating in Detention?*"

I stifle a chuckle, knowing the deputy will not be interested in the trashy reality show that debuted this winter. I don't even like it that much. Except for this one couple who are so ridiculous it's like watching an energetic puppy trying to make friends with a sloth.

Deputy Kelley declines from below.

Taryn's jaw sets determinedly as she goes into her room. I try to walk casually and end up shuffling like a freak. I am so not good at this. It's a wonder I pulled off sneaking out even once, much less multiple times.

Pinching the bridge of her nose, Taryn pulls me inside and shuts the door. Whirling away, she opens her dresser and tosses a beanie and an extra pair of socks at me. "Here, put these on. I'm going to grab extra boots from Karen's closet."

Outside it's nothing but raven black. I pull my sister's hat onto my head underneath the hood of my jacket, tucking the hair behind my neck. The thick pair of socks go on next.

Taryn's back in a second, holding out two pairs of broken-in, black boots.

"At least she's consistent," I mutter.

On the nightstand, the lamp flickers. Our power goes out with a snap. The buzzing of appliances and lights gone with a hush, leaving the grumbling of an angry storm in its wake.

"You girls okay?" Deputy Kelley calls. Footsteps start climbing the stairs.

"Yeah, we're good," Taryn yells back. "My laptop has a full battery." My twin's eyes glow in the dark. "Hurry," she mouths, shoving her feet into Karen's boots. Leaping onto her desk, she peels the security sensor off the window frame and sticks it next to the one on the wall so the system won't register it when the window opens.

The storm is so loud it covers the window's squeal as she shoves it up. A flash of lightning illuminates the rain-slicked roof as we scramble onto the shingles. Taryn pulls the window almost shut to keep it from making any more noise. Inside, the deputy's flashlight shines under Taryn's door.

I hold my breath, willing the deputy to pass by without opening it.

"Come on!" Taryn whispers in my ear as rain pelts our coats with slaps I can feel through the thick fabric. We're going to be soaked through in minutes, but there was no way we could have gotten our raincoats out of the hall closet right in front of the deputy without making her alarm bells go off. Taryn pulls on my arm with both hands. "We have to go!"

"I know. I'm coming. Taryn. TARYN." The worn soles of my boots lose traction and fly out from underneath me. The back of my head smacks against the sodden wood shingles as my body slides down the roof, carried on a tide of rainwater.

"Audrey!" Taryn screams, grabbing for my hand and missing.

My scream rips from my throat as I fly over the edge and plummet toward the—

Chapter 29

Taryn

I watch in horror as Audrey flies off the roof and hits the ground. She doesn't move. Oh, shit. My fingers cut into the metal edge of the overflowing rain gutter as I propel myself off the shingles toward the water-logged grass. Karen's boots, which are a size too big, hit the ground and slide in opposite directions. My arms windmill through the thick, wet air, and I just manage to catch myself.

Relief floods my veins when my sister blinks and pushes up on her elbows. "I'm okay, but did I just fall off the roof?"

"Answer this: which designer is Cher wearing when she is mugged in the movie *Clueless*?"

"Alaïa."

"An a-what-a?" I grin. Audrey's okay, but my tongue still feels cemented to the roof of my mouth. "That could have been really bad. Come on, let's get you up before Deputy Kelley busts us. We have to get out of here, for Viv."

Audrey wraps her hands around mine.

We stack ourselves upright and make a run for it. Visibility is terrible in the tempest that batters us. The power outage leaves the road in impenetrable darkness. Wind howls, flinging my coat's hood back. In a second, my hair is a sodden mess against my scalp. A chill works its way through my body.

"Duck!" Audrey yells, yanking me down behind a car parked across the street from our house. We rise on our knees just far enough to see Deputy Kelley come sprinting out the front door, looking wildly back and forth. It's too dark to make out her expression, but frantic energy crackles along her frame.

No cops, I mouth to remind myself why we're doing this.

Audrey and I wait until the deputy stalks around the back of the house, flashlight moving in wide swaths over the marshy ground. It's either too wet to see our boot prints in the grass, or the storm has already washed them away.

My sis and I bolt along the sidewalk, moving as quickly as we can with clothing weighed down by buckets of rain. Water flows through the gutters like angry rivers seeking the ocean and not finding it. It's not long before my entire body is quivering with cold, but we can't stop.

We have to make it to the meeting place as soon as possible, or the Gemini Killer will hurt Viv even more than he already has. In my ribcage, my lungs clench, making my breath short.

A truck careens round the corner, the driver losing control in the rising water, tossing it at Audrey and me in a wet wall. We whirl away, but not fast enough. The tidal wave hits our backs in a smack that makes me shriek. Cursing into the wailing storm, I shake an angry fist after the truck. What idiot takes a corner that fast in a storm that feels like a tornado?

"Come on," Audrey yells in my face. "We have to keep going."

When we finally get to town, it's deserted. The power is out here, too, leaving storefronts like the ghosts of capitalism in the smothering dark. Booming thunder sets my teeth chattering. Lightning illumines our way across the street. I hesitate on the curb, watching the muddy water flow. It's moving, deep and fast. Isn't it a bad idea to try to walk through it? But we're so close to the meeting spot. We can't stop. Viv needs us.

Audrey grabs my hand and holds on tight. "You okay?"

"No, but does it matter?" My throat cracks from yelling so loud to be heard.

She shakes her head. "We can do this. Together. You make the magic, remember?"

"Let's hope so." Tightening my fingers around my sister's, I plunge into the street. And almost get swept away. My leg muscles strain in my boots as we cross through the flood waters. In the middle, a trash can swipes past, almost taking us with it. Only Audrey's additional weight keeps me on my feet.

I try not to think about Esau fighting the destroyed levee at the farm. A pinch in my chest at the idea of him combating swirling water from a ruptured irrigation ditch makes me clutch at the front of my sopping raincoat. I can't dwell on that now. My mind skips to Noah and his family hunkered down in their home near the dairy. Justin and Karen and their rendezvous with Nate and the Gemini Killer. We haven't heard a word from them in hours. Are they okay? Did they capture the bad guy in our story? Or are they injured? Being rushed to the hospital.

Shut up, Taryn. Now is NOT the time.

Pushing across the treacherous street, I grip Audrey's hand. We wade through the rising deluge and climb the curb in front of the newspaper office. Our destination. The glass door rattles when I pull on the wide handle, yanking with all my strength. Locked tight.

Audrey pulls on the elbow of my jacket and points around the building. I follow to the alley. Water streams down the cement block wall on one side. On the other, an icy waterfall rushes over the roof's edge. With a squeal, we duck underneath the frigid curtain and plaster ourselves to the building. Inch closer to the office's back entrance. Audrey tests the knob, and it turns. Her eyes push up to mine. "You ready?" She mouths.

I nod quickly, my need to be somewhere warm overpowering the modicum of common sense that's screaming in the back of my mind. Who cares that whoever snatched Viv said no cops? This is a colossally bad idea. We're alone in the middle of town with someone who definitely means us harm, with no way to contact our guardians or anyone else. Suddenly it hits that this is by far the stupidest thing we have ever done, and that's saying something.

I reach for Audrey, shaking my head. We can't do this. It's a much better idea to get somewhere safe and wait until we can call Karen and Justin. Whoever the kidnapper is, they won't hurt Viv. She's their leverage. My stomach twists at the simplistic terms I'm using to describe one of my best friends. Leverage. A pawn in a bigger, deadlier game.

No. She's not a pawn. She's a vibrant, beautiful girl obsessed with her girlfriend, vintage clothing, and fried foods. I won't reduce her to a mere object. She's important. Vital. And I won't let them hurt her anymore. "Let's go," I mouth to Audrey, pointing toward the unlocked door.

She waits until thunder rumbles to open it, probably hoping the noise will cover our squelching steps. Inside, water ripples around our feet. Hands tangled together, my sister and I wait until our eyes adjust to the dark. Shapes form in my vision. We're at the end of a narrow hallway. Doors open into dark portals on both sides. The other end widens into an open space, and farther, the windows and glass door we found locked a few precious minutes ago. My chest jutters as it rises

228

and falls. The kidnapper, and Viv, could be anywhere.

As if we're sharing a brain, we both take a step. Another. Past one empty, black-holed room. Another.

A big hand lands on the small of my back, shoving me forward. The thin, commercial carpet does nothing to pad my knees as they slosh against the floor. Audrey's eyes are wide where she's hunched beside me on all fours. Twisting to look over my shoulder, my eyes land on our assailant.

My jaw drops. Eyes grow in shock.

An overpowering shadow looms out of the room we just passed.

"Nate?" Audrey's stammered question makes my heart drop with a plunk to the floor.

"What are you doing here?" I yell, crouching. "You're supposed to be with the FBI."

"Wouldn't you like to know. Get up." The gun in his hand is impossible to argue with, so I rise. Slowly. Painstakingly. Giving myself time to formulate some type of plan that doesn't end up with my twin and I being held at gunpoint—again—by a guy with feral eyes and an angry slash for a mouth. One who has already tried to kill us multiple times. Not good. This is Not Good.

The gun's barrel pokes into my stomach. "Turn around," Nate growls. He forces us up the hallway into the last office on the right. A pile of zip ties are scattered over the desktop. A whimper sounds from behind the desk. My eyes find Viv immediately as Nate forces Audrey and me farther into the small room.

Our friend is tied up just like in the photo Audrey got. Darkened, dried blood has formed a crust along her temple and down her hairline. Her eyes are wet and puffy in the gloom. "Mmmph!" She tries to talk, but the gag stuffed between her lips makes words unintelligible.

I pin Nate with the harshest, hottest glare I can muster.

"Zip tie your sister's hands," Nate barks, eyeing Audrey and me warily.

Good. He should be nervous. Because I'm not capitulating. I'm biding my time. I catch Audrey's eye, hoping to send her a subliminal message. When her eyebrows quirk upward in a fearful wiggle, I mouth, "Hospital." We can do the same thing we did to this jack-hole last time he tried to shoot us, in the ICU.

"In case you've got any bad ideas," Nate says, the words splicing through the undercurrent of the storm. Pivoting his arm, he levels the gun right at Viv. "Tie yourselves up. Fast. Or she dies."

Gulping down the anger simmering inside me, I step closer to the desk and pick up a pair of zip ties. The ridges in the plastic dig into my palms as I grip them tight. This cannot be happening. "How did you get away from the agents?"

"And why can't you just leave us alone? We didn't do anything to you." Audrey is furious.

Nate's gaze scrapes over me like a razor blade over vulnerable skin. Veins and arteries pulsing underneath, a hair away from being slashed open and emptied onto the threadbare carpet. "Love."

The single word falling from that harsh mouth makes something inside me break. Love, he said. Love could never make someone do something so ugly, so violent as this. Could it? I shudder.

"Tie her up. Now!" Nate inches the gun closer to Viv, who sobs into the gag.

"Fine! You win." For now. I zip tie Audrey's hands, motioning for her to sit down. I put a zip tie around her ankles and close it. Tighten it on Nate's orders. "Now your own feet."

Mumbling death threats, I comply.

"Wrists too."

Looping one of the ties, I stuff my hands through. Our jailor forces Audrey to tighten it until it cuts into my skin.

There are a lot of colorful words I'd like to shout in his face, but he's got a gun pointed at my friend, and I won't be responsible for her death. That won't be on me. Not if I can do anything to stop it.

Nate snarls down at us from his angry pedestal. "Now you'll get what's coming to you, and so will I." He stomps out, and the newspaper office goes quiet.

As soon as he's gone, I scuttle past Audrey to prop myself on my haunches in front of Viv. Pulling her forward by one shoulder, I work at the knot in the gag, trying not to pull her hair as I work the fabric loose. She spits out the bandana once I'm done. Her chest rising and falling as she pants for breath, running her tongue over torn lips.

"Are you okay?" I murmur, putting my tied hands on her shoulder.

She bobbles her head. "I don't know. I don't... Have you heard anything from your agents?" She sucks her teeth when I shake my head.

"I'm sure they're fine, and they would want us to focus on getting out of here. So that's what we're going to do, okay?"

"She's right. Let's do this." Audrey squirms next to me. "Just like they taught us."

Lifting our arms as high as we can, we yank them down against our stomachs, just like that afternoon Karen and Justin tied us up and left us on the sofa until we figured out how to escape. We thought they were being ridiculous, but now? Now, I'm grinning.

We have an astonished Viv untied in a few beats, and then we creep toward the door to peer out. Nate stands between us and the glass path to the sidewalk. Water flows past, seeping into the office.

Canting my chin toward the back door, I lead down the hall, away from Nate and the gun gripped in his hand.

It's not easy to tiptoe in rain boots without making a sound, but I manage. Holding my breath the entire time. It can't be this easy to escape, can it?

The glass door out front rattles as wind hits it. My instincts are screaming. "Run!" I yell, lunging for the back door and swiping at the knob. Before I can get a grip on the metal, it opens. A solid body blocks our way.

My gaze lifts from the dripping raincoat to the scraggly hair under a bucket hat. Mouth set in a grim line.

"Mom!" Viv cries, throwing her arms around the woman. "Quick, we have to get out of here. I was kidnapped by this guy who said he was with you, and then he tied me up, and…"

My friend's words dry up when she realizes her mom isn't returning her embrace. Isn't even looking at her. No, the woman is staring at Audrey and me with a burning in her eyes that can only be named disgust.

"Turn around," Ms. Miller orders.

Viv blanches. "But Mom, I told you, the guy who kidnapped me is back—"

"Turn around!" There's no more room to argue with the woman when she opens her raincoat and takes a handgun out of a holster at her waist. Shoving Viv aside, she aims it straight at me.

"Don't make me ask again," she says loudly over the thunder. Motioning with the barrel of the deadly weapon in her hands, she steps close enough to press it against my sternum.

At this range, she won't miss if she pulls that trigger.

Audrey gasps, putting her hands up in the air. With singular focus, her eyes zero in on the gun pressed against my chest. With no other alternative, she slowly pivots in her water-logged boots.

Nate is standing at the other end of the hallway, his eerie smile flashing in a bolt of lightning. "You made it," he says, looking past Audrey, past Viv and me, to Ms. Miller.

"Took some doing," Ms. Miller replies. "Turn around, girl."

Horror dawns in six words. Nate wasn't working with Robert Baugh. He was working with Ms. Miller. The only thought buzzing in my head like an over-large mosquito intent on drinking my blood, is why?

The flickering flame of expectation behind my ribcage winks out for a long beat before I nurse it back to life. This looks really, really bad. But there's got to be a way out. There's got to be.

Chapter 30

We spill out into the wider room at the front of the building, stoppered by Nate at the fore and Ms. Miller at our backs. Her eyes are cold and calculating as her attention skims over Audrey and me to land on her daughter. Viv clutches my arm, her broken nails digging into my skin through the raincoat. Sweat trickles down my spine. This is not good.

My friend shudders, taking tentative steps toward her mother. "Mom? Please, tell me what's going on."

Nate aims his gun at her, making her freeze, palms out, eyes wide and shining in the gloom.

I don't wait for an answer, spinning toward Nate. "What happened at the meet-up? With the Gemini—?" I cut myself off when I realize that Robert Baugh was never at the meeting tonight. It was Ms. Miller all along. And if she's here...

Rounding us, the woman pushes Nate's weapon down and away from her daughter, a focused, stern look in her eyes as she stares at my friend. Everyone in this room must know Viv is collateral damage if this goes any more wrong than it already has. "Leave now, darling, and run straight home. Wait for me there."

Viv manages to tear her gaze away from Nate's gun to meet her mom's hardening expression. Her voice is scratchy, the words flying from her throat like bats disturbed into fleeing from their cave. "What? Why? Mom, tell him to put the gun down. We have to get out of here."

Ms. Miller shakes her head slowly, her jaw set. "I can't leave yet. Not until I've finished this." Her hand tightens on Nate's wrist.

The damp, musky odor of loam after a rain fills my nostrils as outside, the storm rails against the buildings. A gust of wind makes the glass front of the newspaper office bow and writhe. Ms. Miller's rain boots slosh as she moves closer, hovering at the edge of the room.

My hand rises to the scar along my cheek, fingertips curling against my marred skin.

Audrey stares at Nate, unable to look away, fear etching along her jaw.

Dropping my hand, I refuse to meet Ms. Miller's eyes. I won't dignify her with it. She's unhinged and doesn't deserve my attention. The tight wire situation between her and Nate feels more urgent, anyway.

I can't ignore the rising waters outside, either. Rain dumps in black, swirling tides that creep upward in a bid to devour the buildings of downtown Hacienda.

Audrey pushes her frizzy, wet hair behind her ears, dragging her eyes away from the boy who used to be a friend. Blinking, she focuses on Viv's mom. Holds out her hands in placation. "Can you, can you tell us what happened to the FBI agents who were in the park? Are they okay?"

The woman's frown deepens as she tears her eyes off the scar bisecting my skin. Her focus skims past us to Nate, head tilting as she considers. Lightning flashes through the window, limning her figure in silver and white. Her eyes snap to Audrey's. "They're dead. Probably washed away by the floodwaters by now. When we left, the park looked more like a lake."

The harsh edges in her voice sever something inside me. A tether that was keeping me in check, on this side of right and wrong. But in this instant, hearing that Karen and Justin are gone—that they've been taken from us by violent hands—any control I had is wrenched away. With a loud bellow that surprises even me, I snatch a heavy duty stapler off the nearest desk and spin, hurling it at Nate. He restarted this—the blood and pain and heartbreak—and somehow got Viv's mom roped into the madness. I'm going to finish it.

Audrey screams as the stapler whooshes past his head and hits the wood-paneled wall with a crack. It drops to the ground, but I don't see it. I'm already throwing myself toward the desk. Running my hands over the surface. Groping wildly for something else to throw. Pens. Sheets of paper. Notepads. Where is one of those completely useless, hefty paperweights when I need it? Bellowing in anger, I whirl to face him. The guttural, furious cry scrapes at my throat as it comes, leaving it bruised and raw.

Nate appears unbothered by my outburst. And why would he be? He and his accomplice have weapons. All I have is a ceramic mug full of dull pencils and pens. Raising his voice to be heard over another boom of thunder, Nate says, "Let's finish this, like we planned. I'll kill them quick. Then we've gotta get out of here before the water cuts us off."

My mind is spinning off its anchor. A singular thought strikes in the dark, slicing through the stench of fear and fury. Sheriff Lamb didn't know what to make of the note with the letters. *D, Y, T, L.* He speculated that they were the initials of the girls who died in the 80s. The case Noah has been researching. What if those deaths are somehow connected to our attacks? Nate isn't old enough to know anything first-hand about them, but Ms. Miller is closer to the right age. A sinking in my gut forces me to scrutinize the woman still standing a few feet away, studying me like a bug under a microscope. Unfazed by my violence. She has the gun.

There weren't any similarities or individuals in common between the 80s case and ours, but maybe Ms. Miller was there. Maybe she knows why the psychic killed those girls. Knows what happened when Lydia Freeman disappeared.

"D, Y, T, L. Did you put Nate up to writing that note? Were you there? Were they your friends?"

Ms. Miller's lips curl. "No questions. You won't understand."

Her vehemence is the answer. "You *were* there. They were your friends. Did you see them die? Do you know where Lydia is?"

The woman blanches. Fingers tightening on the gun's handle, she glares at me. "Shut. Up."

Audrey steps closer, eyes wide in question, chest rising and falling rapidly.

I press a little harder. "Do you know why Mistress Maxine killed them? The sheriff never found a motive, not counting her dog's death. But that never made sense to me. Why kill three, possibly four teenagers, over a dog?"

Ms. Miller seethes. "That had *nothing* to do with it. You don't know what you're talking about."

My eyes widen at the nerve I've struck. She knows something, is afraid of it. Her expression is pure fear. Pure anger. Mixing hot and pressing on her shoulders. Tightening her fingers around the gun's handle.

"You're lying." As soon as I've said it, I know I've pushed her too far. She's going to kill us, right here. Right now. It'll all be over in a bloody blaze of death. Taryn and me. My parents.

All of the people the Gemini Killer annihilated. Four girls who met their ends too early, twenty years ago.

Ms. Miller's entire body goes taut, her mouth flattening. Eye contact zeroed in on my face. "I have to do it. To beat him. He took everything from me. I'm just returning the favor."

Some favor, if it ends with bodies on the ground.

Black, turgid ripples are pouring under the glass door more quickly as the water level outside rises. Some sharp piece of debris scrapes the entire length of the office's front window as it drags past on the murky floodwaters. I gulp, hoping beyond reason that Esau and Noah and their families are safe. Hoping they survive this hellish night with their families intact. Audrey and I aren't so lucky.

"Mom, let go of me. You can't do this." Viv screams, but her mom doesn't heed.

"We don't have time for this!" Nate roars, shocking Viv and her mom into looking at him. In a sudden and brutal move, he lunges forward and grabs Audrey by her hair, yanking her back against him and pressing the barrel of the gun against her temple. She cries out, trying to meet my eyes. The brutal angle at which he's holding her head prevents my sister from seeing much but the dingy drop ceiling. "Enough. I'm tired of waiting. Let's finish this so we can go."

Ms. Miller puts a hand on his arm, but it doesn't relax him. He only tightens his grip on my sister, his lip curled in a snarl. Her voice is high and reedy. "Just a few more minutes, baby, then we'll go."

"Baby?" Viv and I say in shades of incredulity and disgust.

Audrey puts it together before Viv or me. "She's the one you were meeting at the hotel that time? But she's so much older than. . ."

238

The way Nate is looking at Ms. Miller sends chills down my spine. Her expression as she returns his gaze sends warning bells buzzing between my ears. Something about this is intensely wrong. He's looking at her like... he loves her.

Love. That's what he said when we asked him, in the hospital, why he was doing this. I didn't understand then, but Viv's mom is looking at him like she could have loved him, if circumstances were different. From the shining look in his eyes, he doesn't see the difference.

"Shut up," Nate growls, yanking my sister's hair mercilessly. "Age is just a number. It doesn't matter to us. We love each other."

Viv stills beside her mom, who she has drifted toward in the last few minutes. "He, he's the guy you were sneaking off to see? Is that why you wouldn't tell me? Because he's my age?" Each word climbs higher than the last until they're shrill, piercing arrows. Her face aghast in a wide-mouthed gape.

I fight with my lungs, wrestling them into a less erratic pattern. But seeing Nate's unyielding hand tangled in my twin's hair, the way he drags her chin higher. The cold gleam of the metal barrel against her skin. Fear settles in its nest in my stomach, making its home in a place from which I'm not sure I will ever be able to evict it. "Let her go. She hasn't done anything to you," I plead, eyes locked on Nate's. "Please. You know what it's like to lose someone you love. Don't do this to us. We used to be friends. Remember?"

His scoff is full of hate. "Some good it did me, being friends with you. The Gemini Killer did all of this because of your sister. He used her social media to choose his victims. Admit it. This entire mess is as much your fault as it is his. And I'm going to make sure none of you ever get to hurt anyone else." His hand is rock-steady on the gun's handle. My eyes move from it to where Ms. Miller is forcing Viv to stay behind her, shielding her from the weapon.

I hook my eyes back to his. Swallowing, I try to keep him talking. To buy ourselves more time. But the clock is running down, and if what they say about Justin and Karen is true, if they are— There might be no rescue on the way. "It was you who shot at us those times, wasn't it? The FBI never found the rifle."

Nate's chin lifts. "My dad used to take me hunting. He taught me everything he knew about tracking. Showed me how to find hiding places where I could shoot without spooking my prey. I had no idea that it'd come in handy hunting you monsters, but look at that. It has."

Us monsters? "You hate us that much? For something we couldn't control?"

"You won't kill us," Audrey grinds out.

"Won't I?" Nate snarls. "You want to know how I met Anna? During the trial, she wrote some articles on it. My sister got an email asking for an interview. Kate didn't want anything to do with it, but I was so angry. I thought, here's a way to tell everyone how they should be blaming you two instead of fawning over you. I saw the way they offered you book and movie deals. All of that attention made me sick. So I met with Anna. We got to talking. I could sense right from the beginning we had something in common. We both wanted someone to pay for what had happened to us. You." With a flick of his thumb, Nate releases the safety on the gun pointed at my sister.

Audrey wails, pulling at his arm banded around her stomach. "I'm tired of being blamed for all the bad things that happened. It's not my fault. It's not our fault! If you want someone to pay for all of this shit, go find Robert Baugh."

Nate snarls at that, tearing at her hair. Making my sister

scream. "He has nothing to do with this."

I manage to stifle a gasp. He doesn't know about Albert and Robert's switcheroo. The arrests. Any of it. And I'm not going to tell him, not against the risk it'll make him even angrier. Even more deadly. But I can't say nothing. Maybe reminding Nate of his sister will soften him, like Audrey softens me.

"Don't. Don't do it. What would Kate say?" Anguish builds inside me until I can't hold it in. It spills out in hot, angry tears. I swipe at them with the back of a hand, not willing to lose sight of my sister. She locks her eyes on mine, entreating me silently to do something.

For the barest second, Nate wavers. I can see the ignition of doubt in his eyes. His face swivels between my sister, Viv, and me.

Ms. Miller moves, drawing my attention. Achingly slowly, she puts a hand on Nate's arm. "Baby, let's not forget why we're really here, okay?"

He sneaks a look at her from the corner of his eye. "How could I forget?"

A throat clearing makes me jump, my hand covering the thudding organ in my chest. Terrified to see who's back there, but unable to keep myself from looking, I spin in the floodwaters.

Paunchy belly. Neatly-trimmed beard. Crooked nose that has definitely been broken at least once. Harsh, narrowed eyes under a dripping baseball cap. My insides recoil in abject dread. I know this face, its lines. Its furrows and divots and creases carved by time and anger. The specter glares, an impossibly large hunting knife brandished in the space between us.

"Yes, let's not forget why we're here," Robert Baugh drawls, a single finger sliding lovingly along the blade in his hand.

Chapter 31

Robert Baugh stands, stroking the edge of his blade absently. Seemingly content to wait to get in on the action. Why is he so calm?

I gasp, the knowing, the loathsome understanding coursing through me.

He's content to let Nate and Ms. Miller completely uncoil before he acts. The man is biding his time, like a true hunter. Waiting for the most opportune moment to spring. Forcing that terrifying thought away, I focus on Nate. In this single, solitary instance, Robert Baugh is right. Nate is a ticking bomb about to blow. And he's got my sister at the center of the blast radius.

I turn my eyes toward Viv's mom and Nate. Their handguns that have a wider killing range than the murderer's knife. I am so irrevocably sick of guns.

All color drains from Viv's face as she turns to gape in horror at the devil at my back. I steal a glance over my shoulder. Nate goes from shocked to furious. Yanks Audrey in tighter. A human shield against evil.

Face contorted by the fingers of darkness, the Gemini Killer tilts his head. Completely ignores Nate. "You did all of this for me, didn't you, Lydia? Just like last time. When I got your message, I knew what you weren't saying. That you missed it—the control. The power you felt as you watched your friends die. That's why you did all of this, to bring me back here. Back to you. So we could finish this together. After how we left things, I was touched."

Oh, oh crap, he's *pleased* by what he sees. My stomach lurches in disgust.

Wait, Lydia? With stunning clarity, I find another piece of the puzzle. Viv's mom is Lydia Freeman, the girl who went missing all those years ago. Something about those attacks forced her to flee. To change her name. And now she's back, trying to hurt Audrey and me. I can't see the bigger picture, still missing so many of the jagged-edged pieces.

Ms. Miller's lip curls. Angrily, she spits, "You tried to slice my neck. You arrogant bastard. You're right. I did want you back here, but I wasn't trying to help you. You took everything from me. My friends. My family. Now it's my turn to return the favor. By killing your prey right in front of you."

Nate stares at the unfolding tableau with a horrified expression. Struck speechless by the back and forth between the woman he loves and the killer who likely haunts his nightmares.

Robert Baugh's voice is slow, soothing in a way that sends tingles of nausea rippling through my stomach. The man sounds just like I'd imagine a snake would. "What are you talking about? Killing Dana, Yvette, and Theresa was your idea. Remember how badly they treated you? How they excluded you after you confided in them what your father was doing to you and your mother? They weren't really there for you. They didn't support you. I did. I gave you the means to get back at them, and the encouragement to follow through. You didn't know if you could do it, remember? But I believed in you. And I was right. You killed all of them. You watched them die, and you enjoyed it. It made you feel alive, just like it does me."

The woman flinches at each of her former friends' names. Her fury shrinks as he talks, as if she believes everything he's saying. The bastard. He's gaslighting her right in front of all of us, and she's buying it.

"What is he talking about, babe?" Nate asks, looking like he might be sick.

Ms. Miller sniffs hard, wiping hair out of her eyes. Musters a glare at the Gemini Killer. "No. You're lying. None of it was my idea. You're the one who put it into my head, how easy it would be. You showed me how to do everything. Everything, Bobby. I wouldn't have done it if it hadn't been for you." Her attention is fixed on him, as if she's forgotten the rest of us are even here.

Viv's white, bloodless face peeks out from behind her mom, eyes fixed on the man whose evil heat is prickling at the back of my neck. *Bobby?* She mimics without thought.

Everything in me screams to run, get away, but I can't bring myself to move. If I do, will it snap the spell that has fallen, reminding them that Audrey and I are here and ripe for the killing? I can't risk it. Clenching my fists at my sides, I give the smallest head shake I can. Viv bites down viciously on her lip.

Water swirls around Nate's shins as he snaps, yelling and pleading with the woman he loves. "Don't listen to him. Let's kill them, and go."

Robert Baugh watches me with a feral gleam in his eyes. My heart skitters when he pivots toward Nate. It's as if my pain alone isn't raw, real enough to hold his focus. There's a flicker of something behind his gaze that almost looks like irritation. Good. He's getting frustrated. Justin said once that perps tend to make mistakes when they're emotional. Clenching my fists against my thighs, I pray he was right. Still, these three monsters have Audrey, Viv, and me in an uncomfortably tight spot.

Viv's mom is wrestling her daughter behind her, away from the gun and the knife and the pall of death that fills the room like a colorless, odorless—but no less deadly—gas. From the Gemini Killer, who is slowly inching closer with his knife out held. Feet wide in a killing stance. The tension in his body, the hungry look behind his eyes. I've seen them before. Watched in nightmare after nightmare as he approached, ready to loose the blood from my veins.

Fear grips my chest, choking off my breath.

Shaking his head, the devil smiles. The hint of teeth makes my stomach roil. Completely ignoring Nate, he speaks to Ms. Miller. "We both know that's not true. Don't deny the choices you made, Lydia. It's true I gave you the encouragement to be who you already knew deep down you wanted to be. A killer, just like me. And you've proved me right, going after these girls. You wanted to kill them, didn't you? And you even convinced this young whelp to help you."

Nate scoffs. "Shut up. We love each other. Don't we?" He looks at Lydia, but she doesn't acknowledge him. Doesn't even seem to see the hurt in his eyes when he realizes she's practically forgotten he's standing right there. She only has eyes for the man standing unbearably close to me.

Robert Baugh tosses his knife between his hands. "Tell me, boy. What did she promise you to get you to help her? No, let me guess. She told you that you two could be together. That you could leave town and start over somewhere else. Just the two of you."

"The three of us. With Viv," Nate counters hotly.

"Why does that sound familiar?" Robert Baugh's eyes

twinkle. He loves this. Relishes it. He runs a hand over his beard. "Oh, yes. It sounds familiar because that's exactly what I promised her, twenty years ago. Before I tried to slit her throat. She was using you, boy, just like I used her way back then. She doesn't care about you, just like I didn't care about her. You are nothing. So was she."

"NO," Lydia screams.

Nate flinches when Lydia's gun goes off, the bullet flying wide of where Robert Baugh is standing, feet wide set. A ready stance.

Releasing Audrey without thought, Nate's focus narrows on the other man. The originator of the Anderson family's pain, mine and Audrey's, and so many others. His threat is stone cold. "You're dead, old man."

Audrey drops to the floor, whimpering.

I lunge for her.

A steel arm bands around my waist. "I don't think so," the killer's sickening voice purrs in my ear. "Lydia may have lured me here, but I'm not going to let you slip away. I promised myself I'd come back to finish what I started someday, but I hadn't planned on it being so soon." His nose makes my hair stick to my neck as he takes a deep inhale. "I can smell your fear. You're drenched in it, and it's too delicious to pass up. Besides, you and your sister have made it very hard for me to further my mission, do you know that? So I'm going to take you apart, piece by piece, while she watches. And then I'm going to kill her. How about we start with something easy, eh? Like maybe a finger?"

I fight and kick and scream, but he has my hand gripped in the vice of his palm as he forces it upward toward the blade of his knife. "I admit I'm looking forward to this. In the past, I didn't have so much time to spend with my victims before I had to leave them. But with you, tonight…" He clucks his tongue. "It doesn't look like we're going to be interrupted, does it?"

Fat tears spill down my cheeks as he presses his sharpened knife at the base of my fingers, just enough to make my blood pump like a torrent through my body.

Forcing my eyes open, I latch onto Audrey, who is in a heap on the ground, peeking at me through shaking fingers. "I love you," I mouth. Trembling, she tells me the same.

"Get up," I reply with all the force I can muster. "Run."

With a sniff, Audrey pushes up to all fours, her eyes never leaving mine. "No," my sister jerks her head. With effort, she peels her gaze over her shoulder to where Nate is pleading with his girlfriend to leave with him. Ms. Miller is crying, shaking her head.

"Please, Anna, baby. I know he was lying. You don't mean any of this." Nate reaches out to her. "He was the reason for all this, why we started working together. Don't lose sight of that."

She jerks away, forcing Viv to press tighter against the window. Silent tears course down Viv's cheeks, but I don't think she's aware of them as she braces her elbows against the glass.

"Lydia," Robert Baugh barks, his grip tightening on my waist, making it harder to breathe. "Get rid of that brat so we can finish this."

Ms. Miller's resolve hardens, the muscles in her face flattening. Her frown twists into a hard, wet line. The gun in her hand steadies.

Nate looks from my captor to the woman in front of him, his eyes widening in disbelief as her fingers coil tighter around the gun's handle. Nate's mouth twists in an avenging smile. "She won't listen to you, old man. You're done here. It's your turn to die."

The gun flashes as Ms. Miller fires.

I jolt.

Nate's body drops without even as a splash, a blackening stain widening in his stomach. Deep red mixes with the flood water drowning the carpet.

Sulfurous, burnt gunpowder makes my nose wrinkle, but I can't look away from the trauma playing out on the watery stage where I watch from a front row seat. Robert Baugh has just manipulated Ms. Miller into mercilessly killing the boy she was seeing. He's an unintended victim in this deadly game. Who will be next?

My rain boots splash in the icy water as I shift, searching for a steadier foothold and find nothing but slippery, soaked carpet.

Viv screams uncontrollably in horror, her hands pressed to her ghostly cheeks. "Oh my God, Mom. What did you do? You just killed him! I can't believe you—"

Her mom's vicious slap brings Viv up short.

Stunned, my friend falls silent, her mouth open in a betrayed O. She presses back against the glass, heedless of the rising level of the floodwaters clawing at the transparent barrier.

Robert Baugh snorts, pleased. "Good. Now we can really talk."

Any light, any hope I had buried deep down inside me dies when Ms. Miller meets his eyes. Lowering the steaming gun, she nods. "Okay, Bobby. Let's talk."

Chapter 32

The sluicing liquid climbs higher, eddying around my calves, up to Audrey's elbows where she's still on all fours. My eyes dart from her to the nearest desk and back. Trying to warn her without speaking to get to higher ground. Eyes widening in understanding, my sister, inches away from where Nate's body floats in the rising tide. She clambers onto one of the desks and crouches, eyes never leaving the scene we're playing out in the river's grasping flow.

"I've wanted to say this to you for a long time," Lydia says slowly, her arm gliding through the air until the gun is pointed directly at me. And the demon who has me in an iron hold. "You ruined my life, Bobby. You took my friends, my father, and even my mother from me. I knew it was only a matter of time before they figured out Mistress Maxine didn't kill those girls. And then, they'd come after me. It took me a long time to realize you were so careful, back then. You didn't leave any trace that it was you all along. I was the one who planted the evidence in Maxine's house. I cut Theresa's brakes. I lured Yvette into the cemetery. You were so careful, I knew I could never expose you. So I waited, knowing that a monster like you would eventually come out of hiding. You can't help it, can you?

"I built a new life, had a beautiful daughter. Do you have

any idea how hard it is to live looking over your shoulder? Knowing eventually there will come a knock on the door when your time is up? I do. For the past twenty years, I waited for that knock. It was hell, living like that. I won't go back to it. This ends tonight." The barrel of the gun grows so large it blocks out the rest of my vision, leaving me staring down the steel tunnel into the lightless maw of death.

Robert Baugh shakes his head, his scratchy beard catching in my hair and making me recoil. It's apparent in the taut cord of his voice that his patience is ebbing. "I'm afraid you don't have a choice. The police think my simple brother was the Gemini Killer. And he's dead. What do you think they'll do when they find you here tonight, with all the bodies? You're going to jail, Lydia, and they'll never let you out."

The hypnotizing current in his words is eerie, making my flesh cringe away from every point where he touches me. With renewed vigor propelled by fear, I claw and kick, trying to get free. If I can just—

His grip tightens on my hand, making the tiny bones grind together. "Patience, little one. Your turn is coming."

My blood runs cold. We're not going to get out of this.

Ms. Miller wails a strangled, wretched sound. The gun swings in her hand. "No! You can't blame all of this on me. I'm the victim here. I didn't kill anyone."

"You killed Nate. Justin and Karen. You said so." Audrey lobs the accusation at her, pushing to her full height on the desk to tower over us.

The devil chuckles, a full, molten, burning laugh. "Haven't you realized it by now? This woman is an unapologetic liar. Now. Let's stop pretending. You say you hate me, but I don't think you do. You're putting all of your shame and guilt about the deaths of those girls on me, and we both know that isn't fair."

Ms. Miller thrusts the gun through the misty air toward us. "It is fair. I'll tell them. They'll have to believe me when they find you here. I'm not letting you go this time."

"Lydia, be reasonable. How about we strike a deal? You kill that one on the desk; I'll kill this one, and then we'll go. We can go somewhere far away, where no one will find us. You can stop looking over your shoulder. I promise."

"Don't believe him!" Audrey yells. "He won't take you with him. He'll kill you too. And Viv. Your daughter. If you agree to go with him, you're killing her."

"I'd stop talking if I were you." Robert Baugh pushes my finger harder into his knife. Burrowing toward my bones. "Ready to lose your first finger, little monster?" The Gemini Killer's taunt rips through me. I'm unable to stop the scream that shreds my throat as my worst nightmare in the flesh makes the first cut. My vision tunnels until all I can see is the blood welling on the knife's edge.

I use all of the force in my body to fight, to pull away from that cruel blade, but it's hard to think past the pain throbbing in my hand. Hot, thick blood seeps down my palm to my wrist, and drips into the black water.

"Want to watch me remove your sister's fingers, one by one?" The absence of emotion in his voice makes Audrey go still. Her eyes are glued to the knife pressing into the bones in my half-severed pinky.

Viv shakes her head vigorously, mouthing "No" over and over. Her hands fly up to cover her eyes. She peeks out between two fingers, entire body shuddering.

I'm quaking too, from fear or adrenaline or the freezing waters climbing my calves, I don't know. Lightning outside illuminates a boat drifting along the street past the building.

Wait, that wasn't lightning. Relief courses through me as I stare out the window, begging the boat to come back. Whoever's in that boat might be able to help us, if they spot us grappling in the inky gloom. Maybe if we can distract Robert and Lydia, we can—"

"Lydia? Lydia, look at me. Do we have an agreement?"

"Yes." Ms. Miller swings the gun to point at Audrey.

"Viv, move!" I yell. Something in Viv's brain comprehends in that instant, because she lurches away from her mom toward the desk where Audrey's standing. Thunder rumbles outside, drawing closer. Closer. Louder.

Viv's mom screams, but I can't make it out over the clamoring thunder. Light streams through the building's floor to ceiling windows, blinding us. My eyes snap shut.

"What the—" The woman's cry is cut off by a resounding crash. The building shakes. Glass shatters. Water floods into the room, jostling my body back against the Gemini Killer's. We tip toward the inky black swirls. I try to steady myself, to keep from being sucked under the extended arms of the tidewaters, but the demon won't let me go. The last thing I see before I hit the water is Audrey leaping toward the shallow bow of the fishing boat that just crashed into the building.

The icy water is a shock as it engulfs me, making my muscles sluggish and rigid. Something sharp pierces the side of my neck, slicing my skin. One hand flows up to touch it, just as Robert Baugh twists in the water. Strong, unyielding hands force me down deeper as he uses my weight for leverage to stand up. Then his hands are gone.

I surface, coughing and spluttering. Water clears my vision as I blink. The boat sits idling in a gaping hole in the front of the building, bobbing on the churning waters. Flashlight beams in my eyes make it impossible to see who's driving it. But I don't need to see the driver to recognize the boat. And Karen thought the idea of buying a boat was stupid. Panting, I wade toward it.

They're alive. Ms. Miller was lying when she told us she'd killed them.

"How did you find us?" Audrey yells, beating me to the boat. She scrambles over the side.

"Trackers in all of your coats," Karen barks. "Taryn, get over here. Hurry."

I push through the water, dragging my legs along the floor, battling to stay upright. Something hits my kneecap and almost makes my leg buckle, but I keep moving.

"He's getting away!" Audrey screams from somewhere behind the light.

I spin to see Robert Baugh clawing his way toward the back door. No. I'm not letting him escape. The water resists as I inch away from the boat, toward the Gemini Killer. Swinging my arms helps me gain ground. My fingers clench around a lamp that I swipe off one of the water-swept desks.

"Taryn, come back!" Karen orders.

I don't listen. I struggle forward, determined to stop the Gemini Killer before he slithers out the back door. I have to do it. He can't walk away from tonight.

"I can't let him get away," I snap, fighting through the waters up to my thighs.

"Come back! We'll catch him. Just get over here."

Images flash through my mind. Karen and Justin taking down Albert Baugh and arresting his brother, John. Driving us to the courthouse and making sure we got inside without being accosted by over-eager reporters. Dinners at the diner. Cake tasting. The visit to the vineyard. Their welcome presence in the back of the theater during hours upon hours of play practice. Every step of the way the two of them have been right beside us, whether Audrey and I were aware of it or not. Protecting us. Still, I can't look away.

Robert Baugh reaches the back door, yanks the handle with force. It doesn't budge. Another pull. Another. The door flies open, water rushing inside. The man yelps as he's tugged under the surface. It churns in the doorway, shoving inside, waves rippling onward.

Blood rushes in my ears as I watch. A single breath. Two. Three.

The Gemini Killer doesn't surface again.

Without any hesitation, I turn carefully in the frigid water, fighting the current as it shoves at my hips. Waves of murky liquid gush through the broken window, rocking the boat.

"We have to get out before the water gets too high," Justin calls, hands clenching around the anchor's chain as he pulls it up.

"Come on Taryn. Just a little farther." Karen leans over the side, craning her arm toward my outstretched fingers. I inch closer, shuffling through the water.

Something large and slimy flicks past my leg, making me jump. "I think there's something down there!" I squeal, flinging myself into Karen's outstretched arm. Wrapping it around me, she tugs me over the side into the ski boat, ordering Justin to get us out of the building.

The boat rocks, knocking us to the floor. Clambering up, Karen uses a length of fishing pole to help push off so Justin can reverse the boat without slamming into one of the walls.

After we're free, Karen grabs my hands, inspecting my finger that's sliced to the bone. Taking a wad of gauze out of the first aid box on the bench seat, she presses it against my palm. "Are you hurt anywhere else?" Her hands glide over my arms and legs, checking for more injuries, stopping once she's satisfied.

Audrey hands me a dry towel, and I cocoon myself inside the thick terry cloth at her feet. The boat's engine rumbles as Justin slowly eases the vessel backward. It lists to one side, forcing Karen to scramble to the opposite edge for counterbalance. Outside, the storm lulls. Even the clouds are holding their breath to see if we'll make it out of the building.

I exhale in relief when the boat putters out into the waters over the street. A gasp wrenches my jaw at the extent of the flood's damage. Feet of water cover the street and sidewalk. The storefronts are flooded. With the power out, the downtown appears as an abandoned city overtaken by churning tides.

My teeth chatter so hard I'm not sure they'll ever stop. Audrey wraps her arms around my shoulders and presses a cold cheek to mine. "I'm so glad you're okay. Taryn, I don't know what I would do if—"

"Me too," I say fervently, wrapping one of my hands around hers. I'm a mess of cold and expended adrenaline, my body shivering as it tapers.

Justin maneuvers the boat toward our side of town. Karen slides out of the passenger seat and takes three careful steps to where we're huddled in the back of the boat. "You did good, Taryn. Audrey. We're so proud of you. And now you don't have to worry about Robert Baugh anymore. Odds are he never resurfaced, but we'll look around tomorrow, just in case." She rubs my shoulder reassuringly before doing the same to Audrey and Viv.

"How far does the water go?" Ms. Miller asks in the dark. I'd forgotten she was with us, sitting in the opposite corner of the boat. She's alone, crying silently as she stares at the

256

devastation down Main street.

No one answers.

I glance between Viv and her mom, wondering if they'll ever be able to get past all of the crap that was dragged out of the dark kicking and screaming tonight. If they'll ever have a good relationship again. Watching Viv's stiff lips and quivering chin, her sharp turn away when Ms. Miller shifts in her seat, I'm not so sure. A tear skids down my cheek, over the scar that begot all of this.

Chapter 33

Two Hours Later

Taryn

Temporary floodlights illuminate the high school as we approach on foot. Toward the center of town, the water got shallow enough that we couldn't ride any farther in the boat, so we got out and walked. Karen led us to the school, keeping Ms. Miller in front of her the whole way, her hand on the woman's cuffed arms.

As soon as we hit the parking lot, a deputy comes sprinting over from a tent they've set up near the gymnasium doors. Others come and go. "You found them," Deputy Sykes says, smiling when he sees it's us. Taking up his radio, he speaks into it. "Sheriff, Kelley? They found them."

Lamb circumvents the table and walks toward us. His cowboy hat has been abandoned under the tent, and the man's hair is in dire need of a comb.

I brace for a snide remark when the sheriff stops in front of us, looking like he's had a long night. The older man surveys Audrey, Viv, and me before moving to assess Ms. Miller. "Anna. Can't say I'm glad to see you again tonight." He orders Deputy Sykes to take her to the temporary holding cells they've

258

set up in the ag wing.

Karen thanks him, handing over custody of Viv's mom to the deputy and filling the sheriff in on the night's events. Immediately, someone is dispatched to the newspaper office to see if they can retrieve the bodies.

Once that's done, Sheriff Lamb focuses on my twin and me. I take Audrey's hand, ready for whatever dressing down he's going to spew our way.

My jaw drops when Sheriff Lamb smiles. "It's a relief to see you two in good shape. When I found out that you'd both gone AWOL this evening, I thought for sure that would be the end of you. Glad to be wrong for once."

My face contorts in confusion.

"I thought you hated us," Audrey stammers.

Sheriff Lamb has the audacity to chuckle. "I admit you've given me your fair share of headaches, but no. I don't hate you. You weren't my favorite people a few months ago, but the way I reckon it, none of the responsibility for this mess falls on you two. And I won't hold being teenagers against you, seeing as I have one at home. I do know a thing or two about seventeen-year-old girls, despite everything."

Karen chuffs into her palm.

Lamb lifts an eyebrow. The exchange makes me immediately curious about the sheriff's daughter. I may have to do a little social media stalking later to see if I can find her. Without the actual stalking, of course.

"Why don't you five go inside and warm up? We've got the generators up and running, so it's almost toasty in there."

We're halfway between the tent and the parking lot when Audrey stops and turns abruptly. The sheriff meets her eyes when she calls his name. My twin shoots him a smile and a quick thank you, to which the man winks before turning away to talk to one of his deputies. Seeing him this affable is strangely okay.

Justin lags behind, letting us know he's going to hand over the boat keys in case one of the emergency responders needs it.

When the rest of us step inside the school, mats on the ground have been set across the door frames to keep water from getting inside, but they haven't been effective. Trails of muddy water streak the linoleum floor all the way down the hall. Emergency lights along the ceiling put spots in my vision as my eyes adjust to the brightness. Deputy Kelley comes marching toward us, a stern look on her face. "If I'm ever tasked with watching you two again, I'm using those toddler leashes. But I'm glad you're both safe."

With a tight smile, Kelley leads along the dirt-smeared corridor and ushers us inside the gymnasium, where people are huddled in groups all around the room. Some have only blankets and towels while others have backpacks and duffle bags clutched in their hands. Wrestling mats have been laid out in the far corner, and some of the elderly are using them to rest. A tiny girl in footie pajamas rolls a soccer ball toward an older boy, giggling when he nudges it back.

"We're using the school as a temporary shelter during the flooding," the deputy tells us as she leads us past the gym to one of the classrooms. "We thought you might like to keep these two separate from the crowds for a while, so we set aside this room for you. I'll send in one of the doctors for your hand as soon as I find one that's free."

Karen thanks and dismisses the woman before turning to us. "I should be absolutely furious with you two."

Audrey bites her lip but doesn't retreat. She's come a long way in the past few months. Where she used to be quiet and affable, she's more likely to speak up. To defend herself. My chest puffs up with pride.

"Maybe you should be, but are you?" I cross my arms, calling Karen's bluff.

Her shoulders lower as she shakes her head. "Yes."

"Liar."

Stomping over, she throws her arms around us. "You two are going to be the death of me."

I can't help the laugh that bubbles out of my chest. It's a cocktail of slackened tension, relief, and pure happiness. We made it. We're standing, mostly unscathed. There is no longer a bogeyman out there, waiting in the dark to attack when we eventually let our guards down. He drowned in the flood.

Chilled by that thought, I focus on how great it feels to be in a warm room, wrapped in a group hug with my twin sister and my favorite FBI agent.

Justin comes in, drops his still-dripping coat onto a chair, and grins. "It's group hug time, eh?" He plows into us, making Audrey and me laugh as we're squished between the two adults. "Viv, come on in." Justin extends an arm. Viv hesitates a beat before she throws herself into the mix. Justin's warm breath fans the crown of my head. "I'm so glad you girls are okay. You cut it pretty close tonight. I hate to admit it, but for a second there, I was afraid. Can't say I enjoyed it much."

"You, afraid?" Karen quips, eyeing him over our heads.

"A tiny bit," he smiles, sheepish.

She smiles back. "You're such a softy."

"You love it."

"Okay, enough flirting please," I say. "Save it for the wedding, which we still have to finish planning."

"In less than three months," Audrey adds. "Wow, that snuck up on us, didn't it?"

"We'll get it done. Simple, remember?" Karen says,

breaking our huddle.

A woman comes in wearing a grimy, tan raincoat smeared with various fluids I don't care to identify. "I was told someone has a hand that needs stitches?"

Justin checks the woman's credentials before allowing the doctor near me. They push two desks together, and I find myself sitting across from Doctor Cassidy while she cleans my cut finger and stitches it to my hand. I stare as she works, unable to look away. Once it's clean and bandaged, the doctor straightens. "If I leave some antiseptic and bandages, can the two of you handle their other abrasions? There are other patients I need to see." At Karen's nod, the doctor hurries out.

Justin helps Audrey and Viv with their cuts and scrapes, while Karen works on the cut on my neck.

"So, how much of town flooded?" I ask.

She purses her lips. "Well, you saw downtown. And the neighborhoods between that and the river are flooded. Plus, Dell'Osso Farms and the properties on that side of town. It's pretty extensive. But the town's been rebuilt before. There was a huge flood in the 90s that did a lot of damage, and they got through it. We will this time, too."

"The farm? Have you heard if the workers and everyone are okay?"

Karen shakes her head. "But I'm sure Esau is fine. He seems like a resilient boy."

My eyebrows wing upward. "Did you just compliment my boyfriend?"

"I like him. He's been good for you."

"Even with the sneaking out?"

Karen studies me a beat before selecting a large, square bandage and placing it on my cut. "Even then. He stuck by you. I can respect that."

I'm beaming. From someone as buttoned-up as Karen that's an undeniable stamp of approval. "So, can I go out without a chaperone now?"

"I want to talk to Ms. Miller first, and then I promise we'll talk about that."

"Deal."

All of us take turns washing our hands in the sink in the back of the room, flicking dry because there are no paper towels to be found. Justin knocks his fists together. "Now that everyone's all patched up, you three head to the cafeteria. I was told they're serving hot meals. Karen and I need to speak to Anna Miller for a few minutes."

"No way," I protest. "If you're going to interrogate her, I'm coming."

Audrey agrees. Viv, on the other hand, starts shaking her head, her skin a ghastly white.

Karen gives my friend a sad smile. "Uh, I'll take you to the cafeteria, okay, Viv? Then the rest of us can go."

We all agree, shedding our wet coats on a rack by the door.

Chapter 34

Taryn

Anna Miller sits in a student desk, her hands cuffed to the metal pipe that connects the desktop to the base beneath the plastic chair. She's hunched over, her forehead resting on one arm. The greenish light from the overhead fixture makes her skin pallid and sickly, clashing with the dark, muddy clothing she's wearing. Behind her, the wall is covered with posters on crop growth cycles and animal husbandry.

One of the deputies walks past the doorway where Audrey and I are standing. I shift my weight from one foot to the other, remembering the last time my twin and I stood in an interrogation room. The day Albert Baugh was killed and Sheriff Lamb questioned his brother, John. *Mr. Baugh.*

This better be more illuminating.

Justin re-enters, holding out a handful of steaming pizza pockets on a plate. "Anybody hungry? If Deputy Sykes asks, you did not eat these."

I'm about to say no thanks when my stomach growls.

Justin gives me a look as he nudges the plate against my arm.

I take one, its flaky crust searing my fingertips. "Thanks. Nothing like a gourmet meal after almost dying."

Audrey takes one, thanking Justin too.

Ms. Miller perks up in her chair, swiveling toward us, her stomach complaining.

Justin offers her a savory pastry, which she eats quietly.

Nibbling on my pastry, I wait. Staring at Ms. Miller. Karen told us she'd normally let the woman sweat for a while before she goes in to question her. Give her time to think about what she wants to say. How much she wants to share. The longer they're made to wait, the less important they feel. The more they want to talk. It has something to do with a lot of criminals being narcissists, apparently. Making them wait hurts their egos, so they're more likely to spill to make themselves look important.

Audrey bumps my shoulder with hers. "What're you thinking?"

I shrug, whispering, "Hoping Karen's narcissist theory is right."

"She usually is."

I hum in response, glad Audrey believed my half-truth. I was thinking about Karen's theory, but I'm also wondering why Esau isn't here yet. When I called him after we arrived at the school, he didn't answer, so I left a message. It was a blink-and-you'll-miss-it overview of why Audrey and I snuck out, who we'd run into, and our current location at school. And can he come see me ASAP?

A hole opened in my chest when he didn't pick up, and every minute longer it takes for him to show up makes my worry grow. Leaves me spinning. Doubting he's coming at all. What if the flooding at the farm was worse than even I can imagine? What if he was hurt? Nate's body sinking under the turgid water makes me shudder. Esau is fine. He'll be here.

Thinking back, I acknowledge I've put him through a lot.

265

From his broken arm to having to pretend I had died. Lamb assured us it was the best way to lure the bad guy. Make them think they've partially succeeded and puff up their confidence. I knew Esau would hate it as soon as they told us the plan, but I went along with it.

Licking my greasy fingers, I toss the empty wrapper in the trash by the door. I want Esau here with me more than anything. With Ms. Miller sitting in handcuffs, this thing that has taken over my life and transformed it into something I don't recognize, feels almost powerless. Like fate's monster mounted one last attempt to murder me and failed. But without Esau here? It feels unfinished, like fate could still rise up and slap me.

If I can just see Esau, I believe we'll be okay. That we'll arrive in a better place in our relationship after this. My throat tightens when I think about never spending time with him again, just the two of us. If, when this is over, we're never able to get back to the feisty couple we were before.

Karen enters, wearing her serious FBI agent face. Like a stealthy panther, she circumvents Ms. Miller's seat and leans a hip against the teacher's desk, facing her.

Ms. Miller sits up straight, wincing when the binding handcuffs pinch her wrists. "Can you take these off?"

Karen doesn't move a muscle. Next to Agent Biel's calm, powerful demeanor, Viv's mom suddenly looks small. Afraid. I feel bad for her, and don't like it.

I whisper to Justin, "Was Viv okay when you left her in the cafeteria?"

He leans closer, whispering back, "The McCallisters were there. She's with Erin."

Sighing, I turn back to the front of the room. Viv isn't alone, wondering how this is going. When I ask, Audrey shoots off a text to let Viv know she can talk to her if she needs.

Karen must decide Ms. Miller is no longer a threat, because she releases her from the cuffs. Viv's mom drops her hands into her lap, rubbing at the skin around her wrists.

Being a hard-ass, Karen plunks into the teacher's chair, not saying a word. She's so cool and collected it looks like she's got all the time in the world. And why not? She's got the only villain still standing in custody. The woman's partner already confessed to sending the notes, which means that Taryn and I are safe. We're *safe*. Today, evil lost.

Hell, maybe Karen does have all the time in the world.

Ms. Miller nods when Agent Biel asks if it's okay to tape their conversation. Pressing a button on a recorder I recognize, she sets it face-up on the desktop. Leans forward, arms folded. "Please state your full name for the record."

"Anna Marie Miller."

Karen nods, writing something down on a yellow pad she found on the teacher's desktop.

Audrey bounces on the balls of her feet, the hot pocket forgotten in her hand. "Ask her. Ask her. Ask her," she mouths. *Yes*, she fist pumps when Karen does.

"Is that your birth name?" The eraser on Karen's pencil taps the pad.

Ms. Miller shakes her head. "I was born with another name, but I haven't used it in a long time."

"And that name is?"

Ms. Miller shifts in her chair, glancing back at us as if she can sense our eyes on her. The cold emptiness in her stare cuts to the bone. She's not looking at me. She's looking through me. I hold still, resisting the desire to flinch. She can't hurt me anymore, and she doesn't deserve even another pinch of my fear.

Audrey curves her fingers around mine, latching us together. Taking a deep breath, I pull my shoulders down.

Karen tries again. "Your birth name?"

Ms. Miller shakes herself, lowering her eyes to the wood-veneered desktop. "Can I have some water?"

"Stop stalling," Audrey whispers. Glances at Justin. "Think she'll tell us what happened?"

Justin ushers us out into the hallway so we can talk. "It's hard to say. Anything can happen in an interrogation. One time this five hundred pound dude, seriously this guy was built like a brick house, accused me of tossing him around, even though there's no way I could have. Plus, he knew there was a camera recording the entire time."

Snagging a water bottle from a passing deputy, Justin takes it to Viv's mom. She drinks it slowly. Lifts her face to Karen. "Thanks. My birth name, it's Lydia Joyce Freeman."

"Why would Lydia Freeman come after us instead of going after Robert Baugh directly?" Audrey asks. "I still don't get it."

I crack the knuckles on my clammy hands one by one, thinking. "Maybe watching her friends die broke something inside her. Maybe when she saw us with Viv, it flipped a switch or something."

"That sounds a little far-fetched," Audrey replies. "What kind of mother tries to kill her daughter's friends? And anyway, she didn't go after Erin, or Fiona, or Marisa."

"You're the true crime nerd, and I'm not a psychologist." She dodges my prodding finger, and we focus on the conversation through the doorway.

"You weren't there. You don't know what it was like, watching them die. Every day for the past twenty years I've tried to forget. I consoled myself with the conviction that they got what they deserved. They had it coming to them for what they did."

Karen writes on the pad. "Why do you say that? What did Dana, Yvette, and Theresa do to make Maxine kill them?"

Ms. Miller shakes her head. "You're asking the wrong questions. It wasn't about what we did to Maxine. It was what they did to me. Their supposed best friend. I needed them, and they weren't there for me. That's why they had to die."

"Maxine killed them because of how they treated you." It's a statement designed to provoke an emotional response, but Karen sounds so disinterested. So flat. How does she do that?

Viv's mom starts to get visibly agitated, running her hands through her clumpy, soggy hair. "No. You don't understand. Maxine didn't kill them. I did, but that's not exactly right. He made me do it. It wasn't my fault. I didn't even know where a car's brake line was. He had to show me. I wouldn't have done it without his goading. He didn't think I could do it. So when I saw his name in the paper, I knew I had to. Because it wasn't really their fault. We were all so young and scared." The woman gets more choked up as her rambling increases, the story she's telling making less and less sense.

Karen taps her pencil tip on the desk, reeling Ms. Miller's attention back to herself. "You said he made you do it. Who are you referring to?"

"Bobby." She spits out the name, clearly upset. Karen seems to sense that she's nearing the edge of how far Ms. Miller will let her push, changing topics deftly.

"You said your friends deserved to die, but then you said they didn't. Can you tell me what you meant?"

Ms. Miller wrings her hands in her lap, squirms in her chair. "I don't know if I can. I never told anyone, after they died."

Karen leans forward and waits until the other woman meets her gaze. "You can tell me. I'm trying to help you."

The clock on the wall tick, tick, ticks. Audrey might be holding her breath, she's so still.

Ms. Miller sits forward. "My dad was mean. When he got angry, he'd lash out. Hit us. I told my friends about the... abuse, but they convinced me to keep it quiet. They thought if it got out, if everyone in town knew, it'd make him even angrier. They said they were worried. Then I caught them together. I don't think they were worried about me; they were worried about what the town would think. That's when I knew: they weren't my friends anymore.

"My boyfriend, Bobby said they deserved to be punished for leaving me out. He twisted me around, telling me horrible things about my friends, until I thought I had no choice but to kill them. It was his idea to pin it on the town psychic. It was all him, really. I only did what he told me to. Once they were dead, we were going to run away together. We were going to get married. But then he tried to kill me. He took one of those huge butcher knives they used to slaughter their pigs, and tried to slit my throat. That's when I realized he never loved me. He used me to kill them, and he got away with it. So I ran." Ms. Miller sniffs as a tear slides down her cheek.

Karen shifts in her seat. "What brought you back to Hacienda?"

"My mom died. I came back to bury her, sell the house. But a few weeks passed, and the bad feelings I always carried about this town didn't bother me anymore. By then I had changed my name. Had my daughter. No one I grew up with was still around, except for Jack, but he was easy to avoid. So I decided to stay and raise Viv. We were happy for a long time."

Karen waits for Ms. Miller to fill the wistful silence.

"Then last fall, Viv started telling me about a new friend she'd made at school. Megan. She was really upset when we found out about how Albie and Jack kidnapped those twins. How Albie was a killer. I didn't believe it. I knew it couldn't be true. If one of those boys was a serial killer, it had to be Bobby. He'd done it before, and I'd helped him. I thought if I finished this, it would all be over."

"So you tried to hurt the Thomas girls to get to Bobby?"

Ms. Miller nods sloppily, covering her anguished expression with her hands.

I frown, not believing it. She's a grade A actress who had everyone fooled, even her own daughter.

The woman's shoulders quake. Maybe she's faking it. "Do you believe her?"

Justin's hand slips off my shoulder. Tipping my chin up so I look at him, his brown eyes warm. "She confessed. A lot of the time, it's more than we get. Most people don't take responsibility for their actions even when we have them on video committing the crime. Believe it or not, this is a good thing."

Karen asks Ms. Miller, otherwise known as Lydia freaking Freeman, for some proof the girls' deaths twenty years ago were caused by Robert Baugh. She goes into a long-winded explanation about planted evidence and the Baugh boys' abusive parents.

I turn to Justin, trying to be cool. The two men who tried to kill us are dead. Ms. Miller won't get another chance to attack Audrey and me, because she's going to be in jail for a very long time. "I want to go. Can we go?"

Down the hallway, voices rise. Someone is yelling. "Let me back there. I have to see her. Taryn!"

My chest lifts like a hot air balloon. I know that voice. A

grin I can't stop splits my face as I turn toward the commotion. "Let me just—"

"Sit tight. I'll go get your loverboy." Justin winks over his shoulder as he leaves.

Butterflies do high kicks in my stomach. Esau came. He's here. Despite everything. Despite the flood and the pretense and the bickering. He's here. For me.

"You're so cute right now," Audrey sing-songs, batting at my arm.

"Shut up, you."

She points a finger in a circle over my face. "You're bright pink."

"I am no—"

Esau appears at the other end of the corridor, and my words dry up in my throat. His hair is disheveled like he's been tugging at it with wild, unrestrained fingers. His chest rises and falls on short breaths. The white tee and jeans that hug his frame are painted with streaks of mud. His work boots are crusted with it. He was fighting the flood. He was fighting for his uncle's farm, and now he's here. Esau's entire body relaxes when his eyes find me.

Justin jostles past him to join Karen in the classroom, but Esau doesn't even flinch. His attention is solely on me. Analyzing from top to bottom and back up.

"Hi." It comes out more breathy than I thought it would.

Esau's throat bobs as he swallows. "You're alive."

My heart threatens to pound right out of my chest as I take a step toward him. "I'm alive."

He moves so fast I don't register it before he tugs me into his chest and holds on so tight I imagine he won't ever let go. Big, warm, comforting hands spread over my spine. Burying his nose in my hair, he inhales deeply. "This day has been hell without you."

My boyfriend's scent is a balm soothing the sore parts of my body and soul as he cradles me close. My name is a whisper on his lips, making me hold on tighter. "I texted you earlier, and when I didn't hear back, I was worried. But then the levee broke and the river flooded. My uncle needed every hand he could get to sandbag the farm. We fought it for as long as we could, but the water rose so fast we had to get out of there. It's such a mess. And I still hadn't heard from you. I was *freaked out*, Taryn. I didn't know if you were still alive, or if the flood had gotten to you. It made me realize how much I need you. We'll make it work when I leave this fall. I won't have it any other way." His hands ripple up and down my spine, as if to verify that each inch of skin is intact. I shiver under the touch.

Reaching up, I press the pad of my finger to his mouth, quieting his worried words. "Other than a cut finger, I'm okay. I admit, it got a little hairy for a minute, but Justin and Karen got there in time. And I'm so sorry I didn't tell you before we left. I wish I could have, but there wasn't time, and I was worried Viv—"

"I know. Lamb was out front, and he told me what happened to her." Esau loosens his grip, running his calloused palms from my shoulders down to my hands to tangle his fingers with mine. The warm touch is like the sun's rays on my skin, making me glow.

"He did?" My eyes roam over his expression. Giddiness bubbles up at the way his attention slips from feature to feature like he can't take in enough of me at once. And despite Lamb's assurance that he doesn't hate us, I'm still pleasantly surprised the sheriff defended me to Esau. Old man must be going soft.

"He said you thought you didn't have a choice." Esau's thumb coasts over my lower lip before his eyes dart behind me.

"I'm glad you're okay, too, Audrey."

Behind me, my sister laughs. "Thanks."

Esau's eyes find mine again. I tighten my grip on his fingers. "Still, I'm sorry about this. I can't imagine what this day was like for you. Fighting to protect your farm, and then not being able to get ahold of me. If it makes you feel any better, they caught the bad guy. It's done."

Running his fingertips along my jaw, Esau burrows into my hair. "Glad to hear it. I'm going to kiss you now."

I peep along the hallway. Audrey is a few feet away, talking to Deputy Kelley. Several more people dot the space.

"In front of an audience?"

"I don't care." Pure, unfiltered joy overwhelms my system when Esau's mouth lands on mine. It's a short kiss, a promise, and it's exhilarating, like jumping into the ocean's waves and trusting them to carry me to shore.

Chapter 35

Half an Hour Later

Audrey

The cafeteria is bursting with people. Every table is full. My lungs constrict as I realize how many of them won't have a home to go to tomorrow, when the storm clouds have blown away and the sun has risen. Where will they all go while they're waiting on aid?

Justin shuffles toward the food line, but I hang back. Karen waits beside me, patiently studying my face. "So, our house? Did it flood?" Based on what she told me, it should be okay since it's on the opposite side of town. The dairy is there too, and I'm hoping that since she didn't mention it, it's come through the storm mostly unscathed.

"I haven't been back in hours, but it's not in the flood zone, so it should be fine. Wouldn't be surprised if there was some wind damage, but nothing we can't fix."

I smile, surprised at how glad I am to hear that the old building is likely intact. "That place used to creep me out. It makes a lot of weird noises."

Karen laughs. Gestures past my shoulder with her chin. "It sure does, but you get used to it. Looks like you've got

275

company."

My heart palpates with excitement. "Noah?"

"Join us when you're ready." She moves toward the table Justin has claimed.

I spin around. The boy standing a few feet away, drinking me in with fierce brown eyes behind black frames, makes my heart flutter. Noah looks like the best thing I've ever seen with his wild, looping curls, his Henley hugging his lithe body. "Hi." I wave shyly, sliding toward him.

I stand awkwardly an arm's-length away, wanting to tackle him, but not knowing for sure if he'd be okay with that. My mouth goes dry, wishing he was mine. That I could step into his arms without hesitating. I should have taken Taryn's advice and had a define-the-relationship with my favorite boy before this. It would be a lot easier if I knew where we stood.

Noah's pupils blow wide behind his glasses, his lips splitting into a bright smile. My name floats between us on an exhale. The look he gives when our eyes meet devastates my insides. "Audrey..." His eyes brush over me in a reverent caress.

He's here. Noah is here. Came to see if I was still alive, by the look of concern scrawled across his brow. "I'm okay. We're all okay."

Noah shifts, and his mud-caked shoes bump mine. "Are you sure? Do you mind if—Can I touch you?"

It's the only sign I need. The barrier between us is demolished. He laughs when I fling myself into his arms and wrap my own around his waist. My clothes are just as wet and dirty, so a little more mud isn't going to stop me.

When we finally part, his palms skim from my wrists up to my shoulders, and rest there, bringing his face closer to my own. "I'm so sorry I couldn't get here sooner. It was a long night." He rakes a hand through his hair. "But from what I've heard over the radio, your night was pretty wild too. You don't have to tell me what happened if you're not ready, but answer me this: Are you really okay?"

I sigh, swaying closer. For the longest time it bothered me when he'd ask me that, because I was never okay. Because it seemed like I never would be. There were always open questions hanging in my mind like ripe fruit weighing down a tree's branches. But now, all of those questions have been answered. No more living under those drooping boughs. I'm ready to step out into the sunlight.

"I'm okay. Really." Taking his other hand, I inch closer until there's barely any space between us. Look up into Noah's sweet face. "Before anything else happens, can I ask you something?"

"Yeah?"

"Be my boyfriend?"

Noah nods, his mouth a happy curve from ear to ear. "I've wanted to be yours since almost the day we met. So yes, I'd love to be your boyfriend."

The first light of the morning sun shines through the cafeteria windows, making it glow as I lift up on tiptoes to brush my lips over his. Joy is like a warm breeze across my skin as he kisses me back.

Noah doesn't let go of my hand for the entire length of the food line, and when I take a seat next to Karen and Justin at our table, he drapes an arm over my chair. If this is how it's going to be between us from now on, I am unequivocally for Noah as my boyfriend.

He waits until I've gotten some food in me before he scoots closer, elbows propped on the table. "So, will you give me an overview of what happened tonight?"

I hesitate for a second before I realize I am ready to tell him. Now that everything is done, I want to talk about it. Get it all out in the open so there aren't any unknowns between us going forward. Taking a deep breath, I start at the beginning. The messages from the unknown number that turned out to be Nate, letting us know he'd kidnapped Viv. The reveal that he was working with Ms. Miller. The bombshell that was Robert Baugh showing up at the newspaper office. All of it. I swallow the tightness in my throat as the memory of the Gemini Killer disappearing under the water floats to the forefront of my mind.

Noah sighs, tucking his chin over my shoulder. "How's Viv?"

"She's okay, physically, but I imagine she'll need help coping. Esau might have to cave and let her make those adjustments she wanted to the play costumes."

Noah chuffs. "I saw him and Taryn ducking into a closet when I got here, so I'm guessing he's gonna be in a pretty good mood today. You should ask him about the costumes next time you see him."

Grimacing, I stuff a fry into his mouth. "Don't be gross."

He mumbles an amused, "Sorry," as he chews.

Chapter 36

Taryn

"Is it okay if we stay here for a bit? I promise to meet you in the cafeteria as soon as we're done catching up." I bat my eyelashes at Karen, projecting my most innocent expression. She doesn't need to know I want to pull Esau into one of the empty classrooms and kiss his handsome face senseless.

One of Karen's eyebrows arches as if she can read my mind. Pointedly, she looks down the hallway, marking the handful of deputies and first responders who are taking care of other people displaced or hurt by the flood. "Ten minutes," she says. I agree, and she leaves.

"I thought she'd never leave," Esau says. He must have the same idea crowding out the rest of his brain cells, because he pulls me down the hall, away from the emergency personnel. He swings open what appears to be a supply closet and herds me inside. It's pretty dark in here, even with the illumination from the tiny, bald light bulb hanging from the ceiling. Shelves filled with cleaning supplies and paper goods bracket the space. The door closes behind me, and I blink, eyes adjusting in the dim light. Grinning, Esau crowds me toward the back wall. His broad hands settle on my waist as he draws me in. His mouth hovers over mine.

I smile against his lips. "What has gotten into you? Didn't get enough of me in the hallway, huh?"

"One more kiss. I need it. Then we can go get some food."

I can't resist teasing him a little. My hands twirl in the hair at his nape. "You need it, huh? I don't know. I'm awfully hungry. And I bet my breath stinks. I haven't brushed my teeth in a while."

Esau's hands flex on my sides, his voice coming out more like a growl. "Taryn, I swear."

"Okay, just one." Rising up on tiptoes, I skim my lips over his. It's all the encouragement he needs to slide his broad hands to the small of my back to hold me securely against his chest. His mouth seals over mine, wrapping me in his heady warmth from top to bottom. I sink into the kiss, grateful I'm here with Esau. My pulse kicks up. Earlier tonight, I thought I'd never see him again.

With a nip at my bottom lip, he lets go.

I mewl softly in complaint. "Wait, wait. One more? Please?"

Esau's mouth turns sly. "You don't ever have to ask." He kisses me again, and this time his caress carries me away from the lemony chemical smell, the broom handle digging into my back, and the pile of toilet paper rolls on the shelf next to us. I could stay in this tiny space all night.

My stomach is the only thing that makes us finally leave the supply closet—my new favorite room in school—and head toward the bustle and promise of food. "We should probably get back. It's been at least ten minutes."

A soft smile curves his mouth up. "You're probably right."

"Say that again."

Chuckling, Esau leans in as we walk, putting his soft lips to my ear. "You're right, Taryn."

I try to stifle a smile, needing to know one more thing. "What you said, about when you're gone. Did you mean it?"

Esau stops in the middle of the hallway, hand gripping mine. Deep brown eyes fasten on me. "That we'll make it work next fall? I meant every word, because I love you. So much. We are magic."

Nodding, I wrap my arm around his and snuggle in until I can't get any closer to this boy. "I won't ever forget. I love you, too."

We meander toward the cafeteria, letting the hum of activity around us fade away under the promises we've just made. Too soon, we reach the caf, and my boyfriend gently untangles himself from my arms. I don't protest. Much. It's okay; I only just decided that I'd stay in his arms all night if he let me. No biggie.

Esau smirks at my put-out expression before scanning the room, looking for someone. He holds out a hand in offering. "I want to introduce you to someone. Okay?"

He waits until I put my palm in his.

Steering me between the crowded tables, he ushers me toward the back of the room where his aunt and uncle—both as muddy as Esau—are sitting with another middle-aged couple. The man has on dirt-crusted denim overalls and a shearling coat. His black hair is short, but the intense eyebrows and sharp jawline are all Esau. The woman's joggers and matching sweatshirt are solid mud from feet to elbows. Looks like all four of them went into battle when the levee broke and the flooding started. Her black hair is in a messy knot at her nape. Soft, sable brown eyes rise to meet Esau's before swinging to mine. "Mi hijo? Es esta ella?" she asks.

Esau smiles, nudging me forward. "Mamá, this is Taryn.

Mi novia."

She smiles, standing up and circling the table toward us. Holding her hands out until I take them, she grins up at me. "I am so pleased to meet you. We were very curious to meet the girl who drove this one so crazy last semester. He had a lot to say about you, but you're even lovelier in person. Miguel, come meet Esau's Taryn."

"Wow, thanks!" I smile wide as Esau's mom beckons his father closer without letting go of my hand. Her palm is warm and soft in mine. I like her already.

"I've heard a lot about you, young lady," Mr. Chavez says as he gives me a hearty side hug. "I always knew my boy would need someone to keep him on his toes."

Laughing, I nod. "I do my best."

"Whatever you're doing, keep it up. He sounds so happy whenever he calls to check in with us. And we're looking forward to seeing both of you in the play, too." Mr. Chavez smiles, putting an arm around his wife.

Mrs. Chavez squeezes my fingers before letting go.

Esau takes possession of my hand, holding it snuggly in his. "I'm going to get Taryn back to her family, okay?"

They both nod, rejoining his aunt and uncle at the table. They go back to the cafeteria pizza squares they were eating when we came over. Seeing adults eating it makes me giggle. Esau steers me across the room to where my family is sitting around another table, eating their own early morning breakfast of cafeteria pizza.

Chapter 37

Day 345, Wednesday

Taryn

Marisa and I are in the middle of running a scene in my living room when the front door opens. Marisa stops in the middle of her line. Fiona leans forward on the couch, craning to see into the foyer. We fall completely silent when Viv steps into the room, clinging to Erin's hand. The other girl gives her an encouraging smile as she ushers her forward. Dark circles shadow her drooping eyes. There's a stain on the front of her sweatshirt. She doesn't look like herself, and I can't hold that against her. Her mother is still breathing, unlike Audrey's and my parents, but Viv has lost her as surely as we lost ours last spring. All the crap Anna Miller has done is irrevocable. And she's not the only one who will have to live with that. Viv will carry the memories for the rest of her life. I make a mental note to slip her the info for Audrey's therapist.

Viv toes at the old shag carpet, avoiding our eyes. Erin puts an arm around her, whispering in her ear. Erin's ginger hair is swept up in a messy bun on top of her head. Her skin looks washed out in the late afternoon sun. She looks like she hasn't gotten much more sleep than Viv.

I can't imagine how difficult it is for Viv to stand in front of us right now, knowing everything her mom did. Deep down in my gut, I know that Viv had no idea the darkness her mother was hiding, but it's still awkward.

Marisa, Fiona, Audrey, and I don't move. Fiona's arms are locked around the pillow in her lap. Marisa rubs at the front of her sweater, eyes on our injured friend and her lady. A few days ago at school, when Viv was once again absent, the rest of us got to talking about how scarce Viv had been since the night of the flood. We all agreed to let her come to us when she was ready, and to let Viv say what she needs to before we jump in. We agreed to listen, to let her get it all off her chest without us putting words in her mouth or feelings in her heart. Today appears to be the day Viv has chosen to share her pain with us, as much or as little as she wants.

It takes physical effort for Viv to lift her chin to look at us. Takes several deep, steadying breaths. Her body moves sluggishly, wearily, as if she's already lost the battle she came here to fight. I shift in my seat, wanting to grab her and hug her tight, but that's not what I agreed to do.

With a shudder, Viv speaks. "I just wanted to tell you I'm sorry for everything my mom did. I had no idea she was—but I should have. I should have known, somehow, that she was trying to hurt you. But I didn't, and I'm sorry."

Something snaps, and we're all on our feet. Rushing Viv and Erin, tangling them in a vortex of limbs and smiles and tears. We're a writhing, warm ball of friendship, each of us pushing closer to Viv to let her know that we don't blame her. Not for any of it. Her mom's decisions are not her fault, and we won't hold them against her. Under Fiona's armpit, I catch my sister's eyes. I blamed her for so long for everything that happened to us, and I am so freaking glad I finally let it go. I hope Viv can let it go.

Kate Anderson is going to have a difficult time letting go of everything that happened. Audrey and I insisted on going with the Sheriff to let her know that her brother's body had been found after the flood. That he'd been helping Ms. Miller attempt to murder us. By the time we left, our old friend was a sobbing mess, incapable of looking anyone in the eye. I hope she gets the help she needs to heal from the soul-deep wounds the past months have inflicted on her.

I'm still tangled in a mass of friendly bodies when gravity starts to pull at us. Marisa squeaks as she falls. Audrey goes, her arm still linked with Marisa's. Erin trips over Marisa's legs and goes down. Viv keels over, scrambling. Fiona gives up, flopping down onto the pile of girls in the floor.

"Aww, what a cute puppy pile," I tease them, wagging my finger.

"Oh yeah?" Fiona sweeps my feet out from under me. Oof. I land on top of the heap in a fit of giggles. Somehow Marisa's elbow is buried in my hair, making me wince when I try to sit up.

"Just give in," Erin says, splaying a leg over my waist.

"It's better down here anyway." Viv smiles from her spot pinned under Fiona.

Karen does a double take when she comes into the room. She snickers. "Everything okay? I thought I heard—Oh. I didn't know you were playing Twister in here."

"Very funny. Help us up?" I hold out a hand, which she uses to haul me upright.

When we're all up straightening out our sweatshirts and messy ponytails, we plop down in a bunch on and around the sofa. Erin sits against Viv's knees, running her hands over the carpet. Marisa gets Viv talking about her progress on the play costumes, which perks her up. She starts waxing poetic about the fabrics she talked Esau into letting her use. Audrey cuddles in next to me and pulls a fleece blanket over us.

Karen lifts a phone to her ear. "What pizza do you guys like?"

"Cheese!"

"Pesto!"

"Veggie lovers!"

Nodding, Karen orders a lot of pizza—way more than we can possibly eat—before perching on the edge of the plaid chair across from us.

Audrey's head tilts forward on my shoulder in that direction. She sits up. "Is there something going on?"

Our guardian adjusts the pillow at her back, relaxing further into the cushy seat. "Nope. For once, I have nothing to report. Which is why we're celebrating with pizza."

Justin comes in the front door, leaning against the frame. "Looks like a party in here. Anyone in the mood for dessert?"

A cheer goes up from our girl pile.

Justin looks out the door. "Two dozen cupcakes, coming up. Guys? Come on in."

A bunch of heads swivel to the door as Justin steps aside. Esau, Noah, and Dariel come in, arms laden with pink bakery boxes. Esau winks at me over Noah's head, and I smile wide. Cupcakes sound amazing. Popping up, I follow the guys into the kitchen.

Noah greets me with a smile as he slides his pink box onto the counter. "How's it going in there?"

I shrug. "I think we're all going to be okay."

"Glad to hear it." He ducks out, probably drawn to where my sister is cuddled up on the sofa. Yep. He slides into the spot by her, and Audrey happily shares her blanket. They're way too precious together now that they're officially dating.

"It's been hours since I've had pizza, and I'm so ready." Dariel unloads his pink box on the countertop, patting my elbow in greeting as he lopes past, joining everyone in the living room.

I watch him settle in next to Fiona, my attention moving back to my twin and her super sweet boyfriend. "It's so nice that we've been drama free long enough for them to actually date. Eep."

Esau must have put his pink box down when I wasn't paying attention, because he snatches my hand and pulls me out the back door. It snicks closed, and he turns the intensity of his attention on me. The heated look in his eyes warms my fingers and toes, which is good because I don't have shoes on and it's freezing out here. His eyes sweep over me when I shiver. "I should have asked. Want to go in?"

Shaking my head, I move closer to him. "You'll keep me warm, won't you?"

Inclining his head, he unbuttons his coat. I trace his progress with my eyes, assuming he'll take it off and throw it over my shoulders. I turn to give him my back, expecting the weight of the shearling to cloak my frame.

Esau draws me against him, my back to his chest, tucking my arms over my belly and wrapping his coat around both of us. He leans against the wood siding of the house, taking me with him. I rest my weight on him, knowing he'll hold me up.

Sniffing at the lining of the coat that's tickling my nose, I bury my face in it. It smells good, like him. Plus it's warm. I'm in heaven.

"Getting high off my smell?"

"As a cat on catnip."

His arms tighten over my chest, keeping the flaps of his

287

coat closed over us. His nose draws a line from beneath my ear down to the collar of my sweater, breathing deeply. "That smell. You know it drives me nuts, right?"

My mouth splits in a grin. "I might have noticed, since you bury your face in my hair every chance you get."

I can feel him shrug behind my back. "Won't apologize for it."

"I didn't ask you to. I bet you're glad you got your cast off, finally. How's your hand?"

He flexes it before snaking it over my stomach again. "Pasty and gross, but not bad."

I drop my head against his shoulder, completely relaxing in his arms. It's the first time I've been able to uncoil the tension that's been building in my chest for weeks. The moon ascends over the tops of the eucalyptus trees that span our backyard, marking the edge of the property. A rustling in the branches draws my eyes. A raccoon shimmies down the trunk of one, followed by two of its babies. "Cubs? Kids? What are baby raccoons called?"

"Don't know. Don't care."

"Unhelpful."

"Speaking of parents." Esau's arms tighten around me. I can feel his throat bob as he swallows.

"What about them?" I tilt my head to catch his profile.

His eyes lower to mine. "They want to have dinner with you and your family tomorrow, to celebrate opening night on Friday. You up for that?"

After the flood, we postponed the play's opening for two weeks to give everyone some time to breathe. Many of our classmates were displaced as cleanup on Hacienda began, but at this point everyone in drama is excited to finally be putting on the show we've been working on since January. Nodding my cheek against his chest, I smile. "That sounds really nice."

We go quiet, watching the night and its denizens wake from their slumber. In the distance, a coyote howls. Its brothers and sisters answer.

A shiver of cold goes through me. My sweater is no match for the wintry air. Goosebumps rise along my skin. I rub my arms with my hands to try to warm up.

Esau hauls himself up straight, pushing me upright too. Opening his coat, he spins us until I'm the one pinned against the house. He moves closer. Crowds me against the wall. Heat from his body permeates my skin. I pull him nearer by the lapels of his jacket. "I blame you for making me cold."

"You should. My fault you're out here. How can I make it up to you?"

I hum in my throat, grinning. "I can think of a couple ways."

My boyfriend's attention dips from my eyes to my mouth. A pulse pounds in my throat. "Yeah?"

I nod. Fisting his coat, I pull his face closer. "Are you nervous? About opening night?"

"Yes." His lips barely skate over mine when the back door opens and Justin pops his head out. "Pizza's here. Come on inside."

"We'll be in in a minute." I say, knowing that my cheeks are probably red, and not just from the cold.

Justin looks between us, his eyes settling on me. There's mock somberness in his expression. "Do I need to get out my gun? Give some version of the 'you behave yourself because I have a shotgun and a shovel' talk?"

"No! We'll just be a second."

"I'll be watching the clock," he says with a jaunty wink. The back door closes behind him.

"Busted," Esau whispers, his hot breath fanning my skin. I hold him in place when he tries to put space between us.

"Just one more minute."

"I should say no. Don't want to get shot." His chuckle works its way through me, pulling my smile wider. We kiss, enjoying the quiet for a stolen minute. I make good use of it, mussing up Esau's hair with both hands. When I finally let him pull away, a giggle breaks out of me. He looks like he just walked through a wind tunnel. I love it.

Sweeping my palms off each other, I grasp the knob. "Job well done."

"If I get held up at shotgun point, I'm blaming it on you." Esau holds the door open so I can go in first.

"Fair. Let's get some pizza."

Chapter 38

Day 347, Friday

Audrey

In the past two weeks, a ton of work has been done in Hacienda. Hundreds of people from neighboring towns came with tools and supplies to help begin the repairs on waterlogged storefronts and homes. It's been pretty inspiring to watch. Noah and I have spent a couple of afternoons after school helping clean up the grounds around the senior center where Mrs. Lopez works. It's incredibly satisfying hearing the seniors living there remark about how much better the courtyard looks after we spent a bunch of time replanting pretty plants and mulching the flower beds that were destroyed in the storm.

As of today, everyone has moved out of the gym—either back into their homes, local hotels, or other places. Campus is quieter during the day, but after school the cast spends hours upon hours in the drama room, going over the play until it's ingrained in their brains. My friends are so entrenched in it they quote it constantly.

I'm backstage with Taryn, hanging out while she gets ready. Last night, we had dinner with Esau and his family at the diner, and it went really well. Justin and Mr. Chavez spent most of dinner talking about the work Justin needs to do to repair his boat. Karen got drawn into a conversation with Mrs. Chavez about cooking, and when Esau's mom found out Karen can't cook, she strong-armed her into agreeing to lessons. So that'll be entertaining.

"Fifteen minutes to curtains up. Everything okay in here?" Fiona balances on the door frame, leaning halfway into Taryn's dressing room. Taryn sits at the mirror, putting the finishing touches on her stage makeup. Her blond hair is already pinned in an up-do that she, Viv, and Esau agreed on for her character. It fits perfectly with the play's historical setting. Somehow, her nest of curls makes her look both younger and more timeless, as if she stepped out of the mirror, a traveler from Victorian England.

"We're good." My sister smiles at Fiona in the mirror. Getting up, Taryn strips out of her button-up shirt and pants, trading them for one of the beautiful gowns Viv updated for the play. "Zip me up? Thanks."

She grins at me over her shoulder. "Tonight is going to be climactic. I can feel it. I might pop if we don't start right now. You know?" Turning to face me, she wiggles her hips. "I'm itching to get the show going. Speaking of, have you seen Esau? I'm dying to know what his costume looks like."

"You know I haven't. He and Viv haven't let anyone see. It makes me wonder if he's going with the emperor's new clothes or something."

Taryn laughs. "Not likely. But why all the secrecy? It's just a costume."

I shrug. "Maybe he's embarrassed?"

"A distinct possibility. But that doesn't explain why Viv hasn't spilled the beans. She's usually so effusive when it comes to costumes, but this time? Not a peep." It's true. When Viv is excited about something, she's a gusher. But for some reason, Esau's costumes for the play are a secret they've guarded like the script for a hotly anticipated superhero movie. So naturally, the entire cast is morbidly curious about how our illustrious director will be attired.

The dressing room door opens and slams, making us both whirl toward it. "Geez, Fiona, I thought we still had—" Taryn's breath dies as it hits the air, the words sinking like bricks to the ground.

Robert Baugh stands in front of the closed door, blocking our only exit. My eyes are locked on his weapon of choice. The shrewd, protracted knife held confidently in his hand. "Just came by to say, 'break a leg.' Isn't that what you theater types say to wish each other good luck?"

Taryn's hands are buried in her skirts. Eyes latched on the killer. Her tone is quiet, but firm. "How did you get in here?"

The man snorts. Advances toward us, herding Taryn and I until we're hemmed in against the back wall. "They were letting anybody in the other night, during the storm. So I came in. Had a warm meal. Found a hidey hole and waited. I knew I'd get my chance, sooner or later. That pixie-haired costume girl hasn't been here all week, so the costume room was a convenient place to hide. It's practically a jungle in there, perfect for a patient man like me."

"They'll realize we're missing," Taryn says. Behind her back, a single finger forms into a point. I try to pinpoint what she's gesturing at without being obvious. Makeup is strewn across the vanity's surface. A hairbrush rests on its side. The curling iron she used to transform her hair into beautiful curls blinks red. It's still on. Still hot. Genius.

"They will, but not for a few minutes. Plenty of time. You know how long it takes a body to bleed out, if it's cut in the correct place? Minutes. By the time someone comes back here looking for you, I'll be gone. And you'll both be dead."

My sister shifts, leaving me room to inch along the vanity. She's giving me the chance to grab it. I can't hesitate when she distracts the man who came here to watch us bleed out on the floor. Trying to harness my fear, turn it into something useful, I take slow, tiny steps closer to the only weapon we have.

Taryn squares her shoulders to block the man's view of my hands as I grope for the appliance behind my back.

"You don't have to do this," she says. She sounds so composed, so sure. "If you leave now, we won't tell anyone you were here. You can get away. Go somewhere else. Start over."

Immediately, it's obvious that this was not the right thing to say.

The Gemini Killer bristles, his eyes blazing with angry heat. "I don't want to start over," he spits. "Ever since I was a teenager I knew what I was supposed to do. My mom and dad were shit parents, pitting me and my brothers against each other at every turn. They made being a twin miserable for me and for Albie. It was obvious they should never have been parents at all. They didn't know what to do with us. Then I hear from Albie that he's made friends with a girl who's a twin. That her parents are shit, too. It made me realize that most parents of twins are rotten. Nature didn't make parents good enough for twins, so I decided to do something about it. My parents died before I could make sure they got their punishment, but there's lots of other twin parents out there for me to find. To teach their lesson. But you two... You two are just as rotten as your parents. It's because of you I lost my brothers. I can't stand by and let that go."

Righteous fury glows in the man's eyes as he gains ground. The dressing room shrinks until it feels like we're trapped in a too-tight box, gasping like fish dragged up a rocky shore and left to die.

I suck in what air I can, my ribcage expanding, then hold my breath. Tiny plastic tubes shift under the tips of my fingers. None of them is the one I need.

There.

My hand seizes the cord before painstakingly slowly inching upward. My fingers shift around the handle, trying to get a firm grip. My wrist is twisted at such an odd angle I'm not positive I'll be able to hold it long enough to use it.

Robert Baugh's nostrils flare as he works to calm himself down. He resets his grip on his blade, eyes not leaving us. "Hiding your fingers? Don't worry, little monsters. I don't have time tonight to take you apart piece by piece. In fact, since the show is about to start, I'll make this quick. Tell you what. I'll let you decide who goes first. Personally, I'd say it's the easier way. I wouldn't want to watch one of my brothers die." His eyes home in on my sister, fluttering over her cheek in a grotesque caress. "Since you're already scarred, let me finish the job. One stab is all it'll take."

The metal in his hand glistens as if hungry for blood.

I can do this. I have to do this. Taryn is trusting me to save us; I won't let her down.

"No thanks," my sister says, her fingers white in the folds of her skirts. "I have too much to accomplish to die tonight. Rain check?"

"No can do." He lunges, his bulk blotting out the edges of my vision until all I see is him. The whites of his blazing eyes. Large hands. A gleaming blade thrust toward Taryn's fitted bodice.

With a battle cry, I whip the curling iron around and hook it under Robert Baugh's chin, burying it in his reddish beard.

Burning hair smell fills the dressing room. He screams, pushing away, clawing at his burnished throat. "You bitch," he growls. "You'll pay for that." His arm swings out, his blade cutting through the air toward me.

The dressing room door is thrown open, its wood frame splintering against the brick wall.

My hands hold up the curling iron like a sword as Karen hurtles inside, sizes up the situation in a heartbeat, and shoots Robert Baugh in the back. He gurgles as his face registers the shock. Slowly, his hands sink to the ground. The knife drops to the floor with a clang. A weird convulsion flows over his body, and then he goes still, unresistant.

Crimson oozes around him on the vinyl floor. I don't look away. I've had enough of blood for a lifetime, but seeing this, proof that the Gemini Killer won't rise again, is worth one more bloody vision imprinted on my brain.

Taryn pries the curling iron from my clawed fingers. Switches it off and sets it on the vanity. Wraps her arms around me and pulls me close. "You saved us. You did *good*. Never forget that."

Returning her hug, I take in my first full breath in what feels like eons. "Zero out of ten, do not recommend. But I'd do it again if I had to."

My twin's cheek curves in a smile against my shoulder, and I smile too.

Epilogue

Day 365

Three hundred and sixty-five days ago, I woke up in my bed at home. I took a shower, got dressed, ate toaster pastries for breakfast and left. Walked to school for the last time with Taryn, my twin sister and best friend.

Three hundred and sixty-five days ago, I stayed late after class to ask a favorite teacher about the camera I was dreaming of buying with money I'd saved up. If I hadn't forced my sister to hang around campus waiting while I gushed over lens options, playback features, and a movable view screen, I wouldn't have been late getting home.

That extra fifteen minutes changed my life. Took something from Taryn and me that we can never get back.

Three hundred and sixty-five days ago, when Taryn and I got home, our temples sweaty from toting our backpacks through the neighborhood like pack animals, the beat-up car I'd seen way too often around town was parked outside our house.

Inside was a macabre tapestry of crimson stains and the moans of chest-rattling death. No matter how many days pass, I won't ever forget walking into that kitchen. Seeing my parents eviscerated and bleeding out on the tile floor.

I will never forget.

But with every new day, the sharp pain slicing between my ribs lessens. My lungs are able to take in just a little more air without being pierced and deflating. The nightmares come less often, fewer nights end with my chest heaving, flailing as I try to wrest myself from brutal hands and tangled blankets.

The memories of Mom and Dad that surprise me now—in something Taryn says, in something Justin or Karen does by way of their tentative grasp on parenting—don't steal my breath or leave me gaping and dizzy like they used to.

I'll never forget, but I will go on living.

Taryn and I are building new lives for ourselves with Karen and Justin. With Esau and Noah. With Fiona and Dariel and Viv and Marisa. With photography and theater and milkshakes. Justin has promised to teach us to water ski this summer, once the boat is repaired. Karen has been drilling us in self-defense on the off chance we ever need it again and don't have a hot curling iron within easy grabbing distance.

The time-lapse I took of the milky way last night came out close to perfect.

Which is why, when Karen and Justin approached us, mumbling that there was an opening at the wedding venue—a cancellation that would allow them to have their special event on this day—a top contender for one of the worst days of my life—I didn't say anything. I listened, waiting for the sting to rise. The pain to cut. When it did, it was manageable. I could handle it.

They asked Taryn and I if it would be okay to get married one year after my parents had been killed, on the dot. Taryn and I met each other's eyes, a long look connecting between us. We told them yes.

Karen looks fantastic in the white silk pant-suit she

decided to wear instead of a dress. Taryn watched a couple of tutorials online and figured out how to pull our agent's hair into a chic chignon at her nape.

My twin and I are wearing knee-length dresses in a pretty eucalyptus green. I'd be lying if I didn't admit it was inspired by the tall, graceful trees in the grove behind our house. A place I spend a lot more time in, taking photographs and listening to music, now that I'm not worried about a shadow watching from behind every tree. Taryn's blond hair is up in a crown braid. She whirls around, breathless with excitement. She adores weddings.

Gauzy white curtains covering the large window to the bride's room dance in the air conditioning, granting me glimpses of the emerald lawn outside where Justin, Esau, and Noah wait in their suits. Two rows of chairs face the white-painted arbor draped by a vining rose bursting with peachy flowers. Noah says something to Esau that has him straightening the tie at his neck. My boyfriend takes his glasses off and cleans them on his coat before slipping them back on. Justin asked them to stand up with him, not for the lack of potential groomsmen he had back at the FBI, but because of what this day means to Taryn and me. Noah catches my grin through the window and mouths, "Wow." It's my favorite compliment he ever gave me, because it was the first. It's one he repeats often when he and Esau pick Taryn and me up for double dates. Okay, date singular. It was a blast, but Taryn and I don't have to do everything together, not anymore. Especially not dating our boyfriends. Sometimes a girl just wants time away from her mirror image, especially when it involves milkshakes, anime, and a cute guy. Am I right?

I slide into the mirror a few feet behind Karen, making sure my hair is holding the style Taryn crafted. My brown tresses are up in a crown that matches my sister's, a few wisps loose around my temples. Crisp, spanking new Converse adorn my feet. A gift from Justin and Karen for our special day. Because they've made it clear that this day isn't just about the two of them. It's about the four of us officially becoming a family. Justin and Karen? They're adopting us. Making it legal as soon as the courts say they can. So pretty soon, we won't be a family just in our own hearts, but on official government paper too. I smile up at Karen from my spot on the ottoman when she turns from the mirror. "How do I look?" she asks, her quiet smile in place.

"Fantastic. Gorgeous. Justin will faint dead away when he sees you." Taryn slaps the back of her hand against her forehead, staggering back as if physically struck by the sight of the bride's elegance.

"You two are too much." Karen shakes her head, amused, and beckons. She takes one of my hands and one of Taryn's in a firm grip. "I never saw myself as a parent. Never wanted to have babies of my own. Especially in my line of work, it was difficult to picture going home from the office to kids who needed me. But I want you girls to know that this past year has been, well it's been a challenge"—she laughs—"But I'm so grateful Justin and I were assigned to your case. I'm so glad I've gotten the privilege of watching you two rebuild your lives after something no child should have to experience. I want you to know I love you both, so much.

"And I know this day might be hard for both of you, so if you need to step away, that's okay. I wouldn't have agreed to do this if I thought it would hurt either of you, even a tiny bit. I'm just so ready to be married. It feels like Justin and I have been dancing around this for a long while, as partners in all ways, and it's time. I hope you understand."

It's a surprise to see the shine of happy tears in her eyes. I give her a quick squeeze, and then Taryn does. All three of us wipe at our cheeks, laughing.

"Stop making me cry," Taryn orders. "Marisa will be furious if the makeup she worked so hard on doesn't last through the ceremony."

I swipe the wetness from under my eyes, moving toward the door when someone knocks. The wedding coordinator announces it's time to start.

The three of us link arms as we take the steps out into the vineyard, rounding the house toward where stringed music plays. Taryn starts up the path first, grinning at all of our friends as she passes, a single rose cupped in her hands. She stops at the top of the aisle, whispering something to Justin that makes him laugh. With a wink at Esau, she takes her place.

Three hundred and sixty-five days ago, my family was shattered. Irreparable. I never thought I'd have that again.

I was wrong.

So when I start up the aisle toward my new family, joy spills through my body like helium, making me feel lighter than air. I promised Taryn I would stop counting the days since our parents were killed, and I'll keep that promise.

Because today isn't just day three hundred and sixty-five.

No, today is so much better.

Today is the start of something brand new. Something I never thought I could have again.

A new family.

A permanent place here in Hacienda with friends I've come to love.

A house that has become a home I call my own.

Today? It's day one.

Acknowledgements

Whenever I sit down to write a new book, the difficulty of it catches me off guard. You mean I have to make up a story? Construct characters that make readers actually feel things? String together events that, when taken together, create an engaging thread that makes sense? It blows my mind.

This, my thirteenth book, was much the same. Lucky for me, I got to journey forth with characters I know and understand. Even so, I still got it wrong sometimes, which my lovely beta readers Sarah Lusby Johns and Christina Kobel pointed out to me in comments varying from, "This sucks," to "FLIPPING FANTASTIC." Thank you, ladies, for reading this story so painstakingly, and helping me patch the holes. Thank you for rooting for Audrey and Taryn, Esau and Noah, and the rest of the Hacienda gang. This book would not be what it is without your help.

Thank you to each of my writer friends who encouraged me on the days when I wasn't sure this book would ever get done. Autumn Krause, you rock for spending hours writing and brainstorming with me in our local coffee shop. Chelsea Ichaso, thanks for lending an ear when I have silly questions. Diana Urban, thanks for your entertaining reels that made me smile on the days I contemplated giving up.

Deepest thanks to each and every one of my readers,

bloggers, booktubers, bookstagrammers, and booktokers for talking about this book. For posting about it on the endless void that is the internet. For adding it or reviewing on Goodreads. Each and every one of you is invaluable to me.

Lastly, I could never write another word if it weren't for my husband, Adam, who works his butt off for our family while I chase my authorly dreams. I couldn't do this without your love, support, and teasing about how long it takes me to put out a book.

About the Author

Emily lives in sunny Southern California with her husband and daughters. When she's not writing, she enjoys cuddling with her two dachshunds, Nestlé and Kiefer, making homemade ice cream, watching television, and enjoying the sunshine with her daughters and their flock of backyard chickens.

To learn more about Emily, visit her website: www.emilykazmierski.com